Death By Decree

A novel from the Inspector Stark series

Keith Wright

Book 6.

*If you are affected by an issue in the book, contact:
The Samaritans or check local charities.*

'Death By Decree'

Could you become the target of evil? Could your world be turned upside down and inside out? How could such a thing happen to you? It can't, can it?

Have you ever stopped to consider the transient nature of your life? Do you think that nothing will ever change? That it will always be like this? I hate to be the bearer of bad news, but I'm afraid it won't. Maybe that is a good thing. Maybe it is not.

Look at that crowd of people hurrying through the shopping centre: Three are engaged, twenty are divorced. Two have cancer; six have a cold. Ten have depression, and four are criminals. One is a Bishop, and three are queens. Four are flush; two are bust, one is a busted flush. Eight are younger, ten are old, and one has a secret never to be told. But one of them…one of them, is going to die.

Is it you?

Single mum Jane Cooper is forced into an altercation with a woman in a supermarket. Big deal. But it escalates, and despite Jane's best efforts to calm the situation, the aggressor is knocked to the floor.

The problem is the woman happens to be the wife of one of the most feared gangsters in England; Dougie Brown and his maniacal brother Len 'the bitch' Brown.

His wife is more seriously hurt than first thought, and they feel that their name and reputation has been weakened because of the humiliating episode. So, Jane Cooper must be found, and an example made of her. Everyone connected to her is now in danger.

As Stark and his team battle psychotic criminals and sinister forces within their ranks, things get out of control.

Can Jane survive this? How can she protect her daughter and elderly parents? Will the Brown's get their hands on her? If so, how extreme will her punishment be? Jane never wanted it to get this far. It is all too late. She is trapped. The wheels are in motion. The Brown brothers have decreed she must die.

In his sixth gritty crime thriller, award-winning author Keith Wright again regales the stark reality of crime, derived from his hands-on experience as a CID detective sergeant working in an inner-city area. Keith's books are set in

Nottingham in the 1980s – a time before political correctness and mobile phones. It was a different world.

Crime novels in the Inspector Stark series by Keith Wright:

One Oblique One

Trace and Eliminate

Addressed To Kill

Fair Means or Foul

Murder Me Tomorrow

Short story anthology by the author –

Killing Dad and other crime short stories

Co-opted contributions to short story anthologies-

City of Crime – Edited by David Belbin

Perfectly Criminal – The Crime Writer's Association anthology – Edited by Martin Edwards

To Serve, Protect and Write – Cops Writing Crime – Edited by Andrew Patterson

1

'Do you ever wish you had a second chance to meet someone for the first time?'

Unknown.

Could you become the target of evil? Could your world be turned upside down and inside out? How could such a thing happen to you? It can't, can it?

You think you are exempt, don't you? You believe your lovely happy time is a forever thing that the status quo will remain forever. Wrong. A minute sooner or later and maybe, but not today, today is a catalyst; the planets are aligned, and it is time for change.

Perhaps you will happen to find yourself in the wrong place at the wrong time, and boom, your life, your precious fucking life and your dreams and aspirations too, they're gone, I'm afraid. All gone.

It's not just you; it's your loved ones, too, everyone in your orbit. You are going to drag them into your hell as well. Consider that. Imagine being the cause of such horror to your loved ones. To your little child, even. The people you are about to encounter don't give a frog's fat ass about you. They are evil. They don't think like you. They have no morals or scruples. They find this shit funny. And you are in their web, running through treacle and shouting for help in a school for the deaf. They will kill you, but you need to suffer first, you need to be made an example of, and they know what it takes to destroy you. They have done this before.

On such a day in the Autumn of 1987, fate had Jane Cooper in its crosshairs as she walked across Slab Square in the centre of Nottingham. She could never

have dreamt what was about to happen, how her life was about to change over the simplest of misunderstandings. In the next hour, a chain of events would focus the most dangerous members of society on her and her family. Before nightfall, these bastards would be plotting ways to hurt her, make an example of her, and get to her through her family. To frighten her. Intimidate her and eventually kill her. She had never hurt anyone; she was a kind, loving person, but, sad-to-say, her death was now inevitable. It had been decreed.

*

Detective Inspector David Stark sat in his underpants and dressing gown, waiting patiently for his toast and marmalade. He could quite easily have thrown the bread in the toaster himself, and it would probably have been quicker, but his wife Carol had insisted as she handed him a cup of tea. She was like that. This was her domain. Her mother was just the same; Carol was old school in that sense for such a fashionable woman.

However, this meant he was now in a queue behind his daughter, Laura, and son, Chris, albeit their requirements involved only a bowl of Frosties and a seat in front of the telly in the living room.

'Love and Pride' by King triggered David to drum his fingers on the breakfast counter as the music from the kitchen radio enveloped him.

1987 had been a busy year for him and his team; it felt like it would never end. As Autumn approached, so did the darker nights, as if competing with the even darker days that had haunted his team of detectives at Nottingham CID in recent months.

Dave Stark was a handsome man, in his forties and with an almost Italian olive complexion and a temple of grey; he cut something of a dash in a masculine way. He was in good shape despite years of living a detective's life. He would put it down to his ancestry, saying he could fit into his jeans because of his genes.

He could smell the browning of the toast as he continued to tap his fingers on the smooth Formica surface, and he hummed perhaps a little too loudly.

'David, stop tapping. You aren't even in tune with the song. It's painful.' Carol jibed.

'Bloody hell, Carol, who rattled your cage?'

'You did. We're getting low on milk. Are you seeing your therapist later because I could do with you nipping to the shop on the way if you don't mind?'

David replied in hushed tones. 'Shush. Keep it down, Carol. I don't want the kids to know about my seeing Linda. They will think I'm barking mad. It will unsettle them.'

Carol had a glint in her eye as she walked past him clutching two bowls of cereal, her thumb wetted by the milk in one of them.

'Woof!' She snapped at him. Giving him one of her 'looks.'

David slapped her on her backside as she passed, causing a little skip.

'Eh, pack it in. This will go all over the floor.'

The toast popped up right on cue as she hurried back to the breakfast bar.

Stark liked to watch her petite figure scurry around with a finesse of her own. Even after all these years, she kept that. She had always been a beacon of light in the ugly world he inhabited. She was oblivious of course. She was just Carol. She couldn't see it.

'Make sure you get to see Linda, no excuses. Your health is important, David. I shouldn't have to keep getting on at you like this.'

'I will, but don't forget it is only very rare this so-called anxiety. Even Linda gets that. It is few and far between.'

'Still. You have a stressful job, and I worry about you.'

'Stress. Huh. It's a bloody made-up word, I think. Somebody is making a lot of money out of it, not least that bloody Linda.' Stark continued his tapping regardless of his wife's chastisement.

'David, get with the times. The word might be new, but the condition isn't.'

She skidded the plate of toast over to him across the counter. 'Nice. Don't let the Maître D see you.' Stark quipped.

'What?'

'Nothing, dear. I said, "thank you".'

He immediately took a bite, pausing slightly to chew and savour the freshness of the marmalade and the coarseness of the bread, before continuing. 'It is not stress, anyway. It is only when I am talking to a large number of people that I go a bit funny; it will go of its own accord. I'm not frightened of anyone or anything, and you know it.' He pointed with a bit of toast to emphasise his point, but it lost its emphasis when a lump of marmalade fell onto the plate. 'Oops.'

Carol tutted. 'Men.'

'It's true.'

'I know, but…just eat your toast, David. It's because I care, not because I don't. All I ask is that you take the visits to Linda more seriously so you can put it behind you.'

'I know. Come here.'

They kissed briefly.

'Jeez.' Their son, Chris, still embarrassed by such things at fourteen, had come into the kitchen with his empty Frosties bowl.

'Keep your nose out, you.' Carol said, tapping her finger on the said nose. 'You need to get ready for school, Chris, have you seen the time?'

'Yep, thanks for the Frosties, Mum, they're Grrreat!' David groaned. 'See you later, Dad.'

'See you later, son. Be good at school.'

Stark finished his last bite of toast as the phone rang in the hallway.

'I'll get it.' Carol said.

Within a few seconds, she returned, shoulders hunched. 'Work.' There was irritation in her voice. The unwelcome intruder had returned to their world.

'Work? Can't they last five minutes? Christ, I'll be in the office in the next hour.' David said as he sipped his tea.

'Exactly. I don't think they could survive without you.'

Stark walked to the hall and took hold of the phone, stretching the curly plastic lead as he sat on the stairs. The elongated cord was never quite long enough for comfort, and he had to lean forward slightly to speak. Strangely it had never occurred to him to slide the telephone table along a couple of feet to remedy the problem.

'Stark.'

'Sincere apologies, boss, it's Ash.'

'Ash, I'm going to be there soon, won't it wait? Mrs Stark has got the hump again, now.'

'Sorry, sir. I didn't like to ring but…'

'Where's DS Clarke?'

'I think he must be travelling in. I did try him first.'

'Anyway, what's up.'

'I've had info come in, just now, from a snout. He says an armed robbery will take place today on our patch, but he's not sure of the location. I wanted to know what I should do, because if it went down and I hadn't done anything and say someone got shot....'

'Ashley, Ashley, it's fine. You were right to ring. Is the informant tried and tested?'

'Absolutely, it's...'

'Don't tell me who it is, Ashley. Need to know basis, yes?'

'Sorry, yes, boss.'

'What exactly has he said?'

'Blagging with a shotgun somewhere in Hucknall or Bulwell during the daytime. It's on for today, definitely.'

'Is that it?'

''Fraid so, boss.'

'It's a bit thin, isn't it?'

'I know, but I bet you it happens; he's right every time this lad.'

'Okay. Do we know who the offenders are? How does *he* know the info? Are we sure it's not a decoy?'

'No, he doesn't know the offender. I forgot to ask him that bit about how he knows. Sorry.'

'Okay. Look, there's no magic wand with stuff like this, Ashley. Get uniform to park up at banks and building societies and any likely targets when doing their reports. Get in touch with Sergeant Briars at Traffic, give him my compliments, tell him what you know, and see if he can steer the armed response unit towards our area for their patrol. That way, they aren't in the middle of nowhere when and if it goes down.'

'Okay, will do, sir, thanks.'

Stark could sense Ashley was putting down the phone. 'Woah! Hang on a minute.'

'Hello?'

'I haven't done yet. Also, get back to your informant and get some more out of him; how he knows the info, task him to find out more if necessary. We need an offender or a location; otherwise, we will just be responding after the fact. Let's face it he might as well tell us there will probably be a burglary tonight somewhere, and he'd be right.'

'Okay, fair enough, sir.' There was a pause.

'Ashley?'

'Yes, sir?'

'You can do it, now. Look bloody sharp.'

'Oh, sorry, sir, yes. I'm on it.'

'See you in a bit.'

Stark smiled to himself as he quietly placed the phone receiver back on the cradle.

He noticed Carol standing in the hallway, hands on hips. 'Well?'

'Just the normal.'

'It's not going to stop you going to your appointment, is it?'

'No. It'll be fine. Well, hopefully.'

*

Jane Cooper's slight build made the trolley look unwieldy as she negotiated around the supermarket's aisles. In her early thirties, she had a trim figure and a spring in her step. Life was good. It wasn't that super as supermarkets go, as it had only five short aisles of goods; the lights were too dim, and there was just one till operator, who was slowly tapping in the prices. Jane was mindful she had just over eight pounds in her purse, so she needed to keep to essentials.

Yet again, Jane had somehow managed to find the shopping trolley with the bloody dodgy wheel, so steering was a challenge. Despite the irritation, the decision to replace the trolley never quite reached sufficient a level to do so, versus making do with the rogue wheel. It was too much hassle, and she was committed to it now.

Jane always looked well-presented even when in casual clothes, and today was one of those days where despite her brown hair being in a ponytail, and a mere swipe of lippy, she still looked fresh and full of life. Her dress had padded shoulders, and she belatedly discovered to her horror that the floral design was not dissimilar to her mother's wallpaper.

In recent times she had been trying to figure out how to spend more time visiting her parents; it wasn't so much her mother but her dad, who had become forgetful and quite frail in his seventies. It looked like he had Alzheimer's, but her Mother had always been a bit cagey about it. 'We don't know that.' She would say.

Jane was plagued with guilt for not visiting as often as she would like, but she had her own family and responsibilities with which to deal. However, it didn't stop the feeling that she was letting them down—the constant guilt of the child within us.

As ever her mind was busy; monitoring the time, as she had to pick her daughter, Daisy, up from school and so, as always, her activities were marshalled by the ticking hands of her watch. It seemed that before she started doing anything, she had to hurry up and finish. Everything had become a rush, and she couldn't figure out a way to have time to herself, never mind the luxury of a visit to Mum and Dad.

Her eyes flicked at the various wares on the shelves, trying to find something for dinner and thus far had failed, finding herself feeling the slight chill of the freezer aisle. The latest fad was pizza and garlic bread, which was very exotic, but foreign foods were a relatively new experience. In the trolley, it went. Her mother would be shuddering if she could see her; 'Foreign muck,' she would call it. She was a traditional cook – good English grub such as pie and mash, corned beef hash, stew, and fish and chips. In fact that was pretty much the entire repertoire, apart from the Sunday roast, of course.

Jane also grabbed a packet of frozen Chicken Kiev's, which was another new dinner time treat compared to what they had been used to in previous years, certainly when she was a child. She needed milk, some little pots of Angel Delight, and a sliced loaf. Oh, and eggs. 'If you've got an egg, you've got a meal.' Her Mum would say.

Jane was on the homeward strait now and manipulated the trolley towards the till whilst eyeing up the eggs in the next aisle. She could hear banging and crashing and swearing emanating from the next aisle. Someone was kicking up a right old stink.

The woman and her two girlfriends crashed around the supermarket aisles ad hoc, in a bolshy, and anti-social manner. It was a whirlwind of swear words and stomping around in a huff. She didn't seem to care who was in the way, and customers of a meeker persona would hurry to get out of her way. If they didn't, they would feel a barge of the shoulder or stepping on of toes.

The women seemed to have a sense of entitlement, and those in the know steered clear.

Jane was oblivious to all of this.

The woman came around the aisle far too quickly, and her trolley smashed into Jane's head-on, at a fair rate of knots.

'Fuck off out the way.' The woman barked as Jane stumbled backwards.

'Oi! Watch out!' Jane shouted instinctively.

'You what?' The woman had stopped dead, and only her two friends turned toward Jane as the woman stared straight ahead.

'There's no need for that. You nearly sent me flying. Just have some consideration, please.'

The woman turned for the first time to face Jane. 'Are you talking to me, bitch?'

'There's no need to take it out on me because you didn't look where you were going. Be careful. I could have been an old lady.'

There was an audible gasp from the two friends. A small crowd of onlookers had gathered at the ends of the aisle.

'Do you know who I am?' The woman growled.

Jane was getting annoyed. 'Let me guess, the Queen of Sheba?'

The two friends laughed momentarily but then caught it between clenched lips.

'Clever fucker, eh? I am Sharon Brown. Does that name mean anything to you?'

'Nope. Anyway, apology accepted.' Jane began on her way again, shaking her head. She didn't have time for all this, but she had always been brought up to stick up for herself, and she was more than capable of doing that.

Sharon Brown raised her voice.

'Don't you walk away from me, you fucking slag!'

Jane ignored the abuse, but as she neared the end of the aisle, she could sense the woman running from behind at full pelt, and she quickly sidestepped her, with the trolley corner catching her attacker in the pelvic area as she launched herself at Jane. The trolley had wedged against a metal pillar, creating an immovable object, and the corner of the handle might as well have been a sledgehammer swung into her lower abdomen.

Sharon cried out and tumbled to the floor in a mess of arms and legs. As she fell, her shoulders and head knocked into the shelving, and three or four bags of flour fell onto her, one of which split, covering her in a layer of fine white powder. Next came a tray of eggs.

She lay there dazed, and several customers began laughing, and even her friends couldn't resist chuckling at the comical sight. They had no clue that she had really hurt herself.

Jane stared at her open-mouthed and then too gave way to laughter. She reached forward instinctively to help her. 'I'm sorry, but you caught my trolley. It jammed against the beam. I didn't mean it, but what were you thinking of?'

'Fuck off; I've banged the side of my face on the bleeding shelf. You've done something to my stomach; it's torn inside. I can feel it. You have made one big mistake, bitch.' Tears were welling in the woman's eyes, borne from both pain and embarrassment. She was stunned by the collision, and pain seared through her hip as her adrenalin subsided. Her lower stomach was taut and griping with pain. It didn't feel right.

'I didn't do anything.' Jane remonstrated. 'I just moved out of the way. You were attacking me!'

One of the woman's friends tried to help Sharon up, but she was in too much pain, and the fight had been knocked out of her bones. The pain in her lower abdomen increased, and she began to groan. Sharon curled into a ball, pressing at her stomach all to no avail. She writhed on the floor as her friends exchanged quizzical glances.

'I feel sick. I need to get to a hospital.' Sharon said.

Jane took the opportunity to scurry away, grabbing a couple of items on the route to the till. Discretion was the better part of valour, there was nothing to be gained hanging around with that unsavoury group, and it was time to get out of the place. In any case, Daisy needed to be collected from school.

2

'Drink to me only with thine eyes, And I will pledge with mine; Or leave a kiss but in the cup. And I'll not look for wine.' – Ben Jonson.

The view from across the road was a good one. The two men had parked the car facing the betting shop and were only twenty paces away from the door. It seemed quiet in there – 'Squires Turf Accountant' the weathered sign declared. They had only seen three people go in. However, none had come out. The Bookmakers clientele tended to stay longer than a few minutes. Often, they would be in all day.

The front window was filthy and afforded access only to a cardboard effigy of horse and rider in black silhouette against a white background. Once inside, punters were protected from prying eyes and inquisitive spouses.

It was cramped inside the car with two big men rubbing shoulders both with each other and the door frames. The driver wound the window down by a couple of inches and lit a cigarette up, turning his head periodically to blow smoke out of the crack. The smell of tobacco smoke quickly invaded the interior.

Condensation on the windscreen obstructed their view a little, prompting the driver to start up the engine once more, fiddling with the choke to get the petrol flowing through. In turn, he ratcheted the blower on the heater up high. It also created a rattling sound from inside the vents.

The two men were Dougie Brown and his brother Lenny 'the bitch' Brown, the most feared men in Nottingham. People were terrified to have anything to do with them; afraid to be in their orbit or visible on their horizon. These were men to be avoided by the public at large.

However, in parts of the criminal fraternity, people clamoured to be a part of their gang. The badge and the shield that working for the Browns gave a criminal was worth a lot. It was a free pass, immunity from trouble anywhere they went. It gave them VIP status, and the young criminals would do anything, to be accepted as part of this untouchable and 'respected' crime family. The reality was, of course, they garnered fear which was somewhat different to respect. They are not the same thing but are often confused as such.

However, as with all such treaties, it was difficult to get out once in their area of influence. If you were part of the Browns crew, they were with you vicariously wherever you went, you were at their beck and call, but it gave you status and the freedom to take any liberty you wanted.

Lenny got his 'bitch' moniker when he was beating up a cop in the Golden Ball pub, which they had taken over as a sort of base for their nefarious activities from the early days. With each punch, Lenny had used the unlikely phrase 'bitch' at the helpless off-duty young cop who had inadvertently walked into the pub not knowing who was inside. The policeman had locked up one of the kids that hung around the edges of the Browns' little empire. He had been clocked as soon as he walked in. Lennie saw an opportunity for further notoriety and took it.

'Bitch!' Whack.

'Bitch!' Right hand.

'Bitch!' Left hand.

'Bitch!' A kick in the face.

Lenny was arrested and charged with GBH, but thirty people were prepared to testify that it was a case of mistaken identity, and it was an unknown gypsy who had attacked the cop, and Lenny had been heroic in pulling the man away, and that was where the confusion came as the cop regained consciousness. He should be given a medal, not a prison sentence. The naïve police chief eventually sent Lenny an apology for the arrest and a thank you letter under media pressure, which he kept in the toilet for a few years as a talking point. He was also paid £3,000 in an out of court settlement for false arrest. The cop had to retire from the force due to his injuries, spiralled into depression, and committed suicide the following year, which was a cause of great celebration for the Browns once the news was out. This heightened the brother's notoriety amongst the criminal fraternity even more, spreading up and down the country.

The Brown brothers had learned two important lessons over the years as their criminal gang took hold and began to grow. One was that it was far better to have *other* people commit your crimes for you unless it was personal, and secondly, if you threatened someone, you had to see the threat through to the bitter end. Without fail. If the Browns decreed, something would happen to someone. It happened. This was the enduring difference between them and the other members of the criminal fraternity trying to gain status. The Browns never made a threat they did not carry out. This gave them eminence and fear and ultimately was why they were now the crime kings of Nottingham.

However, they occasionally broke the first rule for one of two reasons; if the task at hand was that serious, they could not trust anyone but each other to do it, such as the occasional murder or torture, which they tried to limit. Or if there was a quick win to be had, with low risk and a chance to show they still had the kahunas to dirty their hands. This Betting Shop job was the latter. It was a crime that held limited risk to them as they knew no-one would testify against them for a variety of reasons.

They had been given a tip overnight that the bloke who owned the bookmakers was drunkenly bragging about the amount of money in his safe. Over twenty thousand pounds, he said. They knew the guy, Bernie Squires, a cockney chancer from down south, and he gave them due deference when he saw them. He would often patronise the boozers the Brown's frequented and make a big song and dance with them as if they were lifelong buddies. They weren't, but the Brown brothers enjoyed the ass-kissing.

'No-one's gonna kick off, Len, so don't get trigger happy.'

'You always say this, Dougie. The only time I will pull the trigger is if anyone plays the fucking hero. Then they can have it.'

'I will give 'em an early softener and blast the sawn-off as soon as we get in. To get their attention.'

'I know, Dougie, we've been through all of this. Are you losing your bottle, our kid?'

'Piss off, course not, but we are pro's Len; we need to be running the show the minute we step in there. Lots of noise and shouting the odds, yeah?'

'We will. In, out, shake it all about, leave with the lolly. You ready?'

'Yes, just give it another couple of minutes though, make sure the cops aren't mooching around.'

Len tutted and shook his head.

The Browns would have the princely sum of £20k in their grubby hands within the next five minutes if they played it right. Dougie had the sawn-off shotgun and Lennie had a pistol he had paradoxically bought from the bookmaker Bernie Squires a few years ago, in the Golden Ball public house. He had obtained the shooter from someone in the smoke he knew from way back.

Dougie had set an alibi with the snooker club, where you had to sign in to play, and so should the worst come to the worst, they were covered, but an arrest was unlikely. These men held much more sway than the police and the legal system because they had the ultimate sanction. They could take your life and would.

Dougie threw his cigarette end out of the crack in the window.

'Still ready, Len?'

'Still ready, Doug.'

The door of the bookmakers swung open.

'Everyone stay where you are and shut the fuck up. No one needs to get hurt!'

Dougie shouted out the command with a snarl and immediately fired the shotgun into the ceiling, causing screams and people ducking and crouching on the floor. The noise of a shotgun in an enclosed area is much greater than one might imagine, and it seemed to shake the entire shop. Debris fell from the ceiling as the ringing of the shotgun blast continued in the ears of all present, though the noise itself had left the room.

Bernie Squires, the bookmaker, came charging out from the back office swinging a baseball bat. The two men, indistinguishable under their woollen ski masks, watched the heavyweight cockney blunder towards them.

'Fuck you, you bastards!' he screamed, spittle exploding from his gums, his false teeth rattling as he bounded along.

He knew what was happening, and he was going to batter their heads in. He was old school; he did not take this shit lightly. That was until he saw two guns levelled in his face.

'Hold on, fella. You'll blow a gasket. I'm quite happy to take your knackers off if you don't cool it.'

'Don't press the button, Sally. Just do as they say.' Bernie said quickly, already out of breath. The young girl looked quizzically at him but did as she was told.

'Take me to the safe.'

Bernie sighed and trudged into the back office out of view, still breathing heavily. The crinkly vein on his balding head was throbbing and seemed in danger of popping. He had thought he recognised the voice, and they spoke in hushed tones in the back room.

'My turn, huh?' Bernie said crestfallen.

'Fraid so, Bernie. Don't worry, though; we won't be back; you can relax once you've paid up.'

'Can we negotiate?'

They heard a growl from the main betting shop area. 'Get the fucking cash, bitch. Get a move on.'

'There's your answer, Bernie. Not today.'

'No need to put a bloody hole in my ceiling, Dougie, fuck me, son.'

'It has to be done, Bernie, better a hole in your polystyrene tiles than in some fucker's head. Don't you reckon?'

'Depends on the head.'

'We are doing you a big favour here, Bernie. You can claim it back off the insurance.'

'Thanks a lot. Lucky me.' There was no little irony in the reply.

Bernie's head partially disappeared inside the safe, reappearing with three money bags which he handed reluctantly to Doug.

'It's all there. Twenty large, a nice tickle.'

'You won't be forgotten, Bernie. Add an extra few grand on the insurance calim, and everybody wins. Happy Days.'

'Happy Days. Yeah, sure.'

With that, the two returned to the shop. Bernie was dragging his feet. Resistance was futile.

The two gangsters sauntered towards the door. Dougie turned.

'Don't go pressing no buttons for a couple of minutes, yeah?'

Bernie nodded without saying anything. He was sweating profusely, and his legs were a little unsteady as he slowly followed the assailants out, pausing to lock the door behind them. Bernie leaned with his back against the door; his heart was pounding, and he was short of breath.

Young Sally shouted to him. 'Are you alright, Uncle Bernie?'

'Just give me a minute.' He panted and lowered his hands to his knees, leaning forward and gulping in air.

'Can I press the button now?'

'No, just hang on, Sally.'

The people in the bookmakers remained static for a few seconds as in stunned silence.

Sally was confused. Bernie mopped his forehead with a grey handkerchief.

'What just happened?' Sally asked.

'We just got robbed. That's what happened.'

*

Jane Cooper had been unnerved by the incident in the supermarket. What a crazy woman she was, and now she had seemingly hurt herself. Jane worried she might call the police and that she could get into trouble for it, but she hadn't done anything other than step nimbly to one side. The rest had been providence.

Jane tried to put it out of her mind and get her smiley face ready for Daisy. Daisy had been the best 'accident' that ever happened to her. Daisy's father Simon was in the army, and the letters had long since stopped. He was living in Germany. They were together for over a year, and they called their daughter after the way they met; Jane had been sitting on a bench in Titchfield Park, reading on a gloriously hot summer's day, and this young man approached her holding half a dozen daisies.

'I picked these for you. I don't know why. I just wanted to. You look so perfect.'

With hindsight, it might seem corny, but that was then, and this was now. It was a mutual separation which meant that she and little Daisy faced the world together but without Simon to complete the family group.

Jane joined the long line of Mum's grandparents and the occasional father, who shuffled towards the playground at the rear of the school in time for the bell. The darkening sky gave a somewhat depressing haze to the scenario turning colour to black and white.

Saint Mary's school at Bulwell was a Victorian building with a newer flat-roofed building adjacent, and the pupils moved between them depending on the need. The school grounds were next to Alderman Derbyshire Secondary School and across the road from the now-defunct Adelphi Cinema. Behind that was a hosiery factory, and so within 300 square yards, a child might occupy their entire existence on the planet. Junior school, senior school, across the road to the hosiery factory. One fed the other. The Post Office for pension collection and the cemetery were further away.

The curious nature of school pick-up was that parents usually stood in the same spot in the playground each day. Their own plot of land, of which they were quite protective. It was often a bleak scenario usually dictated by the weather, and today's grey rolling clouds hung a heavy ceiling over the tarmacadam. Despite this, Jane noticed something of a buzz in the air. Apparently, there was some scandal, but she wasn't aware of it, nor indeed that she was it.

'Eh up, Kaz.' Jane slipped into the schoolyard vernacular as she settled in her preferred spot next to the netball post.

'Eh up, Jane, all right?' Karen had the hood of her Parka coat pulled over her head, the faux fur trim animated by the sweeping wind. The hood overwhelmed her thin face and gaunt features.

'Yeah, fine, you?' Jane tried a brief smile.

'Alright, ducky. Have you heard the latest?' She was bursting to tell.

'No. What?'

'About Sharon Brown, it's all-round town.'

'Who's Sharon Brown?' The name sounded familiar.

'Dougie Browns Mrs, you know the Brown brothers.'

'Should I know who these people are, Kaz?'

'Yes, the gangsters, they live up on Highbury Vale, very bad men. Steer clear at all costs.'

'I think I've heard of them. I thought it was all exaggerated, personally.'

'No. It's all true. Someone has kicked the shit out of Sharon Brown in the Co-op supermarket today. Some woman gave her a right pasting. It's all over town.'

Jane felt a nervous feeling building in the pit of her stomach. This sounded all too familiar.

'Sorry?'

Karen continued. 'They will kill her when they find out who it is. I'm not even joking.'

'No, they won't kill her.' Jane laughed.

'Er. I think you'll find they will, Jane; I'm telling you these blokes are crazy, they kill for fun. Everyone is totally shit scared of them. I can't believe you've never heard on 'em.'

'I know who you mean now. Anyway, it's not true.'

'What's not true.'

'The rumour…I…she wasn't beaten up she fell over, that's all.'

'How do you know? Did you see it, Jane? Were you there?' Karen turned to the group of mothers. 'Eh, Jane was there when Shaz Brown got pasted in the Co-op.'

The group started to shuffle towards them.

Jane's face flushed red as all eyes fell upon her. 'I wasn't there. I mean, I was there, but nobody got beaten up. She just ran into my trolley; it was a misunderstanding.'

There was an audible gasp from those assembled. Karen's mouth dropped open. 'So, it was you what done it?'

'I didn't do anything, she started it, and when she had a go at me, she hurt herself. There was no fight or anything like that.'

'Oh, my freaking God! Jane, you're in the shit big time, mate. Rumour is she's damaged her ovaries and been told she can't have kids no more. She's fuming. She's in a right state.'

'It was an accident; she will see that, surely? Honestly, I didn't do anything.'

There was another audible gasp, louder than the first. 'So, it *was* you! Oh my God!'

Everyone moved a few steps backwards as if Jane suddenly had a contagious disease. Karen was stunned. 'You need to get away somewhere Jane, you are going to have your card marked. You are in real danger, mate. Seriously, think about little Daisy.'

Jane began to speak as the school bell sounded inside the building. 'Look, this has been blown…'

The woman next to her held up her palm. 'Don't talk to me; I don't want nowt to do wi it.'

They all began to move away amidst mutterings of 'me neither.' 'Don't get involved.' And the like. Even Karen moved away from the spot she had stood at for the last three years.

Suddenly the classroom doors burst open and out charged all the children, some running, others balancing various cards or artwork precariously. It was a welcome distraction, and as Jane squatted to embrace little Daisy, she couldn't help but feel somewhat concerned about what she had heard. Couldn't have children anymore? Surely it can't be true. That's awful.

'Hello, Mummy. I've made you a dolly from string.'

'Oh, thank you, Daisy. I love it. I really do.'

*

The CID office served as a report writing room, a call centre and sometimes a social club. If there was one thing that detectives liked to do, it was talk, and several of Stark's team were sat around the group of desks with rotund middle-aged detective constable Charlie Carter holding court.

There were three groups of desks around the spacious room, seven desks per cluster, the odd one out being at the head for the detective sergeant to sit at. The desks each had three stationary trays on them, a large blotter usually displaying an array of doodles and scribblings, as well as an assortment of personalised desk junk and mascots, family photographs, random paperwork, and tin ashtrays with various breweries emblazoned on them. These were overflowing with cigarette and cigar butts in the main.

Detective Sergeant Nobby Clarke was in DI Stark's office, so the DC's took the opportunity for a cuppa and a chat, as was their wont.

DC Stephanie Dawson, DC Ashley Stevens and Trainee Detective Steve Aston were chatting; a pall of smoke hanging in a layer above their heads, like their own personal weather system. They were winding up Steph, yet again. It was all good-natured ribaldry.

'Is it wedding bells with you and Nobby Clarke, then, Steph?' The debonair Ashley asked as he sipped at a mug of tea, his gold bracelet hanging loose as he did so.

Steph's' on-off relationship with her Detective Sergeant was a regular focal point for the gossip.

'Not yet, Ash, but you will be the first to know, don't worry. We've got you pencilled in as chief bridesmaid.'

The gang laughed. You had to do well to get one over Steph; she had been around detectives too long to take any truck from them. She could give as good as she got, and usually better.

Charlie had a twinkle in his eye as he lit up a cigarette. 'I'll say this for you, Steph.'

'Go on, what. Let's hear it.'

'Nothing, it's a compliment. You might be a constable now, but I always thought there was a sergeant deep inside you.'

She threw a cardboard coaster at him. 'You cheeky sod!'

'What have I said now?' Charlie was laughing along with the others.

As usual, the quiet Steve Aston tended to observe more than contribute to the banter. He still wasn't in the groove with the detective culture and felt at odds with his colleagues. Somewhat awkward. He allowed himself a wry grin as Ashly whooped at Charlie's joke.

Stephanie tried to bring Steve into the conversation. She was like that. 'Don't you start, young Steven, I can see you grinning; the quiet ones are the worst, believe you me.'

This immediately flushed Steve's cheeks, and he mumbled something indiscernible.

Charlie raised his hand, his face falling serious. 'Hold on, listen in. That's an alarm coming over someone's radio. Shush.'

Silence fell. There was the unmistakable double pip sound intermittently resonating over Ashley's radio on his desk. Then came the tinny voice:

'Control to all units, report of an armed robbery in progress at Bernie Squires Turf accountant, Annesley Road, Hucknall. Panda 3 are you responding?'

'Ten-Four, travelling.' Came the patrol officer's voice then quickly mirrored by another: *'Panda 2 travelling as back up, over.'*

'Ten-Four Panda 2. Panda 3 ETA? Control over.'

'One zero minutes. I'm travelling back from Eastwood, over.'

'I bet this is your robbery, Ash.' Charlie said.

'Sounds like it.'

It wasn't every day that an armed robbery in progress came through on alarm and the CID office at Nottingham emptied as soon as it came over the radio. Stark and Nobby crewed up, as did Ashley and Steph.

Young Steve Aston felt he might have drawn the short straw as veteran Charlie Carter limped and wheezed along the corridor behind him.

'Come on, Charlie.' Steve urged, as he was desperate to be involved in the action.

'Get the car started, Steve; It's in the backyard. I'll be there in a minute.' He threw the CID car keys at him and watched him disappear down the stairs.

'Ouch, ya bugger!' Charlie exclaimed as he flopped into the passenger seat of the Ford Escort. He instinctively rubbed his knee despite everyone knowing that the cause of the exclamation was his piles and had nothing to do with his knee at all.

'I'll ride, shotgun, young Steve.'

'Ha, ha, very funny.'

The car drew out the yard, but Steve had to slam on the brakes to avoid Ashley who screamed past him across the junction having got a CID car from the front of the station.

'No need to kill us, Steve. I'd like to get there in one piece.' Charlie said.

Steve manoeuvred the car and sped off behind Ashley, pumping the accelerator and throwing Charlie around, causing him to wince as he tried to rest on just the one buttock.

There was a slight lull as Steve tried to negotiate through traffic with only a horn as a warning instrument.

'All these drivers think you're a lunatic, Steve.' Charlie smiled at a driver on the nearside who was screaming expletives out of the window. Charlie waved. 'Yes, fuck you too.'

'It is an emergency, Charlie.'

'I know, don't mind me.'

'Eh Charlie…'

'What?'

'I've forgotten my truncheon. What are we supposed to do if they are still inside when we get there?'

Charlie shrugged. 'I dunno. Nick them, I suppose. What else are you gonna do? Give them a kiss?'

Steve smiled. 'I just wondered, that's all.'

'Your truncheon ain't going to help you, mate. You take a deep breath, walk through the doors, and deal with whatever is behind it. No messing about take the bastards down, just remember to duck.'

'Cheers! Thank you for your sage advice.'

'No problem, my pleasure. Up here on the left, Steve.'

Steve swung the car up the pavement and was disappointed to see Ashley's car already there, albeit with the doors left wide open.

Stark and Nobby were also inside. The offenders had long gone.

It quickly became apparent that this was Ashley's armed robbery information from this morning coming to fruition.

There was scant information to put out to other officers; not much of a description, and no vehicle had been spotted. Two men in dark clothing. Steve gave the control room a brief update, nonetheless. The main thing was that nobody had been injured during the robbery.

Control said that someone at Bernie Squires Turf Accountant had pressed the alarm button, and a member of the public had also telephoned in that they had seen two men go into the bookies with a shotgun. They had rung from a telephone kiosk on Annesley Road but didn't leave details. Strangely the panic button had not been pressed immediately that the men went in, so perhaps they mooched around a bit inside before pulling out their weapons? Maybe they didn't have a chance to press it? For whatever reason, there had been a delay of a few minutes between the phone call and the panic alarm.

Bernie Squires rested one hand on the counter and drew on a fat cigar with the other, his gold sovereign rings crowding his chubby fingers. He had regained his composure. Bernie was well known to the cops. Aside from being the only cockney in town, he had always been borderline criminal, but he seemed to have semi-retired in recent years. Rumour had it Bernie had moved north to

Nottingham after upsetting gangsters down the smoke for a reason that never emerged. He had certainly fallen on his feet with the bookmaker's business, and his 'cheeky chappy' persona appealed to the punters. Bernie frequented all the dodgy pubs in the area and was a known associate of many criminals on the patch.

'Mr Stark, for two pins, I would have banjo'd them with my bat, but I thought better of it.'

'Any idea who they were, Bernie?' Stark asked as he took in the layout of the seedy bookmakers and its yellowing nicotine-stained décor.

'No, not a clue. Out-of-towners, I reckon, gov. Irish accent, so no one local as far as I can tell. I know all the big hitters around here, and none of them would dare set foot in here to cause me grief. And certainly not do a blagging.'

Stark smiled. 'Of course not. So, tell us what happened, Bernie?'

'I was in the back office, so I didn't see it all, then all of a sudden, I heard someone f-ing and blinding, and then a huge bloody bang. I thought a bomb had gone off; the whole shop shook like a leaf. Anyway, I ran out with my baseball bat, and there they were, bold as bloody brass, tooled up 'an all they were. Shooters. Proper job.'

'Then what?' Nobby asked as he stood underneath the hole in the ceiling, peering up at it.

'When I saw the shooters, I thought better of it, so I just gave the cheeky little bastards the money. Twenty years ago, they would have been on their arse, shooters or no fucking shooters.'

'Looking at the size of the hole, I'm guessing it was a sawn-off shotgun.' Nobby offered; his days in the army as a Regimental Sergeant Major always helped in firearms matters.

'Yes, a stubby thing it was. They're the worst kind, though; you can't get out of the way of the blast.'

'How much did they get?' Stark asked.

'Thirty large.'

Stark winced. 'Ouch. Thirty grand? Seriously? What are you doing with that amount here, Bernie?'

'I know. I don't trust the banks, plus everyone knows your business when you deal with them. Like I say I don't trust no one. Anyway, it's like Fort Knox to get in that safe. I never thought anyone would have the balls to shit on my manor and do a blagging, Mr Stark. That's why I reckon they're from the smoke. They've got to be.'

'Irishmen from London. An interesting mix. Why choose here?'

Bernie shrugged. 'God knows.'

'Have you been talking? You haven't been shooting your mouth off, have you?' Stark asked.

'No chance. I ain't bleeding stupid.' Bernie averted his gaze momentarily.

'Even when you've had a few beers?'

'No, do me a favour, guv, I'm too long in the tooth for all that. Maybe they just fell lucky.'

Stark nodded, 'Maybe, Bernie. Maybe.'

Nobby seemed doubtful, but he blurted out his next question instead of keeping his powder dry. 'Are you insured, Bernie?'

'Thankfully, yes, but it will still cost me a fortune 'cos the rates will go up. So, I'm gonna get stung either way.'

'Do you get insurance every year, Bernie? Or is it a recent thing?' Nobby asked.

'Oh, here we go. No, I got insured fucking yesterday! It's all a big scam this is; I love holes in my ceiling, it adds to the décor, don't you think? Jesus! Just look around at these punters; they're all terrified. Do you think this is good for my business? No. I've always paid my dues for stuff like that. This is a kosha business; you're out of order, DS Clarke. You're bang out of order.'

'All right, Bernie. No need to get your knickers in a twist.' Nobby grinned.

'Check it out if you like; I've been covered for years, no claims either. God's own truth.'

'I believe you, Bernie. Carry on.' Stark said.

'So anyway, one of them took me to the safe and held me at gunpoint until I gave them the dosh. They were both masked up, so don't ask me what the hell they looked like. They had black ski mask things covering their mugs. Huh, mugs. Looks like I'm the only bleeding mug around here.'

Steve Aston and Charlie spoke to Mrs Eadie, an elderly punter, a regular at the bookies, who was shaking after the ordeal. She was chuffing on a cigarette which she chased with her lips once it was close enough to lock on. The filter was smudged with red lipstick.

'They said for everyone to get down on the floor, I think. They had a funny accent. Welsh, I think Bernie said.'

She looked across the room to Bernie and shouted to him. 'Was it Welsh, you said, Bernie?'

Bernie looked skywards. 'Jesus. She's daft as a brush.' He muttered before raising his voice. 'Irish, Mrs Eadie, they had Irish accents, remember?'

'Oh, that was it, Irish. They all sound the same to me. Anyway, I can't tell you anything more than that. I was just looking away all the time. I couldn't bear to look. You don't want it at my age; I'm seventy-four next birthday, you know.'

Stark and Nobby moved to the back of the betting shop for a conflab. Stark lit up a cigar, and Nobby had his roll-ups.

'What do you reckon, boss? Legit?' Nobby asked in hushed tones standing in front of his Inspector with his broad back masking the conversation from the others.

'Probably. It's all a bit too dramatic for Bernie. Staging a burglary would have been much easier. Plus, there is the person who rang in having seen offenders with a firearm and a bloody great shotgun blast in the ceiling.'

'True, boss. But this is Bernie Squires we're talking about.'

'He does seem a bit cagey, don't you think? I wonder why?'

'Who Bernie? That's him all over, though, isn't it? He couldn't lie straight in bed.' Nobby grinned.

Stark blew cigar smoke out as part of a sigh. 'He's probably working out how to make the best of it, maybe added a bit to the total for the insurance, but I doubt it's a set-up. Let's go through the motions, get forensics travelling, and see what they come up with.'

'Fair enough.'

'I think you're right to question it, Nobby; something feels a bit off. I just can't put my finger on what.'

'Treat it as legit and see what comes up.' Nobby said.

'Exactly. Hang on, is that one of those new CCTV camera thingymabobs in the corner above the till?'

3

'When you have no fear, the possibilities are endless.'

Jeffree Star.

While it was something of a luxury for a single Mum to have a telephone installed in the house, Jane had felt it a necessity with both her parents advancing in years and her father becoming quite frail and perhaps suffering the effects of dementia.

Little Daisy was lying on the floor, switching between her colouring book and the television set. She kept flicking her long brown hair over her shoulders and was talking to herself quietly as she used the felt-tip pens. Blue Peter was on, and it was enough of a distraction for Jane to telephone her mother to see how she was doing and to offload the awful incident in the supermarket. It had been niggling her since the conversation and unnerving reaction by the other mothers in the playground.

Jane ran her fingers over the coarse fabric of the armchair, which seemed to be fraying at the end of the armrests.

'274619.'

'Hi, Mum.'

'Hi? You've been watching too much television, we say hello here in England, or are you ringing from America?' She sounded a bit croaky.

'Ha, ha.'

'I'm sure you just say it for devilment, Jane.'

'I don't, Mum, I don't know where it came from. It's easier to say I suppose.'

'Yes, that extra syllable can be a strain.' She was always able to stick the verbal boot in for such a sweet woman. Years of practice, probably. Nobody would believe it if you met her, she was so polite and well-mannered, but there was a caustic side to her mum that Jane knew was a throwback to her childhood struggles during the war.

'Oh, Mum, you do make me laugh. I take it your cold is improved. Although you sound a bit croaky.'

'Yes, thank you, luvvy, it's about gone now. I couldn't shake the ruddy thing off. How are you?'

'What about Dad?' Jane asked.

'Pretty much the same, maybe…well, you know.'

'Is he there?'

'Yes.'

'In the living room?'

'Yes.'

'Okay. I know you can't speak if he is earwigging. Can I have a quick word with him, just to say hello?'

'Are you sure?'

'Yes, of course.'

A man's voice came on the phone; it came from a dry mouth. 'Hello?'

'Hi Dad, It's Jane. Jane, your daughter.'

He laughed. 'Aye, lass, I know that. I've not lost my marbles, you know.'

'Of course not. How are you keeping?'

'Alright, you know. Eh, can you see that mark on the wall near the cabinet?'

'I can't see it, Dad; I'm on the phone.'

'Oh, yes, of course. Anyway, how are you and how's the little one?'

'Daisy, you mean?'

'That's it, yes.'

'She's fine and sends her love.'

'Ah bless her. I'm going to my dad's later; I think we are. Are we, Mary?'

This was awkward as Jane knew his dad had been dead for a number of years. 'Oh, alright, then. Give him my love, won't you?'

'I will, aye.'

'How's the little one?'

'Daisy's fine, Dad, thanks.'

'You get in front of the telly this afternoon, Dad, and watch a nice film.'

'I will do, but I reckon to fall asleep every time.'

'You might stay awake this time, Dad.'

'I might, aye. I might do that. How's the little one doing? Bless her. Eh?'

'Jane, it's Mum.'

'Ah bless him, he's getting worse, isn't he? I will try to get to see you this week, I promise.'

'It would be lovely to see you, but I know you've got your work cut out, Jane. Don't fret about it, love. We're just glad to see you whenever you can call in; you know that.' She lowered her voice almost to a whisper. 'I'd come over to see you more often, but Dad gets so out of puff nowadays, and I have to watch him like a hawk.'

'It's fine, Mum. Daisy sends her love.'

Daisy looked up from her position on the carpet. 'Huh?' Jane waved away the querying expression.

'Ah bless her. Kisses from mamma.' Jane's Mum made kissing noises over the phone, making Jane smile.

'Mamma sends kisses, Daisy.' Jane directed the comment to her daughter, now engrossed in the edges of the unicorn she was colouring in.

'Huh?'

'Mamma sends kisses, Daisy.'

'Oh.' Daisy put her hand to her mouth and blew a kiss back.

'She's blown you a kiss, Mum.' Jane again fiddled with the fabric on the armchair. It was definitely wearing thin.

'Lovely, isn't she good. Anyway, you didn't answer my question, Jane.'

'What question?'

'How are *you*?'

'I'm fine, well sort of.'

'What do you mean sort of? What's the matter, love.'

'I had a weird thing happen. It wasn't my fault, but the long and short of it was that this crazy woman knocked into my shopping trolley and was then squaring up for a fight, causing a right scene. It was embarrassing.'

'You're joking? In the middle of the supermarket? Which one, the Co-op?'

'Yes, little Co-op on Highbury Vale. I'm not joking. She was rough, you know. One of them.'

'I know the sort. We've all met them. What did you do, Jane?'

'There wasn't much I could do, Mum. It ended up with her charging at me, and I dodged out the way, and she collided into my trolley.' Daisy glanced up at her mother, having heard something finally of interest.

'Oh, my goodness. So, she and the trolley went flying, then?'

'No, the trolley was wedged against one of those steel poles, so it was rock solid when she hit it. The trolley never moved an inch, but she did. She went flying and she knocked all the flour and bloody eggs all over her.' Jane was laughing as she thought about it.

'Ha! Serves her right then. Silly mare.'

'I know, but, Mum, I've since heard that she has really hurt herself and damaged her ovaries.'

'Oh dear, how sad, never mind.'

'Mum! Fancy you being like that.'

'What do you expect? You reap what you sow. Silly madam.'

'Yes, but, Mum, I've heard she is the wife of one of the big gangsters in Nottingham, and everyone is saying I'm in danger and they will come after me. What if it's true?'

'Pah! Gangster my backside!'

'No, he is. I've heard of him; Dougie Brown.'

'I've never heard of him. Just ignore it, Jane.'

'Do you think?'

'Yes, it's just gossip. A storm in a teacup. Wounded pride, by the sound of it. Just ignore them. Don't get involved. You're better than that.'

'I suppose so. It was just the reaction of all the Mum's in the playground: they were suddenly giving me a wide berth once they knew it was me.'

'Ignore it, Jane. It will all blow over.' don't get het up about it either.'

'I hope so. This is all I need.'

'Can I have a word with Daisy? Or is she playing nicely?'

'No, she will come to the phone.' Jane projected her voice over to Daisy. 'Come and have a word with Mamma.'

Daisy rolled her eyes skyward as Jane beckoned her urgently and silently as if to say, 'Get here!'

'Hi, Mamma!'

'What's high? The Sky?'

*

The man's skin was leathery and had an orange hue, perhaps due to smoking roll-ups since the age of ten some fifty-six years ago. The old man sat on a bench pitted with woodworm and innumerable cigarette burns. A notice board behind him bore various betting slips and tiny pens. The paper header on the board was curled and yellow and bore the legend 'Bernie Squires Turf Accountant.' The wooden floor was littered with scrunched up betting slips and fag-ends. The surface was gritty with dust from years of neglect. The smell of cordite still hung diminishing in the air, dissipating with the pall of cigarette smoke, which he added to, lighting a half cigarette with a trembling hand. The man was puffing and panting with the exertion of doing nothing but puffing and panting. In truth, he was a little shaken by the drama but was trying to be nonchalant.

'How are you, Frank?' Charlie asked, sitting down next to him, with Steve perching himself awkwardly on a stool that seemed too high for him.

'Ouch, ya bugger!' Charlie gasped as his backside met wood, causing a shot of agony. Steve was amazed that Charlie seemed to know everyone, and everyone seemed to know him. It came from living and working twenty years on the same patch.

'I'm alright, Charlie, lad. I've seen worse, down the pit.'

'I bet you have, Frank. I bet you have.' Charlie lit up a cigarette himself as he spoke. 'What's happened here, my friend?'

'I don't know. I had my glasses on so I couldn't see nowt.'

Charlie laughed. 'Okay. How does that work, then, Frank?'

'What do you mean? I had me readers, on, so I can't see nowt more than a dog's length away.'

'A dog's length? What's that, a new unit of measurement? It used to be feet and inches. I blame the bloody French.'

'Aye.' He shrugged out a laugh that turned into a cough and a rake of phlegm.

'Surely you could make something out, Frank?'

'All I know is that I could hear a bloke shouting and then a bloody great bang. I about near shit me pants, lad. I'll tell you.'

Charlie laughed again, as did Steve. The old-timer's forthrightness was quite comical.

'What was the man shouting?'

'I don't know, I had my hearing aid turned down.'

'What? Why?' Charlie looked puzzled.

'I was going through the form for the horses, you know, and you can't hear yourself bloody think in here, so sometimes I turn it down a bit or off altogether.'

'When did you turn it up?' Charlie asked, casting a glance at Steve.

'Eh?'

Charlie laughed again. 'When did you turn your hearing aid up because you can hear alright now, Frank.'

Frank paused a moment. 'Aye, well, I turned it up after all the kafuffle, I might be deaf, but I'm not daft.'

'I'll give you that. You certainly aren't daft, Frank.' Charlie knew when someone was absenting themselves, and Frank was heavily into the throes of just that. Charlie watched Nobby and Stark follow Bernie into the back office out of sight from the main betting shop area.

Stark and Nobby sat in the low-slung seats in the office, but Bernie paced around, clearly on edge. His protruding belly forged a path between a pair of red braces, a striped shirt and a red bow tie. It was clear to DS Nobby Clarke that Bernie was nervy.

'Definitely from down south.' Bernie muttered aloud.

'Why down south, Bernie?' Nobby asked.

'It could be anywhere, I suppose. I'm just saying they ain't from around here.'

'How can you be so certain?'

'I know everyone capable of doing a blagging around here. I would have known them.'

'And did you?' Stark asked.

'Course not. Come off it, guv, you know me better than that. Do you think I'd be standing here talking to you if I knew who had come in to wreck my business that I've built up over all these years?'

'Perhaps. Depends who it was.'

The room fell quiet with the distracted Bernie pacing around and chuffing on a cigarette.

Stark seemed thoughtful. There was something in what Bernie was saying, and he tended to agree with him. 'You're right though, Bernie, there aren't many around here that have access to firearms and who would have the balls to do an armed robbery, not least an armed robbery at yours? Everyone knows you have connections, Bernie. There are plenty of softer targets. Have you upset anyone lately?'

'Lots, but nobody who would do this, straight up.'

'There can't be many local candidates.' Stark lit up one of his thin cigars.

'Exactly, that's what I keep saying to you. It ain't anyone local.' Bernie finally slumped into the worn leather chair behind his desk.

'Unless it was somebody local who doesn't give a shit about Bernie Squires.' Stark said.

'What do you mean by that? Like who?'

'Well, there are two people I can think of that qualifies for the description you have kindly given.'

'What? What description? I ain't told you sod all.'

'But you have, Bernie. You've helped us narrow it down perfectly.' The Inspector grinned.

'No, I haven't.'

'Yes, you have.'

'No, I haven't.'

Stark laughed. 'Bernie, I think you are spot on, and maybe they are from out of town, but if they are not, there are only two people that qualify. In my opinion, anyway.'

'Oh yeah, like who?'

'The Brown brothers.'

'That's a point, boss. Good call. They wouldn't give two hoots about our friendly neighbourhood bookmaker.' Nobby said as if flashed with inspiration by his Inspector's observation.

'Fuck off. I would know, wouldn't I? I know the Brown brothers. I'm telling you it ain't them. Don't start spreading rumours like that. It's dangerous talk; people can get hurt spreading rumours like that. The only "brothers" that might have done this are those black fuckers, like Winston Kelly and his lot.'

'So now you think it is a pair of black Irishmen?' Stark raised his eyebrows.

'You are treading on dangerous ground here, Mr Stark.' Bernie padded at his forehead with his handkerchief once more.

'You aren't threatening me, are you, Bernie? Because I get offended ever so easily.' Stark said.

Bernie gave an audible sigh. He was getting himself in a right pickle. 'No, I didn't mean it like that, you know what I meant. If the Browns think that I've fingered them for a blagging, I'm dead meat, so I would be grateful if you didn't go around talking about stuff that is both dodgy and dangerous. It's bang out of order.'

Stark and Nobby laughed. They were enjoying Bernie squirming for once.

'Was it the Browns, Bernie?' Stark asked outright.

'Don't be daft; I've told you I would have known.'

'Even with them wearing a mask?'

'I would know their voice anywhere, and like I said, they had an accent. The Browns don't have an accent, only local.'

'A Welsh accent?' Nobby asked provocatively.

'Yes.'

'I thought you said it was Irish?'

'For Christ's sake, you are confusing me. I did. I mean, it was, but you're confusing me with all this nonsense about the Browns and old Mrs Eadie spouting on about them being Welsh. I know the difference between a Welshman and an Irishman. It's doing my head in all of this. I'm trying to run a business here!'

Nobby was grinning. 'A Welshman, an Irishman and a black man walk into a bookmakers…'

'Very funny.'

'Alright, Bernie. I've got the general picture. I was glad to see that you have a CCTV camera fitted.' Stark said.

Bernie's mouth flopped open, but nothing came out of it until…'Shit!'

'Sorry? It's good news, Bernie. We will have footage of the whole thing.' Stark grinned.

'That's just a gimmick, boss. I don't even know how it works. I reckon it's bust in any case. I'll let you know if there's owt on it.'

Stark pulled himself awkwardly out of the low-slung chair and walked over to the electronic box and screen in the corner behind where Bernie sat.

'It's never seen a duster; I will grant you that. It is working, though, Bernie.'

Bernie winced. 'Great. Fucking brilliant.'

Stark poked his head around the door into the main shop area. 'Steve, come here and sort this CCTV video thing out, will you? If I do it, I will probably delete everything.'

'Sure thing, sir.'

Steve hurried over to the tape machine with all eyes on him. He pressed the 'stop' button and then 'eject.' 'There you go.'

'Oh. That was easy.'

'It's just a video, sir. Nothing complicated.'

'I'm starting to think none of this is as complicated as it might seem.' He shot a glance at Bernie, who looked away. 'Get it seized, Steve. The tape is the first exhibit.'

Charlie appeared in the door frame. 'Scenes of Crime have arrived, boss.'

'Excellent.'

Stark and Nobby walked outside to the white SOCO van. It was getting dark, and there were spits of rain in the air.

'What do you reckon, boss?' Nobby asked. 'Bernie's about to have a heart attack when you mention the Brown brothers.'

'I reckon it's the Browns, and they've put the frighteners on him. Who else could it be? Bernie's more or less told us himself.'

'It could be someone from out of town.'

'It could be. I'm not feeling it, though. Unless Bernie has upset someone down the smoke, which, granted, is more than possible. Let's keep an open mind, but it smells of Brown to me.'

'You can say that again, boss.'

*

DC Steph Dawson was chatting with Sally, the girl behind the till. Steph was aware that the girl kept shooting glances towards Nobby Clarke. Steph was oblivious that Sally and Nobby Clarke had met up for dinner during a murder enquiry during one of their 'off' periods in the relationship. There was a rumour that Nobby had 'done the business' with Sally, but he merely said, 'a gentlemen never tells.' Nobby had been playing it cool since arriving at the bookies, even though he could feel Sally's stare following him around the place.

'When did you press the panic alarm, Sally?' Steph asked, pen and jotter poised.

'I think it was when they left.'

'Not, when they came in then?'

'No. I er, was too frightened. They told us all to stand still, and I was a few feet away from it, so it made it difficult.'

Nobby left Stark to walk over to the two ladies of different generations but equally attractive in their own right. Nobby had a muscular frame, paisan features and looked as hard as nails, frankly. This was mainly because he was. Despite being in his forties, he was a force to be reckoned with and the type of person that causes the pianist to stop playing when entering a saloon bar in the wild west.

'How's it going, Steph? Hi Sally.' Nobby's deep voice tingled through both ladies, and both were well aware of his prowess and particular points of appeal.

'Okay, we were just discussing…' Steph began to reply but was interrupted by the young girl in her early twenties.

'Hi, Nobby. How are you?' Sally tilted her head, and there was much fluttering of eyelashes. She was wearing a tight-fitting jumper and began tucking it in at the waist of her skirt, sucking her stomach in and chest out, a display that was not lost on DS Clarke.

'I'm good, thanks. You're looking well.'

'Thanks. You've been a stranger lately.'

Nobby smiled. 'Busy boy, Sally.' He was aware of the pursed lips of Steph and a stare that, if met, would need welding goggles to avoid damage to the retina.

Steph was starting to click that something was going on here. 'Sorry, do you two know each other?'

'You could say that.' Sally giggled.

'Okay, is there something I should know?' Steph put her hands on her hips.

The smile on Nobby's face dropped. 'DC Dawson, is there any new information with regard to the robbery that we should know about?' He quickly switched the conversation to a more matter of fact, official tone.

'Not really, Sergeant Clarke. Not to do with the robbery anyway.'

'Okay. Well, let's have a catch up later.'

'Oh, we will, Sergeant. We will. I have some additional questions for the very young and attractive Sally. We can then have a very detailed debrief. Just you and me.'

Sally faked the sincerity. 'Ah, that's nice of you to say I'm attractive. It's sweet when older women give compliments to us younger ones. It's lovely, isn't it, Nobby?'

Nobby's expression looked as though he had mistaken a lemon curd sandwich for mustard. He muttered. 'Shit.' To himself but was saved by his Detective Inspector.

'Hey, Nobby. Come here a minute.' Stark beckoned him over.

Nobby turned on his heels and felt Steph jab the pen in his arm as he did. He didn't respond but rubbed his arm as he swaggered back toward his DI.

'What's up, boss?'

'We are going for a little drinky poo.'

'Let me guess. The Golden Ball.'

'Ten out of ten.'

It was only a fifteen-minute drive, and the pub's car park showed little sign of life as Stark swung his Vauxhall Cavalier into it, popping some gravel as he did. Late afternoons were quiet ahead of the evening crowd.

'No aggro, Nobby, unless it becomes unavoidable. I just want to shake the bag up and see if the Browns are in, splashing the cash, celebrating or what the general feeling is, okay.'

'Sure.'

The car park lied. There were a good fifteen to twenty people inside. Many were youths in their late teens and early twenties; some dressed in ghastly 'shell suits,' garish shiny tracksuits, and a couple sported neck chains with Volkswagen mascots hanging from them. It was a fad created by the emerging rap group Run DMC, and now every Volkswagen car in Christendom was missing their insignia because of it.

True to form, as soon as the besuited, middle-aged men entered, the raucous laughter and shouts stuttered to complete silence. The air turned to ice.

It was quite a large bar area that arced from end to end. It had a fusty smell of stale ale and cigarette smoke. A hint of cannabis also tickled the nostrils. It would be called 'Dire if you could bottle it as a perfume.'

Stark was at the bar and Nobby a couple of feet behind him. He could see both Lenny and Dougie Brown sitting in the corner on the curve of an upholstered seat that hugged the contours of the wall.

The youths parted to give a view between Nobby and the Browns. You could cut the atmosphere with a knife. Two young skinny, spotty faced youths came up towards Nobby, seemingly trying to sprout muscles, judging by the way they splayed their arms out from the side of their bodies. They oozed a somewhat misplaced confidence, clearly feeling they were untouchable in the presence of their heroes. One of the youths started to 'oink, oink.'

Nobby gave him a sideways look. 'Aren't you late for Maths? The bell must have gone by now, kid.'

The youth flushed slightly and sucked in saliva through his teeth. It was something he must have been practising in his bathroom mirror. Nobby was tempted, but he had promised his DI he would behave.

'Two pints of bitter, please.' Stark smiled.

The old guy behind the bar hesitated and looked towards the corner where the Browns held sway. This was their pub in all but name.

Dougie nodded his consent to the barman and stood up slowly. He approached the two detectives. He ignored Nobby and stood at the side of Detective Inspector Stark.

Dougie was about the same height, slightly broader and stretching his Fred Perry T-shirt a little too much. A thick gold chain and expensive watch adorned the gangster.

Nobby tensed and formed a fist. He would take the guys head off his shoulders if he made a move.

Dougie slid sideways, a little too close to Starks personal space. 'I don't think I've had the pleasure. I thought I knew all the Feds around these parts.' He put out his hand. Stark hesitated slightly but met the offer with a firm handshake; he could play that game. That's fine by him.

'Detective Inspector Dave Stark and this is Detective Sergeant Clarke.'

Dougie nodded over at the man-mountain. Nobby appeared insouciant. Solid and immoveable.

'Dougie Brown.'

'I know who you are, Dougie.' Stark said.

'So, you're the famous DI Stark, are you? I wondered when our paths would cross.'

Stark grinned. 'Today's the day, Doug.'

'Today's the day. Lucky me.'

'Yes, it's your lucky day by the sounds of it.'

'I'm surprised to see you come in here, Inspector. You've got some balls ain't ya? This pub's got a bad reputation, you know.'

'All the more reason for us to come in then, Dougie, don't you think?'

Dougie winced slightly.

'Let me get you, gentlemen, a drink.' Dougie took out a wad of cash nearly three inches thick and thumbed off a ten-pound note to the bartender.

'£1.72 please, Doug.'

'Keep the change.'

'Thanks, Dougie.'

'Looking a bit flush today, I see. That for my benefit, is it?' Stark said.

'Not at all, we do okay. Anyway, we had a bit of luck at the bookies, didn't we, Len?'

Len shook his head. 'Dougie!'

'Relax, Len. These cowboys don't mean us no harm, do you?'

Stark turned and faced him head-on. 'That all depends on whether you've been naughty boys, Dougie.'

'It's not a crime to get lucky at the bookies. Is it now?'

'It could be. Are you a betting man, Dougie?'

'Always.'

'I like a flutter occasionally. Funnily enough, my instincts, my hunches are always right. It looks like it's the case here too.'

'Hunches don't mean too much, though, do they, Inspector. I mean. They're nice and all that, but they don't count for much. Not in my experience anyway.'

'I only have to be lucky once, Doug. You have to be lucky every time, my friend.'

'That is true. Very…erm, what's the word?'

'Astute.' Stark said, shrugging out a laugh.

'That's it. Astute. Me and my brother are big supporters of the law. We like to look after the boys in blue, don't we, Len? Always very accommodating to the right sort of detective, especially a Detective Inspector. A very useful companion for us. I am a very generous friend. Mr Stark.'

'Don't waste your breath, Dougie.'

'Well, it's always there. I'm always looking for new friends.'

While this verbal fencing was taking place, Stark was in two minds. Not in the sense that he was uncertain, but he had developed the ability to respond on the surface while hosting a myriad of thoughts in the back of his brain. In this instance, he was simultaneously considering his options. Should they arrest Dougie and Len? They potentially had cash from the bookmakers blagging. What if the notes had Sally's fingerprints on them to show their origin? It was a bit thin. What about the discharge of the shotgun? One of the brother's clothes would have cordite traces on them or their hands. But they weren't dressed in black as described by the witness ringing in. They must have changed. It made sense. What grounds were there to arrest? It would all be on a wing and a prayer, and with the Brown brothers, they needed more than that. It was difficult because, with an armed robbery of cash only, there is little to attach them to the scene or show the origin of the notes. Maybe they still had the shotgun in their car? What car? Which was there's? Did they come in a car? There was nothing to be gained by arresting them without sufficient evidence and then getting refused at the charging desk. That would be a loss of face. It would piss them off, though.

While Stark was rapidly assessing all these options and questions in his mind, his Detective Sergeant remained in clearer waters, merely considering the best order of persons that he would punch if they started to get too leary.

There was a momentary lull as Stark passed Nobby his pint of beer, and he and his DS took a gulp. Aware that all eyes were on them.

Dougie clicked his fingers at one of the young men and gestured for him to bring his drink over. The lad jumped to it, double-quick and gave it to Dougie with an extended arm and a sort of half-bow.

'I hear there's been a bit of noise down at Bernie Squire's shithole.' Dougie said.

'Is that right?'

'You tell me.'

'Come off it, Dougie. You know everything that happens on this patch, and nobody would do Bernie without your say so. We both know that.'

'I think you mistake me for someone else, Mr Stark. What people do is their own business. Nothing to do with me.'

'Don't be modest, Dougie, you and Len run the show around here and no one in their right mind shits on your doorstep unless you sanction it first.'

'Nah. That's telly stuff. It ain't real life.'

'Oh, well, thanks for educating me on that. Fancy me being wrong all these years.'

'Fancy.'

'Fancy.'

Stark took another drink of his beer.

'Most cops see this pub as a no-go area, Mr Stark. You know, a dangerous place to be caught with your pants down.'

One of the youths stood in the doorway, blocking the exit. His eyes were wide. To Nobby's estimation, he was agitated, probably on drugs – twitchy and dilated pupils. He looked ready to kick off, and Nobby shifted the order in his list of people to batter. He was flexible like that.

'A no-go area? Really? I must have missed that memo. And you will be glad to hear, Douglas, that I wear both belt and braces, so my pants are really secure. Lucky me, huh.'

Dougie laughed. 'Yeah. Lucky you. Lucky I'm in a good mood.'

Stark raised his hand to his mouth in a fake yawn.

The two men met each other's stare, and Dougie was surprised at the brass neck of this detective to walk into the middle of his empire without batting an eyelid. He must have a death wish.

The telephone rang at the end of the counter, and the barman answered it in hushed tones.

'Dougie! It's for you. It's Sharon. She sounds upset.'

Dougie took the call, and Nobby and Stark settled at the bar. Nobby was trying to hear the conversation.

'What!'

'The supermarket? You're shitting me!'

'Are you sure that's what the doctor said?'

'Who? I want to know who it is!'

Dougie glanced over at the detectives. 'Stay there. I'm coming home.'

Whatever the news was, he seemed rattled, and the receiver slid from the cradle as he put it down, and in temper, he pushed it off the bar and left it dangling down.

'Len, come on. We've got to go.'

'Why?'

'Just, come on, bro.'

The two brothers, complete with entourage, hurried out the bar. Stark spoke as Dougie passed by.

'See you again soon, Doug.'

He received no reply.

It fell very quiet after the gang had left.

'That's better. Some peace and quiet.' Nobby began to relax at last.

'Something's up at the Brown household, Nobby, by the sounds of it.'

'Yeah, I couldn't quite hear what was going on, but you're right. Something is definitely up. Mind you, these low-life fuckers shift from one crisis to another; they thrive on it.'

'Just another day, Nobby. Anyway, we've got work to do. Drink up.'

'Bloody hell, I was just getting settled.'

Stark threw two-pound notes onto the bar.

'What's that for?' The barman asked.

'For the two pints.'

'Yeah, but, Dougie...'

Stark shouted over his shoulder as they left. 'Keep the change.'

4

'We're born alone, we live alone, we die alone. Only through our love and friendship can we create the illusion for the moment that we're not alone.'

Orson Welles.

DC Cynthia Walker was annoyed she had missed out on the action and had to belatedly rally and get up to the scene of the armed robbery to help out. Cynthia was a 'half caste' young woman, as was the vernacular of the day, and she was relatively new to Stark's team. She was the only mixed-race detective in Nottingham CID, which came as no surprise to her as there had only been two children of colour in her entire Secondary School.

Cynthia had made a promising start in Stark's team, and she was well thought of. She had a feline grace and a maturity beyond her years. She also had a crush on her much older Detective Inspector, one David Stark.

It was typical that there was an armed robbery on the one day she had a dental appointment. She had attended several such raids as a patrol officer but never as a detective, where your role was to find out who had done the damned thing. As a uniformed officer, first at the scene, it was all about preservation, obtaining details, and waiting for CID to take it over. On this occasion, she *was* the CID, and it felt good. This was the business end of serious crime, and she couldn't get enough of it.

In the absence of Stark and Nobby, who had disappeared off to the Golden Ball pub, Charlie had asked her to team up with Steve Aston and 'knock on a few doors.'

Being on the edge of town, Bernie Squires Turf Accountant was surrounded by several ad-hoc houses which, over the decades, had melded to become known as Annesley Road Estate.

It was something of a disappointment to Cynthia as it was the least glamorous aspect of the investigation and something uniform could have done. Still, it needed doing and she approached it with cheery optimism. They started farthest away from the bookmakers and worked their way down the street, but the enthusiasm was waning somewhat by house number fifteen. The Autumn air was turning cooler, and Cynthia had not put her overcoat on, so she was starting to feel the cold. The only saving grace from the tedium, was the eclectic nature of those answering the doors, everyone different and everyone eliciting some conversation point between the two detectives. 'Weirdo.' 'Fit as a butcher's dog.' 'Daft as a brush.' 'Thick as pig shit.' That sort of thing.

The next house the two embryonic detectives approached was somewhat unkempt with dirty windows and even dirtier net curtains. A battered old van was on the weed-ridden drive. It had one wheel entirely removed.

'This is it, Steve. We've found it.'

'Found what?'

'The hub, this is the hub of all activity.' She pointed at the removed wheel.

He groaned. 'Bloody hell, Cynthia, you've spent too much time with Charlie Carter, coming out with lame jokes like that.'

'Just getting through the day, Steve. Only a few more to do.'

'Thank God.'

TDC Aston knocked on the door using a key from the bunch he had been nursing all along. Keys worked much better than fist and didn't hurt his freezing knuckles so much. The two fledgeling detectives turned to face the street as they awaited an answer.

The door swung open. A man in his thirties, in a white vest and worn-out slippers, presented himself and his potbelly. 'I've told your lot before I don't believe in that shit.'

Steve held up his open wallet and produced his warrant card. 'CID.'

'Oh, I thought you was them Jesus folks. I get sick of 'em.'

'Jehovah's witnesses.'

'That's em.'

'No, we are the police Mr?'

'Cranshaw. Wayne Cranshaw.'

'Mr Cranshaw, we are investigating an incident just down the road at Bernie Squires bookmakers, do you know it?'

'Oh aye. What's gone off?'

'I can't say just now, but we wondered if you had seen anything unusual in the last few hours.'

'Like what?' Wayne sniffed up a load of phlegm and, hoiking it from the back of the throat, dispatched it on the grass as a spit.

Steve continued undeterred. 'Anyone hanging around, unusual cars, that sort of thing.'

'No. I've been out on the drive sorting the motor but not seen owt, duck. I've just come in for a cuppa and to get the chill out of my bones. I would have seen if owt had gone off.'

'Okay, thanks.' Steve began to turn away.

'I would say ask Dougie Brown, but he ain't going to help you guys now, is he?'

'Sorry?' Cynthia asked.

'Dougie Brown, you must know the Brown brothers. He would be a dead cert; he would have seen something.'

'I'm not with you?'

'I haven't seen nowt, but Dougie Brown might, cos I saw him and his brother hanging around the bookies earlier on. They were a lot closer to it than me so they would be your best bet, so to speak.'

'You saw Dougie and Lenny Brown hanging around Bernie Squires bookies earlier on?'

'Yes. You could ask them if they've seen anything, but I can't see them wanting to help. They were much closer to it than me. Sorry, I can't help you any more than that but try them. Good luck, you're gonna need it with that pair. Cheers, then.'

As he was closing the door, Cynthia put her hand out to stop it.

'Hold on, Mr Cranshaw. How certain are you, it was Dougie Brown?'

'Hundred percent. Why? They aren't going to tell you now. I doubt they've seen anything. Same as me. It was quiet.'

'What were they wearing, can you remember?' She was inexperienced, and adding the 'can you remember' question gave him a get out.

'Oh, Christ. I don't know. I kept me head down. I only know them from the Golden Ball, I don't know them to speak to. I steer clear to be honest. Doesn't everyone?'

'We need to get a statement from you. Can we come in?' Cynthia asked.

'A statement? I haven't seen nowt.'

'Yes, you have, you've seen the Brown brothers.'

'Here, hang on a minute, ducky. I don't mean to be rude, but if you think I am going to make a statement about seeing the Browns, you've got another thing coming, I'm afraid. You can't ask me to do that. They weren't doing anything, and I'm not even sure it was them, thinking about it.'

'You said you were a hundred percent sure.'

'No, thinking about it. It wasn't them. Sorry.'

'Mr Cranshaw.'

'Sorry, duck. It wasn't them.' He closed the door.

Cynthia and Steve looked at each other. 'Now what?' Steve asked.

'Now what, nothing. We can't force the bloke.' They sauntered down the drive.

'What will Stark say?' Cynthia asked.

'We just tell him the truth and see what he wants us to do.'

'Come back, probably. He will want a statement. He's not going to give one, though, is he?'

'You can't force them. He must know that.'

'At least it's good intelligence, Steve. It might not be evidence, but it's something; it's a good indicator. It puts the Browns at the scene and helps steer the enquiry.'

'You've sold it to me, Cynthia. Let's hope Mr Stark sees it that way.'

*

Dougie and Len Brown had access to a lot of money. Actually, they did not physically possess a huge amount, maybe a few thousand hidden in various places, but they had constant access to money as they would go and take it off someone whenever they needed some. They didn't keep it in a bank as they knew it was traceable, so if they were down to their last ten grand or so, they would do another job, or better still get one of the dispensable members of their gang to do it and take their percentage. Most of the time, in their day-to-day lives, they never paid for anything – it was always 'on the house, lads.'

There was big money to be made in illegal drugs, but they didn't like dealing in drugs wholesale too much, as there were dedicated police units fixated on it, and it was a big bowl of porridge if you got caught. They knew that the police had resources, drug squads, to follow you and tap your phone calls if you were a major drug dealer. They didn't want to give the old bill an excuse to listen in on their phone calls at home or from the pub. Anything dodgy they used a telephone kiosk, in any case, but things can get said, and suddenly it is all coming on top.

The Browns had protection money coming in at a fair old rate from many businesses in the town and surrounding area. They would only charge thirty pounds a week, and things were comfortable with the scores of businesses paying up. They rarely had to burn anywhere down or at least get one of their gang to do so. Violence and cash were the jewels in the criminal crown. Sharon didn't need too much as she had her dole money and various benefits to pay her bills. Life was good.

Both brothers had modest abodes—council houses. Len was a few doors down on the same street, Brooklyn Road; their contacts on the council had arranged that for them. Other than their clothing and a bit of flash jewellery, you would think they were broke. Cars didn't interest them. This was because they did not feel the need for status symbols; they were unnecessary; their status was power and so-called 'respect.' They just had a pool of cars to use, usually stolen and churned over after a few weeks. Stealing high-rate cars was easy for their minions to do. They were careful to go out of the county to steal cars. All they had to do was block the owners drive with their rubbish bin as they returned from work wait for them to jump out to move the obstruction. Hop in the driver's seat and away. No need for messy scaffold poles, or parcel straps or coat hangers. They would choose duplicate registration plates from out of town, used by the same make of car but difficult for the cops to check anything out if you told them, it was a recent purchase. Selling them on could make five or ten grand a pop. Sometimes more. So by selling one of the pool cars every week or two, the protection money, the odd blagging, and the twenty percent tax from their gang members who were burglars and criminals, they were earning several thousand pounds a week. It was really more money than they could spend and was sometimes an encumbrance.

All of this criminal lifestyle was fine, but occasionally another lion would walk onto the savanna, and they would have to flex their muscles. This was a pain, but it had to be done. It literally went with the territory. Their ruthless reputation was everything. Without fear, they could not operate much above the status of petty criminals. The fear was their currency, and it had a high exchange rate. Fortunately for them, the violence came naturally to the Browns, and over the years, they had become desensitised to it, and their almost psychotic rages were legendary and vicious. Some of the punishments they meted out were practically medieval in their callousness and creativity.

The one that seemed to make the most impact was when they had a gang member 'disrespect' them by not declaring the crimes they had been doing and not stumping up their dues. The young lad was only in his early twenties, but he was taken to the woods late at night and hanged from a tree. He was forced to tie his own knot to keep the cops at bay and write his own suicide note, which would be dictated to him. Usually, the best murders were faked suicides. The notoriety the killing got was borne out of the disproportionate nature, the overkill, the exaggerated response to some slight. The sentence did not fit the crime, but that was the point they wanted to get over. The Browns must be feared more than any other entity or official authority such as the police.

They seemed untouchable, and they had been at it for years.

Dougie had been annoyed by Stark entering his domain and not 'respecting him.' His normal response would have been violent, but he had to bottle it up on this rare occasion. The mercury in his veins was ready to pop.

As he drove, he was grimacing with rage. He was muttering and chuntering. He hated to lose face, and that Stark character was taking the piss. His knuckles were tight around the steering wheel, and he swore and screamed at anything in his way.

His face got redder and redder as he threw the car around corners. Len knew better than to say anything. He knew his brother, and he knew when he was about to explode. The car was like a coke can being shaken from pillar to post, ready to blast Dougie Brown out of it. Dougie rode the car right up over the kerb and at an angle on the front lawn of his house. By this time, he was volcanic.

Dougie ran up the concrete steps to his house, two at a time, and burst in the door, with Len and three of the lads following on reluctantly.

'What the fuck's gone on? Sharon?' He declared immediately upon entering his domain. His tone was nasty, judgemental.

'She's in here.' Her friend Trixie called to Dougie.

Trixie was heavily built, wore figure-hugging jogging bottoms, and had greasy hair styled in bunches. She inexplicably sported a crude tattoo of Popeye on her forearm. A childhood favourite, perhaps? The sweet name Trixie fitted the cute little baby of twenty-six years ago, but not the creature she had grown into.

As Doug entered the living room, he saw his wife, Sharon, sitting on the armchair, resting her chin on her hand and staring out the window. She had been crying.

Dougie walked up to Sharon, his face contorted with rage. He slapped her across the head. She was ready and ducked, managing to limit the pain of the blow, but only marginally.

'Ow!'

He struck her again. 'What you been doing! You fucking twat!' He rained further blows on her, and she squealed, covering her head. These were now full-on punches, most of which she thankfully dodged with the skill of a professional boxer or, as in her case, the skill of a regularly abused wife.

'Dougie!' Len grabbed at his arm, and Dougie shrugged it off aggressively.

'Don't get involved, Len.' Dougie growled.

'Mate. She's had enough. What's gone off?'

Dougie leaned into Sharon and put his face into hers. 'That's what I want to know.'

'Let me tell you then.' Sharon said, sobbing. 'Stop it, Doug. It wasn't my fault.'

Dougie was agitated and breathing heavily. Violence was always the go-to place when things annoyed him, and the coppers in the pub had riled him and now this.

'Right, everyone out! Not you, Len. All of you in the kitchen and shut the fucking door behind you!'

Trixie was biting her fingernails. 'Dougie, can I just...'

She didn't finish the sentence before Dougie grabbed her by one of her bunches towards the kitchen. He stopped at the door frame to bang her face into the frame. Punctuating his speech with each blow.

'Don't you dare, question me, you fat piece of shit!'

Blood was gushing from Trixie's nose, and she had to swallow blood to get the words out. 'Sorry, Doug.'

He threw her into the kitchen, and she stumbled to the floor, sobbing. She was hurriedly followed by the lads who steered around Dougie at arm's length.

Once the door shut, Dougie kneeled in front of Sharon, and Len sat forward on the settee. It was tense.

'What's gone off, Sharon.' Doug was breathing heavily from the exertion.

She broke down in tears. 'We can't have kids, Dougie.'

'What? What are you talking about, you daft fucker? Says who?'

'The doctor at the hospital, I've got to have more tests, but she's bruised my ovaries, for nowt. What are we going to do? What if I can't have kids no more?'

'Woah! Just stop a minute. Take a deep breath and rewind to the beginning. How did all this come about?' He glanced at Len, whose eyes widened on hearing the revelation.

Sharon tried to gather herself together. She breathed deeply. 'This woman. Barged into my trolley at the Co-op.'

'So?'

'I had a go at her, and she got all leery, and when I went to smack her, she's elbowed me in the stomach.'

'What? Does she know who you are?'

'Doesn't look like it.'

'And her just doing that has caused you to damage your ovaries?'

'Well, one of them at least, but I need to see the specialist.'

'So, we could be, okay?'

'It don't feel right, Dougie, I know something's wrong it's all torn inside. It hurts even to breathe. My stomach is sticking out like a Biafran. It wasn't me; it was her.'

'The cow. Fuck that. Who is she?'

'I don't know.'

'Len. Get on to our contacts. Get the lads out talking to theirs. The word must be out who this twat is. I want her name and address. She's gonna pay, big time. She's gonna suffer for this. If you hurt our Shaz, you suffer ten times more.' So soon after giving her a beating, the irony was lost on him.

Lennie offered his observations. 'Not only that, Dougie, it makes us look the right pair of mugs. It's disrespect, and we can't have people mugging us off.'

*

Jane Cooper sat in the Blue Boar pub alone. She was early. As with many single Mum's, she had a reliable babysitter to give her a small amount of flexibility to have time for herself. She was careful to use this help sparsely and not take advantage because she always treated her with a couple of pounds, and money was scarce, so it couldn't be too often.

Jan was a middle-aged lady with a kindly but weathered face, and everyone called her 'Aunty.' Aunty had no children herself, but she was a Godsend to a couple of local Mums who she helped in a similar manner to Jane and was often available at a moment's notice. She was a kindly soul and didn't seem to have much family interaction herself, and she loved looking after children.

All the silliness over the Co-op incident had disorientated Jane, and she needed a blast of normality. She needed to get back into a routine. It would all be forgotten about, and the low-life women who caused all the trouble would move on to some other ridiculous drama, no doubt. People like her thrived on this sort of thing; it was the only thing they had in their sad, sorry lives. It was pathetic. She couldn't wait to hear what her friends thought of it all. They would think it hilarious, no doubt. 'This could only happen to you, Jane.'

She had met her closest friends Kathy and Amy in the Bowmen every week, without fail, since the hockey team days. It was a chance to catch up on all the gossip and unload the hassles of the week before. They often joked their weekly gathering was like a support network, each dependent on the other for solace and a caring word.

Boy, did she have a story to tell this week? Maybe they could give Jane some advice? She had been thinking about trying to track the woman down to apologise. Maybe that would put an end to it? When you broke it down, all that had happened was that it seems the woman had lost her temper in a moment of madness, and if she has damaged herself, then, of course, that was tragic. She didn't deserve that, even if she had been a bit over the top. She wouldn't wish that on anybody. But then, if there was another argument, and it escalated again, was it worth it? She felt it probably better to let sleeping dogs lie. The woman is probably embarrassed about it herself and regretting what happened. She would realise that it wasn't Jane's fault, and all this fear about the Browns was misplaced. They were human beings, after all.

Jane would be interested to see what the girls said when they arrived. Kathy in particular was always pretty sensible, so it would be good to see what her take on it all was. Maybe she knows the woman; she seemed to know everyone else in the town, which came from her years working in her Mum's corner shop as a child. Everyone knew Kathy Jenson. She had been a good and loyal friend to Jane over the years, and she thought the world of her. They would not be lifelong friends if they didn't have that trust for one another.

The Blue Boar was known for its Sunday evening disco's upstairs, but it was a family pub and a comfortable location for women to meet hassle-free during the week. The only downside was that the door was really drafty in the area they liked to sit, which was like a private little booth. Jane kept her coat on for now to combat the occasional breeze. She had ordered herself a lager and lime to see her through until the girls arrived; she was just buying time. They would be there any minute.

Kathy and Amy would not be there in a minute, nor two. A minute became five minutes, and then five minutes became fifteen. An hour's breeze flowed through that drafty door before Jane accepted, they weren't coming. She had been stood up for the first time in forever. Had she done something to upset them? She hoped there hadn't been an accident or something amiss. Surely it wasn't because of that stupid altercation in the supermarket. They wouldn't be put off by that, surely. She was getting paranoid. Friends are friends, and you don't just abandon them when trouble rears its ugly head, now, do you? They wouldn't do that to her.

*

Dougie had been pacing around his living room for the last hour or more as they went over and over Sharon's story. He was winding his emotions into a tight coil at every telling. The main emotion was disbelief. He had not seen this coming. The woman must be crazy or not know who she was messing with. She will know soon enough. He could not allow this to go past without the biggest display of venom ever shown. If it got out that you could beat his wife and take their chance to have kids away and still survive, they were finished. As well as his wife, his pride had been hurt, and he wanted swift retribution. The others were spreading the word, trying to get a name for the bitch that attacked poor Sharon.

Dougie and Sharon's living room had a curious ambience to it. Everything in it was expensive but at the same time crass. The ornaments and curtains were garish, good quality, but not matching, and too 'busy' to make any sense. The carpet was thick shagpile but had ridiculous crown crests on it, personally designed but vomit-inducing. It turns out taste is not something you can buy. A perfect example was the minibar they had installed in the spacious living room, in the far corner. It had flashing lights on it, but no-one had bothered to replace several bulbs; the top was stained with beer and had scarcely been cleaned. It stunk and looked hideous, yet the Browns thought it was the last word in style. Even the telephone on the windowsill was a proper marble, old fashioned candlestick design, but it was dusty, and the brass discoloured. It surprised everyone in the room when it rang.

Dougie pounced on it and grabbed the earpiece, bending over and speaking awkwardly into the mouthpiece before realising and picking the whole thing up, enabling him to walk and talk.

'Yep.'

'Hello?' A woman's voice.

'Who's this?'

'I'm Kaz. Is that Dougie?'

'What do you want?'

'Dean Smith gave me your number and said to ring. He's one of yours, isn't he?'

'Maybe. What is it?'

'I know who hurt your Sharon.'

'Oh yeah.'

'You just need to know that it is somebody called Jane Cooper and she lives at 126 Squires Avenue at the top. She's got a daughter called Daisy.'

'Has she now.'

'Yeah, she goes to Saint Mary's junior school. That's where she was mouthing off about beating Sharon up. Her Mum was not the kid. She told us in the playground, bold as brass, she was, and everyone heard it.'

Dougie perched himself on the edge of the leather settee, grimacing as he spoke. This woman had some bleeding nerve.

'What? She was bragging about it. Has she got some sort of fucking death wish?'

'I dunno, she's dead snooty. She thinks she's better than everybody else.'

'Does she? Well, I've got some news for her. She's a dead woman.'

There was a stunned silence on the telephone.

Len spoke up. 'Careful what you're saying, Doug.'

'No, I fucking mean it, Len, it ain't an idle threat.'

'It'd better not be, now you've announced it.'

Dougie returned to the call. 'Let me treat you, Kaz. For ringing up, I mean. I appreciate it.'

'No, I don't want anything, thanks, it's alright. I just thought you should know.'

'You sure?'

'Yeah. Thanks anyway.'

'I owe you one, darling. Come to see me if you need owt, yeah?'

'Okay, thanks. Will do. See ya.'

'See ya.'

Dougie threw the telephone across the room, the cord being its only salvation. 'Fucking bragging about it! Right, Len, come on…'

Lennie spoke across him. 'Dougie, did you hear what you said, our kid?'

'What?'

'You've said she was dead, meaning we're gonna do her, so we've got to do the business now. You can't threaten something and not carry it out, Doug; we'd look a right pair of amateurs.'

'I know what I said, Dougie. I'm not having it bro, we can't have this shit. It's got to be full bore. She deserves it, snooty cow.'

'It has to be you and me then.' Lennie said. 'None of the crew, just the brothers, yeah?'

'Yeah, of course. Solid.' He clasped Lens hand. 'Blood, yeah?'

'Blood.'

Sharon spoke up. 'Dougie, can I please ask you something?'

'What?'

'Let me do it.'

'You do it? You can't do it in your state. Don't be stupid.'

'The doctor said the pain will go in a few hours. Anyway, I don't mean kill her. I just wanna mark her. Slash her up. Please, Doug, this is personal. I've got my own pride too, you know.'

'I don't want you in nick again, Shaz.'

'I won't; they ain't gonna put us away, Dougie. Those days are gone. No-ones gonna say a bloody word against us, you know that.'

'I don't think slashing is enough. I want her in cement.' Dougie scowled.

'At least let me do this. Do what you like afterwards. That's up to you. I've never interfered in any of that; you know that Dougie.'

'I will, Shaz. I want her, I want her fucking kid, her family, and everyone who's ever known her to pay for this bastard.'

Len stood up and put his arm around his brother. 'All right, Dougie, let Shaz do what she needs to do. Me and you can do our business. It gives us a bit of thinking time. We need a plan. At least Sharon doing something will be a quick message that it's begun. Everyone will know what's coming. We're just playing with her first. Letting Sharon have her piece. Everyone will know it's us; it's solid, man.'

Dougie waved a finger at Sharon. 'She ain't getting away with this, Sharon.'

'I want her to suffer much more than you, trust me. Just let me make her bleed. Scar her up. Make my mark. I've got my pride too, Dougie.'

Sharon struggled to her feet and put her arms around her husband. She rested her head on his chest.

'You won't leave me, Dougie, will you? If we can't have kids, I mean.'

Dougie glanced at his brother. 'No, of course, not Sharon. Till death do us part, remember.'

She looked up at him. 'What did you say?' He was grinning. She hit his chest. 'You fucker!'

5

'Little pig, little pig, let me come in.

No, not by the hairs on my chinny chin chin. I'll not let you in.

Then I'll huff, and I'll puff and I'll blow your house in.'

James Halliwell-Phillips.

DC Ashley Stevens was a magnet for female attention. It was a matter of fact. Why? He was good looking, tall, slim, drove a Porsche motor car and had a seemingly endless amount of money. Not your usual profile for a young detective, granted. Ashley had had a normal childhood, but then fortune shined upon his family as his father was made redundant from his job at the colliery. Redundancy was not normally a reason to celebrate, but in this instance, his father had ploughed his redundancy money into buying his own videotape rental shop. It was a huge success, and one shop became two, and before long, he had scores of them pitted across the country and had become a multi-millionaire within five years.

Despite this newfound wealth, Ashley politely declined his father's offer to work in the family business. He enjoyed being a police officer too much, despite the dangers. His father understood and was quite proud of his decision but insisted he allow him to share his wealth with his only son and set up a healthy bank account and a monthly standing order of several thousand pounds. So, Ashley was the holder of a princely sum in his bank account and a private income that would be the envy of any young man in his late twenties.

He wore expensive suits and jewellery. He shone like a beacon in the various nightclubs he frequented and had the pick of anyone in there, if truth be told.

He looked a little out of sorts sitting in the greasy spoon café on Piccadilly Road in Bulwell in a three-hundred-pound suit and two-hundred-pound shiny shoes. Affectionately known to the locals as Picco café it made the best breakfasts around with an escalating scale of additions to the plate culminating in the largest breakfast of all, wryly called 'The Heart Attack.'.

Ashley was meeting his informant there as it was a sufficient distance from where the guy lived in St Annes, and it was always quiet just before closing time at 8pm. There was a smell of cooling fat and lard now that the cooking had stopped, and it lightened the appeal a little. Trish had wiped the table for him, but this served to merely coat the Formica with water and make it undesirable to rest arms on it until it dried. The walls hadn't been decorated for many a year and the engrained fat that lingered on them seemed to be holding the building up.

'Big Stu' walked in the door by turning sideways and shuffling through the gap. You couldn't miss him. 6'3" built like a brick shithouse and heavily tattooed on his arms and neck. Stu had been a bodybuilder and a successful one until he got hit with a steroids test, and it all went downhill for him. He was a good lad, though, and he was popular and a name around Nottingham. A big fish in a little pond if you like. He shared an affinity with the young detective as he too was something of a lady beacon himself. They had first got chatting in Ritzy's nightclub and became friendly rather than friends. Ashley had given him a card and was a little surprised when he got his first call a few weeks later about a GBH investigation. Stu had heard who the offenders were in the gym he used. It was a bodybuilder's gym where testosterone and bragging were commonplace, so people would often boast about what they had done or intended to do, and some of this was criminal activity.

Ashley stood up to greet Big Stu and fitted his average hand into the oven glove that was Stuart's.

'What can I get you, Stu?'

'Just a cuppa, please, Ash. Four sugars.'

'Grab a seat, and I'll get them.'

Ashley had sensed a nervousness in Stu as he waited at the counter for Trish to pour the two brews; Big Stu seemed to be a bit more fidgety than normal. He kept peering out of the window and looking around the empty café. He was rubbing his legs and knees; he seemed ill-at-ease.'

Ashley returned with the mugs of steaming tea.

'Four sugars. Thanks for seeing me at short notice, Stu.'

'No problem. Sorry, I couldn't get earlier. I had to take Mum to the hospital.'

'How is she?'

'Not good, Ash, it's her bones; she's in a lot of pain.'

'Not nice.'

'No. She's a tough old bird, though. She says old age isn't for cowards.'

'She's probably right. You want to tell her, a creaking gate lasts the longest, so they say.'

Stuart shrugged out a laugh. 'I will; she'll like that one. She'll probably outlive me. Well, she definitely will if my talking to you ever gets out.' He glanced out the window again and studied a car doing a three-point turn just up the road.

'It won't, Stuart. I've not had it yet; you're safe, don't worry.'

'Some of these dudes are proper misters, though, Ashley, they don't give a shit.'

'I know, you're sound, don't worry. Have you been down the big house lately?'

'Ritzy's? No, probably at the weekend.'

'I'm going Thursday to grab a granny night.'

Stuart laughed. 'You sick bastard.'

'I like the older woman, well, I like all sorts, to be honest.'

'Don't we all.'

They fell quiet for a moment, and Ashley couldn't put off the burning question any longer. 'It happened then.' He said.

'It did, A bookies, I hear. Did you get them?'

'No, we couldn't guess where it might be going down, Stu, but it's fine. I appreciated the call in any case. Spot on, as usual.'

Stuart was cagey, tapping his fingers on the table and shaking his leg up and down at a rate of knots as he sat at the table. 'Do you know who's done it, then?'

'No, not for definite.' Ashley grinned.

'Not for definite. Ain't it obvious?'

'You tell me, Stu.'

He laughed nervously. 'I ain't telling you shit, Ashley. Not on this one.'

'How come?' Ashley lit a cigarette up, pulling the grey tin ashtray closer to him and holding it away from the bruiser sitting opposite. This gave him quite an effete appearance.

'You know why.'

'Do I?'

Big Stu laughed again. 'Yes, you fucking do.'

'Well, unless you can tell us where the sawn-off is, Stu, or maybe the cash, there ain't much else to tell, is there?'

'No.'

'So can you?'

'Can I what?'

'Tell us where the gun or cash is? What's up with you today?'

'Nowt, Ashley, but it's made me a bit nervous knowing who it is. I wouldn't have bothered if I knew it was them.'

'The Brown brothers, you mean.'

'Shush! Fuck me! Ash! Don't say their name, man.'

'Bloody hell, Stu. Who do you they are, Lord God all fucking mighty?'

'No, but they are mad bastards and, well, you know.'

'Can you try and find out for us. Where the gun or cash is, I mean.'

'I don't really want to get more involved with this one. I think I've done my bit.'

'That's not like you, Stuart.'

'I know, but come on, give me a break, man. I like my life. I would like to keep it for the time being if you don't mind.'

Ashley laughed. 'A big lad like you frightened of those idiots.'

Stuart sniffed. 'Course not. I ain't frightened of anybody, but they don't play by the rules, Ash; it's a late-night blast in your head while you're having a piss. I've got enough on my plate.'

'I'm not going to pressure you, Stuart. I wouldn't do that, mate. You've always been straight with me. But it would be handy to just get that little bit more.'

'I know, Ashley, but I'm gonna back off this one if you don't mind.'

'I wouldn't force you into anything, Stu; you've always been sound with me, mate.' There was silence as Ashley wrestled with the conundrum. 'I tell you what, Stuart. Don't make a special effort, but if you do happen to learn where the gun or cash is, ring it in anonymously or give a false name.'

'What name?'

'I don't know. Erm, let me think. It needs to be fairly unique. What about Walter?'

'Fine, but Ashley, don't take this the wrong way, mate, but it only takes some bent cop to drop out that it has come from me, and I am dead meat.'

'It wouldn't happen, Stu. You're safe.'

'Can you guarantee that to me?'

Ashley hesitated slightly before Stuart jumped in again. 'See? You can't, and that's what worries me.'

'Okay. You've heard what I've said, Stu. I'll leave it with you. Anything else I need to know about?'

'Not at the moment I might have something brewing, but it's not gonna happen for weeks.'

'What is it?' Ashley sipped at the mug of tea, trying to be nonchalant.

'A possible drug thing.'

'Cool.'

'Can I ask you a question, Ashley?'

'Sure, what's up?' He sucked on his cigarette.

'We're mates, right.'

'Yes, of course. What's bothering you?'

'I just don't like the thought of being an informant, a snitch, you know.'

Ashley laughed as he lied. 'You ain't that, Stu, Christ, do me a favour. If I wasn't in the job I would help the cops out if I could. Why wouldn't you? It's the right thing to do. What would your Mum say?'

'I guess.'

'To prove we're mates, I will let you buy me a drink next time I see you at Ritzy's.'

'That's very kind of you.' Stu laughed. 'That means so bleeding much.'

Ashley grinned. 'We're still good, yeah?'

'Yes, sweet, Ash.'

They grasped hands as Stuart stood to leave, towering over the suave young detective. Ashley had a twenty-pound note in his hand, which Stu retrieved as they unclasped from the improvised handshake. It belied the conversation they had just had, but Stu needed the money, so, done in such a casual manner, it seemed less official. It was Ashley's own money, but the job wouldn't reimburse him just for an unproductive meeting, so it was fortunate that Ash had the wear with all to fund his growing group of informants out of his own pocket. He was gaining status as the main man with informants in the CID office, and he liked it. This was something he could build on.

Ashley glanced at his Rolex wristwatch; Stark had called an unofficial de-brief in the Green Dragon. He was ready for a pint.

*

Jane Cooper was hurt and confused as she drove her little car home. She'd had better days. Even the radio crackled on every damned station, so she pushed in the tape that was hanging half out of the machine. 'Manic Monday' by The

Bangles. She smiled ironically as she crunched the gears, her mind replaying her emotions.

She had felt such a fool sitting there on her own, fending off glances and smiles from the blokes at the bar. She had ended up staring at the carpet for fear of catching eye-to-eye contact. It was uncomfortable for her, and she didn't like it. She shouldn't have been put in that position.

She would call her friends to try to understand what had happened. She just prayed that they were okay and they had not been involved in an accident. What could have stopped them from meeting her? They had never let her down before, never once. The question niggled her because she knew the answer in her heart of hearts.

Before long, Jane arrived home just in time for the heater in the car to expel warm air instead of the icy blast it had persevered with all the way home. Typical.

Once she parked her car on the dimly lit street, Jane strolled down the alley at the side of her house. As the darkness shrouded her, she felt a little shiver go down her spine. Jane was distracted by a car that swept around in a circle, catching her in the headlights, causing her to squint. She glanced at the windows but could not see who the occupants were.

The back kitchen door was unlocked, and the warmth enveloped her as soon as she stepped inside.

'Hi, Aunty. You must keep that back door locked; anyone could just walk in.'

Aunty craned her head toward the kitchen from her vantage point on the living room settee.

'Oh, ehup, Jane. Sorry, I never bother locking doors at home, not until bedtime anyway. You're back early, luvvy.'

'I know. The girls couldn't make it in the end. I was sat there like a right muppet.' Jane sounded despondent as she took off her coat.

Aunty headed for the kitchen. 'Oh dear, let me put the kettle on. Couldn't they have let you know they weren't coming?'

'I take it nobody has rung, then?'

'No. Not a dicky bird.'

Jane put her coat on the back of a chair at the kitchen table and rubbed her dainty hands together to gather some heat in them. She plonked herself wearily on the armchair in the living room next to the settee, letting out a gasp of relief as she did. 'Probably for the best. It's been a long day, to be honest. How's Daisy been?'

'Off like a light. She's so good. Bless her. She never batted an eyelid. We read a little story, and I stayed with her for a few minutes, but she was gone in no time. Same as I say, off like a light.'

'She's used to you now, Aunty.'

'She is. Bless her.'

Jane stared at the television set as the closing credits to Coronation Street ended. 'I've missed that, now.'

'It was good, Jane. I daren't tape it because I wasn't sure what you'd got on the videotape in the machine.'

'That's okay, I usually set the timer, but I forgot. It's been a funny day. There are rumours that Hilda Ogden is coming out of it. I hope not.'

'Me too. It's not been the same since Stan died, though.' Aunty said as she brought in a mug of steaming tea and gave it to Jane.

'They brought Jack and Vera in as a replacement for them, I think, don't you?' Jane said as she took hold of the mug gingerly. 'Thanks, Aunty.'

'Yes. I didn't like them at first, but I must admit they've grown on me. That Jack's a dopey bugger, but he does make me laugh. Do you mind if I shoot off,

Jane? I'm pretty tired myself, and I like to have an hour's reading before bed. I don't mind staying if you want a chat.'

'Of course not, Aunty. Thank you so much for babysitting.' Jane reached into her bag for a five-pound note. 'Here, this is for you.'

'No, just give me a couple of pounds, Jane, it's not fair, with you being back so soon. Five pounds is a lot of money.'

'Are you sure?'

'Course, I'm sure.'

Jane saw Aunty to the door and gave her two-pound coins. The pound notes the coins were replacing were still in circulation, but not for much longer. 'Thanks again.' They stepped into the darkness. 'What was that!' Jane recoiled.

'What?' Startled, Aunty clutched at her chest.

'I thought I saw someone behind the hedge.'

'Oh, don't say that, Jane, you'll give me the bloody eeby jeebies.'

'Sorry, Aunty, I think I'm going crazy. Give me three rings when you get back, so that I know you're home safe.'

'I will do, Jane. Bye, ducky. Get an early night if you can. It'll do you good.' Aunty's side-to-side waddle made Jane smile as her friend disappeared into the darkness.

'I will, bye, Aunty. Thanks again.'

Jane shivered and quickly shut the door behind her making sure it was locked and bolted, just to be on the safe side.

*

DI Stark's team sat in a large circle in the corner of The Green Dragon pub. It was popular mainly because of its location next door to the police station. It was a quiet night, and only twenty or so punters skirted the bar area with two or three couples pitted around different tables.

The detective's table was overloaded with drinks and ashtrays and a couple of bags of crisps. Smoke chugged from the group like the roofline of a Victorian terraced housing block.

The table was private and set back from the main bar, so they always felt comfortable discussing matters that were not for the public's ears at large. As they went around the table to learn what had been discovered that day, it was clear that it was highly likely to be the Browns who had committed the robbery.

'It's obviously the Browns, so we need a plan of attack.' Nobby said. He had taken his jacket off and rolled his sleeves up, revealing some tattoos he had when he first joined the army. They were quite crude, and he wished he hadn't bothered.

Stark nodded. 'We do, Nobby. There is the slight problem of something called evidence of course.'

Ashley grinned. 'That always gets in the way. Bloody evidence!' He said ironically.

'It sure does, young Ash. So, we haven't got enough to nick them. Not at the moment, at least. Everything is hearsay, and no one wants to give a statement. To be honest, we never will have sufficient evidence unless we get something from forensics.' Stark observed.

Cynthia had managed to manoeuvre herself next to her Detective Inspector once more, and she had already leaned across him to get to her drinks. He had felt her hard bosom against his arm. She nursed the drink with her long, brightly painted fingernails wrapped around the glass.

'Nobody in their right mind will give evidence against them.' Nobby shook his head.

'Would you?' Charlie asked.

'No chance. For them to get off at court. No thanks. It ain't worth it.' Nobby said.

'There you go. It makes you wonder what the point is.' Charlie raised his hand's chest-high as if surrendering, which he sort of was. Surrendering to the ridiculousness of the legal system.

'What do you mean, Charlie?' Stark asked. 'You don't mean give up; that's not like you, mate.'

Charlie was perched precariously on his seat, the buttons of his shirt straining at his gut. 'No, not give up, boss, but when you look at it. You have two robbers who have robbed a bloody robber, who, in turn, will no doubt gain more out of it by fiddling his insurance. There's no way it was thirty grand, not a prayer. He's taking the piss. So, everybody wins, and no-one else gives two hoots or wants to get involved, so why bloody bother? I'm not giving up; I'm just saying. I'm being realistic, that's all.'

'The thing is, though, Charlie, it is the bigger picture. These bastards need taking off the streets, because next time they might kill some innocent who walks in front of them. That's the real issue. That's the danger. Fuck Bernie Squires. It's the poor sod that somehow gets in the way and gets hurt through no fault of their own. It's going to be a tricky one for DS Clarke to solve.'

Charlie shrugged. He didn't seem convinced.

'I'm running it am I?' Nobby asked.

'Yes, armed robbery doesn't need a DI, but I will have more of a watching brief than normal because of who it is, Nobby. The Browns, I mean.'

'Yeah, fine by me.'

'I'm not sticking my oar in, but I've been waiting for an opportunity to get more acquainted with the Browns and that opportunity has now reared its ugly face.'

'No problem. It makes sense. More the merrier, for me.'

Ashley seemed a bit more optimistic than Charlie. 'If forensics come back with the projectile and the wadding, there's a chance, isn't there?'

'Only if we get the shotgun back and connect it to them.' Stark said.

'They might like to hang on to a decent shooter, though, boss. They can be hard to come by. They're not forced to dump it. At least not straight away.'

'Maybe, let us hope so, eh?'

'What about a warrant?' Nobby asked.

'I think it's an option, but we are likely to end up with egg on our faces.' Stark said.

'Not for the first time,' Nobby said, 'Who cares if there's a chance to get them locked up for a stretch.'

'That shooter will be long gone, hidden wherever it was hidden before it was used for Bernie's blagging.' Charlie said. 'Ehup, what have we got here?'

A young man walked into the bar area with highlights in his hair and wearing a white linen suit with the sleeves rolled up to near his elbows. 'What's he come as?'

Ashley enlightened them. 'It's the Miami Vice look.'

'Oh, off the telly, Crocket and Tubbs.' Cynthia chimed in as she leaned forward to put her drink back on the table. Stark gave her a puzzled look, and she smiled at him.

'I can see you in that, Ashley.' Charlie said with a twinkle in his eye.

'Do you reckon? You can be Tubbs, then Charlie. You were made for the role.'

'Cheeky sod.' He laughed.

'Ashley, don't bother turning up at work in one of those suits.' Stark said. 'I wouldn't put it past you.'

'He's been out posed by this guy.' Cynthia said.

'Nah, he's an amateur.' Ashley grinned, lighting up a Peter Stuyvesant cigarette with shiny gold banding on the filter.

'What's that shit you are you smoking now, Ash? Fucking gold bars?' Charlie laughed.

'No. Menthol cigarettes. I find them more flavoursome.' Ashley tapped some ash into the ashtray with an air of campness about it.

'Bleeding puff. What's the job coming to?' Charlie asked.

'You tell me. The guys we joined with will be rolling in their graves, Charlie.' Nobby shook his head. 'The job's fucked.'

'Can we get back to the issue at hand? The Browns.' Stark said.

'So, what's the plan, boss.' Nobby asked.

'We are a bit limited, but it's a rare chance to get at these shit-heads. They've had it too easy for too long. We're going to have to work at it, though. Let's see what the CCTV throws up; see if forensics get anything of note, see what our informants say. They don't have to give evidence. They just need to find out where that bloody sawn-off shotgun is.'

'Judging by the informant I've just seen, they will all crawl back into the woodwork. It's common knowledge it's the Browns. It's not worth it to them.' Ashley said.

'You caught up with him in the end, then?' Stark said. 'Anything of note?'

'No, that's what I'm saying. The word is it is the Browns, so he doesn't want to go near it. I've told him to ring in with a false name if he hears owt.'

'Did you tell him to concentrate on locating the gun, like I asked?'

'Yes. I'm not holding my breath, though.'

'You never know, Ashley. You never know. Anyway, let's see what the CCTV footage shows us. Maybe Cynthia and Steve Aston can go through it and log significant events in the morning?'

Cynthia was first to respond. 'Yes, of course.'

'Take your time, though, because it is important. See if there is anything distinguishable about them or the gun or even their clothing.'

'Will do, sir.'

Steph nudged Nobby. 'Can I have a word, Sarge?'

'Yes, what's up? I thought you'd been a bit quiet.'

'I meant in private.'

'Can't it wait?'

'No, it cannot.'

'Are we okay for a brief chat, boss? Have we done? It will only take five minutes.' Nobby asked.

'Is that all you need, Nobby?' Charlie asked.

'Yep. Twice as long as you, Mr Carter.'

'I bloody wish. I've not seen it for six years.' He grinned.

Cynthia hit him on the arm. 'Charlie!'

'Yes, sure, Nobby. There's nothing else for now.' Stark said, pausing in mid-sup of his pint of beer.

Steph and Nobby got up and headed towards the corner table with their drinks.

'Good luck, Nobby.' Charlie said.

Steph gave him a two-fingered salute. 'Up yours, Charlie.'

'Charmed, I'm sure.'

The two sat down, just out of view of the crowd. Steph did not look happy. She sighed.

'Let's hear it then, Nobby.'

'Hear what?'

'Why didn't you tell me about this Sally girl? She's half your bloody age, Nobby, for Christ's sake.'

'Not quite.'

'You know what I mean.' Steph lit a cigarette. Her hands seemed to be trembling a little, and she was agitated.

'There's nowt to tell, Steph. It's old news. Honestly, love, don't get in a pickle about something like that. It's you and me now, and that's all that matters.' Nobby sipped at his pint and looked over the top of it at Steph. She looked feisty.

'How am I supposed to compete with kids like that Sally girl? She's got tits you could strike a match on.'

Nobby laughed. 'You are not competing with anyone. It was a little bit of flirtatious fun, that is all. Come on, love. She's got nothing on you. If I wanted to be with her, I would be. She's not even on my radar.' Nobby took hold of her hand.

'I don't like the secrecy, that's all.'

'I'm sure you saw men when we split up for those few weeks.'

'I didn't, actually.'

'Yes, but you could have done.'

'I didn't want to. You obviously did.'

'It just happened by accident. In all truth, what would she see in a middle-aged man like me, other than a bit of curiosity.'

'By accident – Jeez. Anyway, we both know the answer to that question, Nobby. And now her curiosity is satisfied she knows what she's been missing, and I don't like it. That's for us. That's private.'

'What can I say, Steph. You're getting yourself all wound up over nothing.'

'You could say sorry?'

'What? Hold on. No, I am not apologising, Steph. I've got nothing to apologise for. Come on. This is silly; we're not kids.'

'No, but she is.'

'She is not, she's in her mid-twenties.'

'Did she cum?'

'Oh, Steph, now you're being totally ridiculous.' Nobby laughed. 'This is crazy.'

Tears began to form in Steph's eyes. 'I'm serious, Nobby. Did she?'

'Just stop it, Steph, you're torturing yourself. You're the only one for me, and you know that. What does it matter either way?'

'Because she will want more, and I need to know if that's the case. It's a woman thing.'

'What do you think?'

'Right, I'm being serious. I don't want you going back in there again. It makes me feel sick just thinking about it.'

'This isn't like you. What's brought all this on? I am the Detective Sergeant running this armed robbery enquiry, and I can't promise not to go to the location that it happened in, for Christ's sake.'

'Make sure I am with you then.'

'You don't mean that, surely? I mean, I'll do my best. Don't let it bother you, Steph. Honestly, nobody compares to you. She's just a kid.'

'Just keep away, Nobby. I mean it. I don't want her thinking she can have you any time she wants.'

'I'm sure she doesn't think like that. Anyway, I am quite capable of looking after myself where women are concerned.'

'Trust me; you have no clue what women are like. I've told you to keep well away. I mean it.'

'The thing that worries me is that if I didn't know you better, I would think you were being serious.'

'Oh, don't you worry about that, Nobby, I am fucking deadly serious. And if you go anywhere near matchstick tits, your wanger will be in the freezer.'

Nobby swallowed hard. Stark shouted over to Nobby. 'Have you got a minute?'

Nobby leaned back on his chair so he could see his DI. 'Coming, boss.' He righted his chair and grabbed Steph's hand once more. 'Come on, let's go back. We're good, yeah?'

'You can be a real shit, do you know that?'

'I haven't done anything, Steph.'

Nobby led the way back. This was all he needed. They re-joined the group. Cynthia grabbed Steph's hand and whispered in her ear.

'Are you alright?'

'Yes, I'm fine.'

'Toilet?'

'Yes, come on.'

The two women got up and shuffled away towards the toilet.

There was a slight lull as the women left the group.

'Bloody women.' Nobby mumbled to himself. He turned to Stark. 'Thanks, anyway, boss.'

'No problem, Nobby. I've got one at home. Anyway, it's your round, isn't it?'

*

Jane had just settled back on the settee and the wisps of the cool air which streamed in when saying goodbye to Aunty, had yet to be defeated by the warmth of her home, when she heard a tapping at the door. Did she imagine it? She grabbed the remote control and turned down the sound on the TV for a moment to listen again. Nothing. As she pressed the sound back up, she heard it again, this time a little louder.

She sighed and hauled herself out of the soft upholstery.

'What have you forgotten, Aunty?'

There was no reply. Jane hesitated as she reached the door. 'Aunty?'

Still no reply, but she could see a figure through the frosted glass. Jane tried again, 'Hello?' She could hear whispering and her heart rate increased. 'Who's there?'

Finally, a response. 'It's Sharon from the Supermarket, I just came to apologise.'

Jane's stomach turned over on hearing the woman's voice again. She paused for a couple of seconds and blurted out some sort of response. 'Oh Hi. That's really nice of you.' She sounded a little breathless, so she tried to compose herself and took a deep breath before elaborating. 'Thank you. I never wanted any trouble. I appreciate you calling around. I'm sorry too.'

Relief flooded through her veins. At last, maybe this dark cloud hanging over her would go away. She was not going to answer the door, though, she did not trust her one bit.

'Can I come in to apologise properly, Jane?'

It suddenly registered with her that this woman not only knew her name but, come to think of it, she had somehow found out where she lived.

'Erm. I'm a bit wary to be honest, Sharon. There is only me and my daughter here.'

Jane tried to make out how many people were on the other side of the door. She couldn't see properly. 'I don't like opening the door after dark. I'm a bit funny like that.' She laughed nervously. 'If we can call it quits, that would be great. Thanks for calling round.'

Sharon's tone of voice changed and had more of an edge to it. 'So, I've gone to the trouble to come around here to apologise, and you won't even open the door. Why do you keep disrespecting me like this?'

'I'm sorry, no offence, but I'm sure you can understand I'm a bit nervy what with everything that's happened. I'm not disrespecting you; I promise.'

'This ain't on, Jane. This is rude. Dissing me like this. It's not easy for me to come around like this, you know.'

Jane had her back to the door, the coolness of the glass chilling her shoulders. What to do? She seemed genuine, and she had come all this way. It was pretty rude. She didn't have to come to apologise. Jane wanted it all over and didn't want to foul things up when it could all be over tonight.

In a flash, she turned, unlocked the door, slid open the bolt, and swung open the door. She immediately recognised the grinning Sharon and the large lady with bunches who had been one of the friends she'd had with her earlier in the store.

'Hello. Sorry, I'm a bit nervy.' Jane was smiling.

'Hello, Jane. That's better. I just wanted to apologise to you, that's all. I suppose you're bound to be a bit scared, and I understand. It's okay.'

'Just a bit. Thank you.'

'Can we come in?'

With a momentary hesitation, Jane answered. 'I am just about to have an early night so…'

Sharon and Trixie stepped into the kitchen.

'Of course. Come on in. I don't know what's wrong with me today. I'm really tired.'

The three walked further into the kitchen area, with Trixie loitering near the doorframe.

'I don't like misunderstandings, Jane. I thought it better we clear the air.' Sharon said in a conciliatory tone.

Jane stopped, and they stood opposite each other. Jane was effusive. 'I am so pleased. Thank you so much for coming to see me. I thought about coming to see you too, but I didn't want to make things worse. I didn't know what to do. I was worried you had been really hurt. Are you okay?'

'I'm fine, apart from the worry of not being able to have children. Apparently, I have bruised my ovaries. So that is not good.'

'Let's hope it's just a scare. I didn't mean to hurt you, I just kind of jumped out the way, and your stomach hit the trolley. I've been worrying about you all day.'

'Ah, that's sweet. Ain't that lovely, Trixie?'

'Yeah, really nice.' She was chewing gum.

'So, are we quits now?' Jane asked.

'Let's have a hug, and then we are even.' Sharon said.

'A hug?'

'Just to seal the deal.'

'Erm, okay. Sure. Why not?'

Jane opened her arms to welcome her in. Sharon reached into her pocket as the two entered the brief and somewhat awkward embrace. As Sharon pulled away, she let her right hand pull along Jane's cheek. She had an old-style folding razor in her hand and the skin and flesh easily separated like a zip on a jacket.

Jane was smiling as the sharpness of the blade delayed any great pain. Yet, her brain realised something wasn't quite right, but she couldn't figure out what, and put her hand to her cheek as blood gushed out.

'Aargh! What's that?'

Sharon went to strike again but Jane instinctively put her hand in the way and the blade slid easily through the flesh of her fingers.

Again, Jane screamed and fell to the floor, more in submission than necessity.

Sharon towered over her. 'Listen bitch. You don't touch any of us Browns and get away with it. This is just the start. Do you understand me?'

'Stop, please. It was an accident. It's not my fault.' There was a lot of blood coming from her face and hands, and it terrified Jane. Was she going to die?

'I said do you understand me, bitch?'

'Yes, yes. I understand.' Jane held out a blood-soaked hand to fend off any further attacks. It dripped heavily onto the floor and Jane's jeans.

'I could snuff you out now, you fucking slag, but you are going to suffer first. You and everyone you know is going to suffer. Is that clear?'

'Yes. I'm sorry. Please don't.' Tears rolled down Jane's face as she pleaded.

'Watch your back, Jane Cooper. This is just the start. We are coming for you.'

'Please don't. I didn't know. I'm sorry.'

Sharon and Trixie were laughing as they headed out the kitchen door and into the night.

Jane was panting, her heart going ten to the dozen. She hadn't figured out how badly she was hurt, but the blood was everywhere. Her hands were sore, and so was her left cheek. She needed to stop the blood. Having got to her feet, she staggered to the kitchen and grabbed hold of a tea towel, holding it to her face as blood trickled down her forearm.

She heard a noise upstairs. It was Daisy. She sounded distressed.

'Mummy?'

'It's okay, darling, it's just mummy's friends leaving. Go to bed, and I'll be up in a minute. There's a good girl.' She was trying to sound as normal as possible so she didn't frighten her.

'Okay. Goodnight, Mummy.'

'Goodnight, darling.'

Jane started to sob but had to hold herself together for Daisy's sake.

The telephone rang. It was Aunty's three rings, but she grabbed it on the second.

'Aunty. Ring the police and an ambulance. Get me some help, please. I've been stabbed.'

'Hello?'

'Aunty, it's Jane, get me the…'

'I didn't expect you to pick up, Jane. Is everything alright?'

'No, Aunty, it's Jane. That woman has been back. I think I've been stabbed. Call an ambulance, please.'

'You think you've been what, ducky, it's a bad line.'

'I've been stabbed. I'm losing a lot of blood. Get help, please.'

'Oh, my good God! Okay. Put the phone down. I'll ring straight away.'

'Thanks, Aunty. Hurry.' Jane replaced the receiver on the cradle of the phone and curled into a ball. She sobbed, and the tears stung as they fell. She would be scarred for life. How could she get out of this hellish situation? How could it ever end? She was scared. Really scared. They were going to come again, weren't they?

*

The house was in darkness when Dave Stark pulled onto the drive. He sat for a moment and rubbed at his eyes with the pads of his fingers. He was tired. He was starting to think that young Cynthia had a thing for him. She must have known what she was doing, when she rubbed her breasts against his arm repeatedly. They were so firm. Incredible. She was attractive of that, there was no doubt. That athletic physique and long painted nails. Long muscular legs and slim waist...

'Stop it! She's a bloody kid.' He admonished himself and muttered aloud. 'There's no fool like a bloody old fool, David.' He would never do that to Carol.

He closed the car door as quietly as possible and tiptoed into the house. He carelessly dropped his keys on the wooden floor in the hall and cursed himself before placing them quietly on the carpeted stairs.

He knew the stairs creaked like hell, so he just went for it and quickly found himself in the darkness of the bedroom, breathing a little too heavily for his liking. He could see the outline of Carol's body on her side of the bed. It looked like she was still asleep.

Sacrificing his suit to the bedroom chair rather than the wardrobe, he undressed in silence and managed to get into bed undetected. Carol had her back to him and seemed fast asleep. He slept naked, but Carol preferred pyjamas. 'The first and last line of defence', she called them.

He gently rested his arm over her shoulders and spooned her. He pushed forward instinctively with his hips as the warmth eased into his muscles.

'Don't bother.' Carol's voice echoed harshly in the stillness of the room.

6

'When you don't take a stand against corruption, you tacitly support it.'

Kamal Haasan.

The DI's office was typically minimalist. Beige walls and beige carpets. Oh, and a beige rug inexplicably placed on a beige carpet. It had some shrubbery in one corner that looked a bit sorry for itself: misshapen window blinds and a couple of pictures and certificates on the walls. Stark's office had a wardrobe and a filing cabinet, which he had purloined during an office move a few months ago and two spare chairs for others to sit at, but all attention focused on his desk. It was bigger than the norm, and it was adorned with a few desk ornaments and a couple of photos of Carol and the kids. Pride of place went to his little Nottingham Forest player with a nodding head which he would occasionally tap with his finger, just because he could. His son, Chris, had bought it him for Christmas a couple of years ago specifically for his desk, so that is where it went.

Stark sat on his high backed, leather-bound, swivel chair which he had bought himself, as the other one was too low for his desk and gave him backache. He preferred to be comfortable even if it did cost him nearly £50.

He struck a relaxed, almost bemused pose as he sat at his desk watching the sweaty Jim McIntyre hurriedly sorting through the array of large clip files. Stark was swivelling the chair a little to the left and right to entertain himself during the hiatus. Jim was trying to find the 'Misper' file - The Missing Persons file.

DC Jim McIntyre was an angry Scotsman who wasn't expressly clear on what he was angry about. Everyone else, it seemed. He had been the CID office manager for a few years now, and in truth, it was the best place for him. His main problem was a mixture of lack of sympathy, 'everyone deserves what they get,' sort of attitude and inherent bone idleness. His quick temper and occasional hissy fits were a mask for his incompetence, along with a dash of sarcasm. The ingredients of a cocktail called 'Old Sweat.'

He was old school, but an old school with a dunce's cap sitting in the corner of the room. There was a difference. There was nothing wrong with bringing along tried and proven skills and traditions long developed, but Jim seemed to have picked up the wrong box from the old school and not noticed it was marked 'bin.'

'This is what happens when you let others do the briefing. Och, look at the state of this, man. For God's sake!' He blustered.

'I can see it from here, Jim. At the bottom of the pile at the side of your left foot.'

'Aye. Got it.'

'Any overnight, Jim? Mispers, I mean.'

'No none, boss. The only live one is that girl Mandy Setter from Bracken House kiddies home, but she's missing every damned week. She doesna' even want to be found.'

'I don't care. If she turns up dead, we're screwed. Make sure uniform are doing at least two tasks or visits a day, minimum.'

'Aye. Trust me, once she's found, she'll be missing again by nightfall.'

'Such is life. I think that just leaves us with serious crime overnight. Anything on the night crime log?'

'They were called to the QMC for a wounding. Some woman from Squires Avenue…'

'That's our patch, isn't it?'

'Aye, it is.'

'Name?'

'IP's name is Jane Cooper.'

'Doesn't mean anything to me. Does it you, Jim?'

'No.'

'When you say "wounding," what do you mean. What injuries has she got?'

'It just says cut to face and hand.' Jim shuffled in his seat. 'I can barely read the man's writing.'

'Who was covering night crime?'

'Jerry Musgrove. He's a right one. Let me tell you that. He couldn't detect his arse cheeks with both hands.'

Stark shrugged out a laugh and shook his head. 'Just tell me the story then if we don't know the extent of her injuries. I can't believe the bloody injuries aren't recorded, surely?'

'It does'nae really say, boss. The bits I can read imply that it was female to female. What the motive was, I don't know. She's not been detained in hospital, so it canna be that bad.'

'Not life-threatening or anything silly like that?'

'No. She's back home. I'm not sure it's anything for us, boss. It sounds like a storm in a teacup.'

'All right. If it needs our input, uniform will send it over, I'm sure. With Jerry using the 'wounding' phrase, I'm sure uniform will be wanting to hot potato it over at their earliest convenience.'

'Och, aye.'

'Actually, nip over the bridge, will you, Jim, and just see if there is a statement or something to get to grips with. It seems a bit unusual, a wounding female on female. It's not the norm is it? I'm just interested in what it was all about and to make sure there are no repercussions.'

'Okay.' Jim scribbled on his pad, speaking aloud as he did. 'Jane Cooper, wounding, motive for DI Stark.' He did that thing where you bang the nib hard for the full stop. 'There, done.'

'Have you read up about the blagging at Bernie Squires?' Stark asked. 'Just in case you can help us with stuff later.'

'Aye. Who is it, the Brown brothers?'

'Looks like it, Jim. Let's keep that to ourselves for now, though, because rumour has it they have a few people in their pocket, even one or two coppers. I find it hard to believe, but you cannot be too careful.'

'Nae worries, boss. Anything else?'

'No, I don't think so. It is a stroke of luck that we can focus on the armed robbery. Thank God it was a quiet night. I would have thought that the Browns will be keeping their head down for a few days at least, so maybe crime will go down for a bit. Or am I being too optimistic?' Stark grinned.

'Crime go doon, around here. You've got to be kidding, boss. It's the bloody pits, man. Animals, the bloody lot of 'em.'

Stark was laughing to himself. 'Thanks, Jim. Bring us another coffee in will you, please? I desperately need to catch up on a bit of paperwork before the day is out.'

*

Jane Cooper was exhausted. She stared ahead, looking at nothing as she sat on the settee in her living room. Lost in space.

Her cheek had a thick pad over it and had required twenty stitches. It would scar, they said, but they had done their best. She only needed half a dozen stitches in her two fingers, which now had bandaging over them also.

Aunty was worried about her as she fussed around and helped little Daisy get her school uniform on. She kept glancing over at Jane, tutting and shaking her head, frustrated at the injustice of the situation and the feeling of helplessness they all felt.

Aunty had been a Godsend and told Jane she would take Daisy to school that morning even though she had been at the hospital with her late into the night and into the early hours. They had got home just after 2 am.

If Jane could just grab another couple of hours sleep, it would take the edge off her tiredness. She felt battered and bruised, but she would survive. She kept going into a trance. It had all been a shock, and she was on autopilot. Only the pain penetrated her malaise. He cheek was very sore and her fingers even more so. They were throbbing, and the pain was sapping her energy. It was a miracle she had managed any sleep at all.

Jane had spent some of the night staring at the ceiling and considering what she should do about the situation she had found herself in. Should she have kept the police out of it? Involving them would only anger the Browns further; she knew that. But what difference would it make? They were out to get her anyway. That horrendous thing, Sharon, told her as much. Who were these people? Why were they allowed to ruin decent people's lives? Couldn't they put them all on an island and let them abuse and assault each other? Leave the rest in peace.

At least the police could protect her. Couldn't they? The policeman said a detective may come and see her at some stage today.

The only path she could see was to just carry on as normal. She was due at work the next day, and she would be there as usual. She had shopping to do; she would damn well do it if she could.

Jane had cursed herself for opening the bloody door to Sharon Brown. She would not make that mistake again. She just wanted it all to be over, and that desire overrode her common sense. It was a foolish thing to do, and she had paid the price for her naivety.

She snapped out of her private thoughts and self-recrimination.

'Has Daisy got her lunch box, Aunty?' Jane asked.

'Got.' Aunty said.

'Schoolbag?'

'Got.'

'Library book has to be back today.'

'Not got.'

'Daisy, nip upstairs and get the book off your bedroom floor for the school library. The dragon one.' Jane said. She then put her hand to her cheek. It hurt to speak. It pulled at her stitches.

Daisy thundered up the stairs.

'Remember, Aunty, that Daisy waits for Margaret Baxter at the bus stop, and they like to walk in together.'

'I know, ducky. We will wait, don't worry.'

'Don't let her be late though, just give her until ten to.'

'I will. Stop fussing, Jane. It's fine. You just worry about you.'

'I know but, I don't want anything to change for Daisy. She is an innocent in all of this.'

'Aren't you all?'

'True.'

The thunder returned as Daisy jumped down the stairs two at a time bursting into the living room with book in hand. 'Got it.' She declared triumphantly with a big grin on her face.

'Well done. Remember to choose another one when you hand it in.'

'Have we got everything?' Aunty asked for the final time.

Daisy stiffened as if coming to attention on a parade square. 'Yes!'

'Good girl. Right then, come and give Mummy a kiss, then, darling.'

Daisy's bottom lip protruded. 'I want Mummy to take me.'

Jane reassured her. 'I know, darling, but Aunty will take you today. I will pick you up, don't worry. Mummy has got a poor paw. Silly Mummy. Come and give me a hug, to make it better.'

The telephone rang, and Aunty answered it for Jane.

Mother embraced daughter, and Jane whispered in her ear. 'Be good at school, for Mummy.'

'I will.'

'Promise?'

'Promise.'

'Cross keys.' Jane crossed the fingers of her good hand, and Daisy copied her awkwardly.

'Cross keys.'

'Come on then.'

Jane clumsily heaved herself out of the settee with a groan and came to the front door to wave them goodbye.

'Thanks again, Aunty. Who was on the phone?'

'Oh, it doesn't matter,'

'What do you mean? It does matter, who was it?'

'It was Mrs Baxter; they can't meet us today.'

Jane sighed. 'Them too, huh?'

Aunty took her hand. 'I'm sorry, luvvy. Don't worry, it'll sort itself out.'

'Will it, though?'

'It will.'

'At this rate, we will be treated like lepers everywhere we go.'

'No, you won't. It'll blow over. Give it time.'

'I keep trying to solve it in my head constantly, but there is no way to solve it, Aunty. All I can do is react to whatever it is they do to me.'

'It's a rum do. It really is. Remember, I'm going straight home, Jane, but I will call in later, ducky.'

'Okay, thank you for everything. I am so grateful I've got you.'

'Don't be silly. I'm old school, Jane. Friends are friends. Give your Mum a ring, yes.'

'I will, but she's got enough on her plate with Dad at the moment. I don't want to worry her.'

Jane squatted down and hugged Daisy again.

'Bye Daisy Do Do.'

'Bye, Mummy.'

'Love you.'

'Love you, Mummy.'

Once they were out of sight. Jane closed the door and sobbed. It all came out of her, and she couldn't help it. She slid down the door into a messy puddle on the floor and, resting her head on her arm, cried until she fell asleep right there on the carpet.

*

Cynthia and Steve Aston had taken over the kitchen area as it was the only room in the police station with a video recorder and television.

They had put a handwritten sign on the door. 'Investigation in progress.' But the desire for tea overwhelmed compliance, and various cops traipsed in throughout the morning as the detectives reviewed the CCTV footage of the armed robbery at Bernie Squires. The gate crashers often paused to give their view on the images on the screen.

As always, Cynthia somehow managed to combine smart professional with sexy, in a two-piece woollen suit and figure-hugging top. In contrast, Steve wore mismatching blue trousers and a brown corduroy jacket with elbow patches. He wore slip-on brown moccasins and sported a knitted tie. He looked more like a geography teacher than a detective.

The kitchen was a Formica palace with plastic moulded chairs and a sink full of used teacups. Only when the mountain overspilled the bowl would somebody take it upon themselves to wash them, usually under duress. It was a constant game of Jenga once the mugs ran out, and you had to extract one without disturbing the rest in the pile.

There were the usual notices which everyone seemed to ignore:

'Wash your pots after use!'

'Do not leave food rotting in the fridge!'

The exclamation mark of despair was always evident but made not one iota of difference to its intended audience.

On the white table was a small wooden board with minuscule holes in it, in long rows, and a handful of spent matches on top of it for the various shifts to use as a marking board for the inevitable game of cards during 'snap' time.

The two young detectives had tried to time the viewing so that they had missed the morning shift breakfast and were ahead of the lunchtime rush. A constant distraction was a howling dog in the kennels adjacent to the kitchen, awaiting collection by the RSPCA. It would cause intermittent wincing and hesitation as the two cops tried to make sense of the video they were viewing.

The first thing Cynthia and Steve did was play the video from start to finish three times and make notes of anything that caught their eye. Noting the time of anything of potential interest. Afterwards, they compared notes.

'So, what have you got, Steve?' Cynthia asked.

'Let's have a look. Time of entry. Description of offenders. Can they be recognised facially? Any distinguishing marks or identifiable features? Any tattoos visible? Who discharges the firearm? What witnesses are present? Is the offence of robbery under section 8 of the Theft Act 1968 fully complete? Can we see the amount of cash handed over? Who the offenders interact with? What time do they leave. That's about it, really. What have you got, Cynthia?'

'Similar, just a couple of other things. We need to freeze-frame when the first offender picks up the money as it looks like he has a distinctive watch on. It would be good evidence if that can be connected to the Browns.

'I didn't see that one. Good shout, though Cynth.'

'Yeah, and also, remember that Sally has said in her statement she couldn't press the button until after they left. That's not true, is it? She could have pressed the panic alarm pretty much straight away. Don't you think?'

'I'd forgotten about that. Maybe, we'll have another look. Maybe she just froze. It would have been terrifying for her.'

'Maybe, it would be terrifying, no doubt. It looks like Bernie shouts something to her, though after he stops dead. He turns towards her and raises his arm as if to stop her. I might be reading into it, but that's what it looks like to me.'

'You've seen a lot more than me, Cynthia.'

'No, not really, Steve. We need to check if the witnesses did what they said they did in their statements, just to check there is no hanky panky.'

'Bernie acts a bit odd, don't you think?' Steve said.

'What? Running out with the bat and stopping dead, you mean?'

'Yeah, but then I suppose once you see they have a sawn-off shotgun pointed at you, it can change your plans in an instant.'

Cynthia smiled. 'Yeah, I would imagine so. I hope I never have to find out. I think once we have sorted all of this out, we can put it into a statement. It might be good to see if we can identify some tasks or enquiries to follow up on from it. Just to show we are thinking ahead.'

'Like what? I can't see that many.'

'There will be, Steve, it is just not glaringly obvious at first glance.'

So the two of them began the 'stopping and starting' for the next couple of hours. Cynthia took responsibility for writing down potential enquiries, which were basically just unanswered questions and, as always, a little disjointed:

1) Can the faces be enhanced to an extent to make identification a possibility despite the masks?

2) Is there anyone outside or shops with CCTV as the Browns approach the bookmakers?

3) Can the car used be identified by reg number or distinguishing features?

4) What evidence is there forensically from the discharge of the weapon?

5) Why does Sally not press the alarm button straight away?

6) Why does Bernie run out with a baseball bat but stop dead when he sees the offenders?

7) The conversation they have seems to last longer than Bernie's statement. What are they talking about?

8) Enhance the still of the watch on the offender's arm. Can it be identified?

9) Identify the makes of the two firearms used if possible.

10) Where are the bags that the money was in? Check the Brown's bins and Golden Ball pub bins.

11) Check with forensic if any footprints on the grubby floor.

12) Obtain Sally's jumper as the offender brushes past her when he goes behind the counter to Bernie's safe and when he returns. Any fibres?

13) Check if the sawn-off shotgun has been used at any other crimes where there has been a discharge.

'Anything else, Steve?'

'No. I think that's enough to be going on with, to be honest.' He was losing interest. 'I think we're in danger of overkill here, Cynthia.'

'Yeah, but I don't want to miss anything. This video is the only piece of real evidence we have. You should be thinking the same. Everything is an opportunity, Steve. We need Mr Stark to approve us for CID in the next few months so, come on. Concentrate.'

'I am, but I can't think of anything else. I didn't think of half of the one's you came up with.'

'That's okay. It's a joint effort. Let's go and find Mr Stark. He wanted to have a look at the video himself before it goes in the property store. He's probably in his office.'

The two young detectives went upstairs onto the CID floor, but it was almost empty. Cynthia clutched her notes and Steve the video. Stark's office was empty and so was the main office apart from Jim McIntyre, the office manager, and a certain Detective Inspector Lee Mole and his Detective Sergeant Carl Davidson, who was chatting to Jim.

'Have you seen DI Stark, Jim?' Cynthia asked.

'Not since the briefing, darlin'.'

The obnoxious DI Mole was never backwards at coming forwards. 'Things are looking up, Jim, in the CID department. That prat Stark always keeps the totty to himself.'

Jim laughed over exaggeratedly.

'I thought Steph Dawson was a nice bit of crumpet, but you take the biscuit, kid.' Mole said.

Jim coughed into his mug of tea. 'Eh, don't let Nobby hear you say that about Steph, sir. He'll take your head off.'

'He's not around, is he?' Mole peered towards the open door; concern momentarily fleeted across his face.

'No, he's out, luckily for you.' Jim said.

'Lucky for him, you mean.'

DI Mole, who covered the neighbouring patch to DI Stark, had the appearance of a used car salesman but with fewer morals. He wore a bright blue ill-fitting suit, which looked two sizes too big for him, and a loud kipper tie with remnants of egg on it. His thin weasel like face matched his sneaky persona. You wouldn't trust him as far as you could throw him.

'What's a pretty little thing like you doing in a shit hole like this?' Mole said, winking at Carl Davidson, who was grinning.

'Hello, sir.' Cynthia smiled awkwardly. She felt uncomfortable as though she had walked into a trap and now couldn't get out.

'What do you want Stark for anyway when you have the A-team here and at your service?' Mole asked, imagining himself to be suave instead of the complete arsehole that he was.

'Oh, nothing really. We need to give him this video from the Bernie Squires robbery.'

'Video?' Mole asked.

'Yes, CCTV of the job going down. The blagging.'

Mole shot a glance at Carl Davidson, who raised his eyebrows.

'Is that the one's the Browns are suspected of?' Mole asked, suddenly serious.

'It is, yes, sir. I didn't think that was common knowledge…'

Steve tried to kick her. 'Come on, Cynthia.'

'Leave the video with me. I will make sure he gets it.' Mole said.

Steve spoke up. 'It's fine, sir, thanks. We can give it to him later.'

'I wasn't talking to you, Aston. Give me the bloody video.'

Cynthia handed it over. Steve and Cynthia knew that the last person on God's green earth that Stark would want to have that videotape was Lee Mole.

Steve hadn't finished. 'You need to sign the exhibit label, Mr Mole. To show the chain of evidence and acknowledge you have taken possession of it.'

Mole had no intention of doing any such thing and, in a temper at Steve's apparent impertinence, picked up the yellow pages telephone directory off Jim's desk and threw it at Steve, who ducked, but it still hit him. 'Get the fuck out! Who do you think you are? Telling me what I do and do not need to bloody do. Get out and do some work, you cheeky little shit!'

Mole threw more paperwork at him off Jim's desk. 'Go on, piss off.'

Jim was perplexed. 'Here, hold on, boss.'

Davidson was laughing as Cynthia and Steve scurried out of the office.

Mole glared at Carl. 'I don't know what you are laughing at. Pick those papers up and meet me at Oxclose Lane Police Station. We've got a video to view. I need to make a phone call to "you know who", sharpish.'

*

Stark sat in the leather-bound chair at Linda Steinbaum's beautifully decorated house. The room she used was not too large but incorporated her desk and two leather chairs with a glass coffee table in front of them. Exotic plants and some sort of water feature trickled in the corner of the room. His mind was far too busy for the nature of the call.

Stark had been masking overwhelming episodes of anxiety when giving lectures or addressing audiences. He would get palpitations and break out in flop sweats, all for no apparent reason. He was not concerned about doing such talks but as the symptoms inexplicably came upon him, it caused him to get anxious about the symptoms rather than the situation, and they grew worse. It was a cycle of stress that left him exhausted. He was desperate to make sure his colleagues or senior officers were unaware of this recent issue as he felt certain it would block him from promotion and possibly from the job itself.

He could not understand why it was just these scenarios that caused the anxiety when he was often in much more supposedly stressful situations, yet he was as calm as you like. He didn't give a damn to supposed stressful situations; he was calm as you like. It was just all the faces looking at him that seemed to trigger something off.

Thankfully it did not affect his work too much as it was a rare event that he would need to address a crowd en-masse, but it was enough to want to get it sorted out as he felt that everyone could see his distress when it happened. Particularly the sweating. It was embarrassing.

Linda was an old friend of his wife, Carol, and while they had enjoyed a few sessions previously, Stark was not wholly convinced it was doing any good.

'Thanks for fitting me in, Linda. Sorry about the other day. I hate letting people down.' He smiled and adjusted his tie pin as he adjusted himself in the high backed chair.

'My pleasure David. To be honest, I am used to people cancelling at the last minute, it goes with the territory.'

'How come?'

'Because the people I see tend to have busy, responsible, stressful jobs or lifestyles, hence the need to see me. And hence the need to cancel fairly regularly.'

Stark laughed. 'I suppose so.'

Linda had long flowing auburn hair and wore a tweed suit and white blouse. She sat to one side of David and had an air of invincibility about her, as if she had all the answers. The only problem was that David was not sure what the question was.

'Shall we start with some breathing?' Linda suggested.

'It's what I'm good at. I've been doing it all my life, and I guess I will until the day I die.'

Linda laughed. She didn't address the coping strategy of him making jokes. It was better to just go with it. 'Okay, eyes closed. We'll do it together. Breathe in two, three, four, five, six, seven, eight and out two, three, four, five, six, seven, eight, nine, ten…breathe in two, three…'

Stark shifted in his seat as Linda continued the tutorial. His balls were a little uncomfortable in his current position, so he tried to surreptitiously adjust himself. It didn't matter as Linda would have her eyes closed. She didn't and smiled to herself as she watched him fiddle around for a couple of seconds.

'Now start to breathe normally and focus on the breath entering your nostrils when it goes in, and on the same place as it comes out. If any thoughts pop into your head just acknowledge them, as 'thinking.' And let them fly away, like a cloud floating away and then gently coming back to your focus – the breathing.'

A thought came into David's head. 'Am I paying for this madness?' He quickly dismissed it. It wasn't a subject he wanted to dwell on in any case.

After ten minutes or so, David did feel a lot more relaxed and clearer-headed, much to his surprise.

'Start to wiggle your fingers and toes, and when you are ready, open your eyes, David.'

Stark opened his eyes. He blinked a few times to dispose of the blurriness.

'How was that?' Linda asked with a radiant smile.

'It was good, actually. Very calming.'

'Do you think you would be able to try that when you know you will encounter an anxiety-inducing activity?' She asked.

'Maybe. It just depends on the circumstance. I can try to.'

'Just go to the loo, David, if you can't find any privacy and get in a cubicle. Nobody is going to stop you from doing that.'

'That's not a bad idea, actually.'

'Practice doing it at home, and you will find you can do it anywhere. The more times you do it, the better. I know it sounds really simple, but trust me on this, it will help, I promise.'

'I don't do it if I feel anxious during a talk, do I?'

Linda laughed. 'I guess you can try, but I can't vouch for the interest levels of your audience.'

Stark laughed too. 'Stupid question.' He glanced at his watch.

'You've only been here fifteen minutes, David.' Linda scolded him.

'I know, apologies, but I can only do half an hour.'

'I know. It's fine. You do what you need to do. Anything is better than nothing.'

Linda crossed her shapely legs extremely slowly and seemed to hutch her skirt up slightly, and David's eyeline lowered. He then remembered what close friends Linda and Carol were, and he quickly looked away. He felt sure she knew what she was doing, the little minx. Maybe he imagined it. She was confident, and this intrigued the Detective Inspector.

'Okay, now we can do some visualisation.'

'Right.'

'I want you to think about the last time you had an attack, but rewind to the hour before, and talk me through everything that happened. What it was, and how you felt. Also, when you began to feel uncomfortable during the lead up to it and then how you tried to combat it.'

Stark leaned forward and rested his elbows on his knees. His gold cufflinks appeared beneath his suit jacket sleeves as he slowly rubbed his hands together.

'The last time? Blimey, it was at the training school, I had been asked to give a talk on the role of the CID for some new recruits, but when I got there, I didn't realise it was going to be the entire intake. Intimate it was not.'

'Good, okay. So, when you learned how many were in the audience, is that when you first start feeling anxious or was it later?'

'No, it was as soon as I heard about it, and then I could hear them all talking, laughing and shuffling chairs in the great hall next door to the staff room.'

'It sounds quite daunting for anyone.'

'Yes, but the point is Linda, I am not just anyone.'

'I'm afraid I have news for your David.'

'What?'

'Believe me, you are just anyone. The same as the Judge, the Barrister, the politician, the butcher, the baker and the bloody candlestick maker.'

*

Jane Cooper had rallied slightly. She had slept for nearly two hours, and aside from the carpet indentation on her face and a stiff neck from the draft sweeping in under the door, she felt a little better, although trembly. She headed for the kettle, and her first sip of tea was heaven.

Once ensconced on the settee, she took a deep breath and dialled her Mum's number.

'Hello?'

'Hi, Mum.'

'What is?'

'Oh, for God's sake, don't start that again.' Jane pulled her feet up onto the settee and swivelling, rested her head on the soft arm of the settee. She hutched her hips up and got herself comfortable as she listened into the green handset. It was a position she often adopted when talking on the telephone.

'That's a bit smart, Jane. What's the matter?'

'How did you guess?'

'It's not a guess. I know my daughter, and I know when something is wrong. What's happened now?'

'She came around to the house.'

'Who did?'

'That woman from the supermarket.'

'You're joking. She's got a brass neck.'

'Unfortunately, I'm not joking.'

'What happened? Did you manage to get it sorted out?'

Jane could feel herself welling up again. 'No, she slashed me with a knife.' She began to sob.

'She did what?'

'Slashed me, Mum.' Jane swallowed hard and did her utmost to gather herself together for her Mum's sake, if nothing else. 'I'm okay, don't worry, but I will have a scar on my face.' She sobbed a little more.

'Oh, Jane, that's too much. Are the police aware?'

'Yes, but they've just taken details. CID is supposed to be coming round, but I've not heard anything.'

'Let me come around. I can be there in an hour.' Her Mum had that harsh tone in her voice, and Jane could just imagine her rolling her sleeves up as she said it.

'On two buses. Don't bother, Mum, honestly, I'm fine.'

'No, Jane, you need your mother there.'

'Honestly, Mum. Don't, I just need a bit of peace and to relax for a bit. I was at the hospital until about two o'clock this morning.'

'Oh, Jane. Who is this horrid creature?'

'Sharon Brown, they call her. I told you, she is the wife of that Dougie Brown, the gangster. I'm frightened, Mum. She said they would be back.'

'Really? You need to ring the police. Speak to the Inspector. This is bloody ridiculous.'

'Let me see if they get in touch today, and if they don't, I will ring them. I promise.'

'We need to get you an alarm fitted. Do you think they will come back then? It's not just bravado?'

'Probably. I think they are that sort. I won't let them in this time.'

'You let them in!'

'Yes, I thought she wanted to apologise. She tricked me. I just wanted it to be over, Mum.'

'I know. I know. You mustn't let them in again, Jane. Just ring 999 straight away.'

'I will.'

'Promise?'

'I promise, listen, don't tell Dad, will you?'

'No. I won't don't worry, he's nodded off. This is all we need.'

'Sorry, mum.' Jane began sniffling again. She was at a low ebb.

'No, I didn't mean it like that, Jane. It's not your fault, my love. It's just frustrating. It is ridiculous. All over nothing.'

'I know. That's the problem, though; it's not over nothing. That Sharon Brown reckons she can't have kids because of me. It's hardly nothing, is it?'

'Surely not. Oh, Jane. What are we going to do about it all?'

'I don't know.'

'Have you had painkillers yet?'

'I'm just about to have some with my cuppa.'

'Are you on your own now then?'

'Yes, but Aunty's been brilliant. She was with me at the hospital all the way and even took Daisy to school for me, bless her.'

'You need to treat her, Jane. Let me treat her. What does she like?'

'Chocolates, I think.'

'I'll get her some. Give her my love, won't you?'

'I will. She's coming back round, later on.'

'That's good. It makes me feel better, anyway. Knowing someone is there with you. What about your friends?'

'I can't see it. Everyone is avoiding me like the plague. Everyone is frightened to get involved.'

'Huh. Some friends they are.'

'It's not that, Mum. People are genuinely scared of these people with good cause. I don't blame them, really.'

'Huh.'

'I'm going to go, Mum; I need to take my paracetamol. My head's thumping now.'

'Okay, Jane. I will be thinking about you. If you are unsure, or somebody comes to the door again, ring 999 and then ring me.'

'Okay, Mum. Thanks. Speak to you soon.'

'I don't know. What a to do. Speak soon, Jane.'

Jane placed the phone handset back on the cradle and having shuffled into the kitchen, pulled down the plastic Tupperware box from the kitchen cupboard. She snapped out a couple of tablets and swilled them down with her now cooling tea. She sighed once more. Where were the police?

She felt vulnerable and alone. It was nice for Aunty to come around, but what could she do if anything happened?

On impulse, Jane took the carving knife out and placed it on the kitchen top next to the door. Just in case.

She ambled over to the living room and, hearing noises outside, went to the window looking out onto the road.

'What the hell?'

There were around ten youths around 16 or 17 years old, standing outside her house. Some were sitting on her wall. Who were these people, now?

One of the youths saw her looking, and he mocked her with a little wave and a grin. The other youths turned towards her, one threw an empty can of Coke which hit the wall next to the window frame, and she ducked out of the way.

*

David Stark, oblivious to the intervention of his nemesis, Lee Mole, happily tucked into a sandwich in the kitchen area. He was feeling good. He'd had a productive morning clearing through a ton of paperwork and then even had a chance to nip and see Linda. The opportunity to go out and see Linda was a bonus, and he would now be in Carol's good books once more. Funnily enough, the world kept turning when he wasn't constantly available to all and sundry. At least he thought it had.

The local news channel was on the television set, and Stark sipped at his mug of tea. There was a young, uniformed officer a few chairs along from Stark, but he hadn't spoken other than mumble 'hello, sir,' when he walked in. Then in walked Nobby Clarke.

'You're hiding in here, boss, are you?'

'If you mean, am I using the kitchen for its intended purpose, of eating a sandwich, then yes. I am not, as you put it, "hiding."'

Nobby sat down next to Stark. 'What's this, a new healthy regime, then?'

'What? Tuna and mayonnaise? Hardly Nobby. Maybe for you.'

'I prefer a hot meal than that crap.'

'Good. I'm glad to hear it; thanks for sharing.'

'You know the Bernie Squires job is going to be the Browns. You know that, don't you, boss.'

'Using my detective powers to their maximum strength…I think…' He put his fingers to his temples. '…Yes, it is going to be the Browns.'

'So, we're screwed.' Nobby shrugged.

'Not necessarily. We've just got to think laterally.'

'What's that?'

'It doesn't matter, Nobby. We will have to try to play them at their own game. It will be tricky, granted.' Stark took a bite of his sandwich and threw in a crisp to back it up.

'The lads are out talking to informants, but while the word on the street is it is the Browns, the jungle drums go a bit quiet after that. Nobody wants to get involved with those nutters, boss. I've told them to concentrate on where the shooter might be kept.'

'Fair enough. What the fuck…?

Stark's attention had been drawn to the television screen.

'Police are investigating an armed robbery at a betting shop in Hucknall, Nottingham. Armed raiders burst into Bernie Squires Bookmakers on Annesley Road. A shotgun appears to have been discharged. Police have released this footage of the attack taking place.'

'What the actual fuck…who the hell has done this, Nobby?'

'Not me. It's the first I've heard of it. We don't want that going out.'

'Aren't you supposed to be running the bloody job?'

'Yes, but Cynthia and Steve were just viewing the footage. Nobody said anything about broadcasting it to the pissing nation. Nobody said to release it to the press. That's the last thing we want at this stage.'

The reporter continued… 'Detective Inspector Lee Mole is appealing for witnesses and in particular is interested in this unusual looking watch that one of the attackers is wearing. There is a freeze frame of the watch.'

'Fucking Mole! That bent piece of shit. How the fuck has he got hold of the video?'

Stark jumped up from the kitchen table, almost knocking it over. He bounded up the stairs, and Jim McIntyre flinched when he heard Stark shouting 'MOLE!' At the top of his voice.

Stark's face was red with rage as he burst into the office. 'Where is he?'

'Mole? He's in with Mr Wagstaff, I think, boss.'

Stark didn't knock. The red mist had descended as he barged in.

'Ever heard of knocking David?' Detective Superintendent Wagstaff stood as Stark rushed in.

'Sorry, sir, but this prat has double sixed us again, and I've just about had my fill.'

Mole stood up. 'To what do you allude?' He was grinning.

'You know damned well to what I fucking allude. You bleeding wet weekend.' Stark pointed a finger at the weasel-faced Inspector.

'What is going on? Close the door, David.' Wagstaff was unusually terse.

Stark closed the door making the shouts from inside muffled to anyone who might listen, such as Nobby and Jim McIntyre.

Stark turned to Mole. 'What do you think you are doing, Mole? Come on let's hear it.'

'I was just trying to help. That's all.' He put his hands up as if in pathetic surrender.

'More like warning the fucking Browns that we had a wristwatch that we could have pinned to them until you got it all over the TV. That will be long gone now, thanks to you. How much will they bung you for that tip-off? Eh?'

'David! Stop it. You cannot march into my office and make scurrilous accusations like that.' Wagstaff barked.

Mole was apologetic. 'All I did, sir, was try to help by putting out the video of the robbery. What's wrong with that? Stark had gone AWOL, and his officers needed some help, and I gave it to them in his absence. I thought we were one big team. Next thing I know, I'm in cahoots with the Browns according to him, anyway.'

'Well?' Wagstaff sought a reaction from David.

Stark was exasperated. 'That's not it. He knows exactly what he is doing. He had no right to do this. It's not even his job, and it's not even his patch. It is bang out of order, and he knows it. He's loving it. Look at him.'

Mole had a nonchalant grin wiped over his face. 'Okay, I won't help again in future.'

'Let's just all calm down, can we, and act like senior officers, not the local numpties after five pints.' Wagstaff urged.

The room fell momentarily quiet, and he and Mole sat while Stark merely paced the floor.

Wagstaff continued, this time in a more conciliatory tone. 'Let's discuss it like grownups. It sounds like Lee has tried to help your team, David. So what is the problem?'

'Because, of... come off it, sir, it's basics, and he knows it. You don't circulate a video when you have suspects in mind. We could have gone around to the house, found the watch, and we would have had half a chance with them. Now they will have disposed of it. It stinks. It's not helping. It's hindering. The only people he is trying to help is the Browns.'

'David, I've warned you about that sort of talk. It's unfounded and dangerous.'

'No. he's fucking dangerous.' Stark pointed at Mole, who was laughing.

'What an overreaction. Have you quite finished? Just because we work differently, you come in here throwing mad accusations around. It's a joke. You're a joke.'

'Come outside and say that you freaking wet lettuce.'

'David, all right, that's enough! Get out of my office and come back when you are ready to apologise to me and Lee.'

'Give me the video.'

'Jim's got it.' Mole said.

'You are going to come a cropper, Lee, trust me. That day gets ever closer.'

Stark turned and left, slamming the door behind him.

'Seems a bit OTT, boss.' Mole grinned at Wagstaff.

Wagstaff shook his head. 'I'm not having this. I'm the detective superintendent, not a bloody agony aunt.'

'It ain't me guv.'

7

'I grew up in a confused house: too much unwanted attention or none at all.'

- **Mary Oliver.**

Time was ticking on, and Jane had to go out now or she would be late in picking little Daisy up from school. They were still there, though; the gang of lads who seemed intent on intimidation were still outside her house. She had hoped that the cold and boredom might have discouraged them after a couple of hours. It hadn't.

Jane decided she must run the gauntlet. She couldn't be late for Daisy. In any case, if she changed her way of life for these warped people, then surely, they had won. Why should she?

Her face was sore, and she was tired. A weight was on her shoulders. She felt in over her head, and the constant feeling of 'butterflies' in her stomach was making her feel nauseous. It was exhausting, and she hated it. She hated feeling this way and the worst thing was the niggling suspicion that she could not protect her daughter from harm's way. That was the biggest terror that was lurking in the shadows of her mind.

Jane took a deep breath and threw on her coat, zipping it up tightly and pulling the hood over her head. She was distracted by the amorphous spectre outside that was the group of lads intent on upsetting her. Jane was frightened, in truth. She was almost running as she flew out of the kitchen door. She was determined to get past the lads as quickly as possible and not even look at them. Before getting out of the enclosed alley, she stopped abruptly. 'It might help if you locked the damned door!' she scolded herself and returned to the door. She hadn't even closed it, never mind locked it.

'Come on, Jane, pull yourself together.' She muttered.

After checking the house was properly secure this time, she took a deep breath and scurried along the passage at the side of the house and out towards the gate.

Upon seeing her, the gang of louts welcomed her with a rousing cheer. She ignored it, turning left out of the gate and away from them as quickly as possible. If they trash the house, so be it. Jane thought.

Only they would not damage the house because they were following her, all ten of them, suddenly animated, excited, that they finally had some entertainment in the form of Jane Cooper.

Jane walked faster, conscious of the gang pursuing her, whooping and hollering after her. She continued head down and into the chilly wind, inadvertently kicking up several crisp brown leaves as she piled through them.

Behind her, the youths shouted abuse, made chicken clucking noises and threw various small items at her such as pebbles and litter they gathered up on the fast-paced walk. It was all petty and childish, and half the time, the lads were that stupid they threw items against the wind that merely blew back into their own faces.

However, it was distressing for Jane, and as she neared the school, she wanted to be rid of them. It was embarrassing, if nothing else. She stopped in her tracks.

'Will you please stop following me?'

A loud and prolonged, 'Ooh.' Came from the youths.

'Seriously, I don't want to have to call the police, and there is a telephone kiosk just up the road,' Jane threatened. She could see and hear herself in a sort of out-of-body experience, and she looked pathetic and weak compared to the confident gang who revelled in just this type of confrontation. It was a mistake; she had broken the invisible barrier between them by engaging.

'Ooh, not the police. Oh, we're scared! Not a telephone box. Please don't.' They were laughing as they mocked her, surrounding her.

They had encircled her now and one of the cowards pushed her and as she turned another did and she became like a ball in a pinball machine pushed from one to another.

It was apparent that she could not reason with these idiots, and so she deftly squeezed through a small gap and continued walking. One of the youths rushed up behind her, put his foot in her stride, and tripped her. She fell onto the pavement with a thud, grazing her hands and tearing the seam of her coat at the elbow.

Again, there was much laughter, but Jane was determined not to cry, though tears were welling. She struggled to her feet and examined the ripped fabric.

'Thanks a lot. I've now got to find the money for a new coat.'

One youth did a flamboyant bow. 'Our pleasure.' He threw a ten-pound note at her. 'Here, use this tenner, courtesy of Dougie Brown. Looking at that shitty coat, you can bring the change back.'

Another chimed in, one of the younger ones. 'You look a scruffy charity case. Unless you want to earn it and suck my dick.' They all laughed and began chanting, 'Suck his dick, suck his dick.'

Jane ignored it at first, staring at the youths, hands-on-hips. She heard herself say, 'No thanks, I prefer men.'

'Ooh, what a fucking slag.' The youth said.

'You fucking dirty cocksucker.' Another chimed.

Jane was getting more and more annoyed. 'Just grow up. You're pathetic. Would you do that to your own mother?'

'What suck her dick?' More over-the-top laughter.

'I mean trip her up and hurt her for no reason. Would you do that to your own mother?'

'No.'

'There you are, so why do it to me?'

'It would be much worse if it was my old cow of a mother. I'd give her a right pasting. Fuck her and fuck you.'

Jane realised that there was no point in reaching for their conscience. They had none. It was just ridiculous. It was a no-win situation, and she was stuck in the middle of it. It was humiliating.

Thankfully as she passed the telephone kiosk, the gang held back, and she was able to enter the school gate alone but flustered.

Jane nodded and said hello to various mothers, all of whom ignored her, purposely turning away from her. Her playground partner, Karen, was not in her usual place and a couple of mothers near to where Jane settled made a point of stepping a few feet away from her as if she had something contagious. Jane sighed and waited for her daughter.

She was worried about the youths waiting for her and what they might do with Daisy. Should she speak to the school? Ring the police? She felt like a condemned man walking to the scaffold, destined to her fate but powerless to change the inevitability of it.

This was all getting too much. She did not deserve this. She hadn't done anything. Why couldn't they see that?

*

The dishevelled kitchen of the terraced house on Ingram Road had not seen a dishcloth or mop in a while. The sink was half full of pots, and an off-white tea towel hung limply on the handle of the oven door.

The worktops sported an array of stains and damage, not least the edge, which had a line of half a dozen or so cigarette burns where they had been unattended too long and melted grooves into the plastic. It was a corrugated monument to neglect.

There was a smell of stale chip fat lingering in the air due to the chip pan, which was a permanent feature on the filthy stove.

An old radio which looked years old was playing tunes, presumably left on throughout the day regardless of where the occupant was.

The debonair DC Ashley Stevens liked how the young woman's breasts bounced as he fucked her against the grimy kitchen wall. She had been quick to rip off her jumper to reveal her prized assets within fifteen minutes of Ashley walking through the door.

Mandy Gregson had been an informant of his for a couple of months now, and she had made it perfectly obvious what she wanted from him from day one. There was no way she was going to get it; she wasn't his type for a start. This time Ashley would be resolute. He wasn't.

It was something of an affliction for Ashley, and he did not understand his incessant lust. Was it an age thing? Was there some weird psychological reason for his large libido? 'Excuse me, Doctor, my libido has enlarged. Do you have any cream for it.'

'Whipping or squirty?'

'Both.'

This was how his mind worked, moving from seeking help and an explanation to imagining a female doctor squirting cream on his dick. He doubted it was normal.

Every time Ashley met a woman, his first thought was whether she was fuckable, and the second was when he would actually have sex with her. He was getting good at guessing correctly. That can't be normal, can it? He could find attractiveness in most women, regardless of age. He once brought a woman in her sixties back to the dorm when he was on a CID course and fucked her on his bunk. In the morning, she was gone, and she had left fifty pounds and her number on his bloody bedside table. That was a low point, until at least lunchtime when one of the lady cooks in the canteen spanked his backside in the queue. Then it was all forgotten. It would be his downfall, no doubt.

Female informants were lethal, and it happened nearly every time that a perfectly decent informant would come on to him or would turn up at a pub he had mentioned or at Ritzy's nightclub. He noticed the warning signs: 'Are you out at the weekend?' They would ask, and lo and behold; they would 'bump' into him at said location. More often than not, he bumped back.

Mandy, however, had bided her time and caught poor, vulnerable detective Ashley Stevens in a weak moment as she followed him into the small kitchen. She stripped off her tight-fitting jumper in the kitchen, revealing unfettered knockers. This caused Ashley to raise an eyebrow and inwardly curse.

'What d'ya think?' She asked.

'Very nice.' Ashley said as he cupped them.

Mandy unzipped his trousers and pulled his pants down. Her eyes widened.

'Wow. I fucking knew it. Jesus.'

She began licking at it, like a lollipop at first, seemingly wary of it before getting both hands on it and masturbating him in between sucking sessions.

Mandy pitted her feverish activity with. 'Fuck, yeah,' and 'You big cocked bastard.' All wonderfully romantic phrases which amused Ashley. He'd heard it many times before.

Ashley thought it rude to spurn young Mandy after taking such a gamble and exposing herself to him. It took courage and was something to be admired, and yes, rewarded. He couldn't leave her hanging, so to speak particularly after she had taken it upon herself to kneel on the grimy linoleum floor to suck his dick. Plus, he now had an erection that would not go away even if you beat it with a stick wrapped with barbed wire. Periodically, Mandy would move back as if to admire it, holding it at the base as it throbbed. Then frantically rub it.

Ashley took hold of her hand. 'Hang on. Mandy, I'll cum in a minute.'

Mandy quickly pulled her knickers off and pulled her tight leather skirt up, revealing a surprising amount of pubic hair.

DC Stevens was committed now and took control of the situation. Despite being small in height, the lascivious Mandy was surprisingly heavy, and Ashley realised that if he were not careful, he could scratch his Rolex wristwatch against the unplastered kitchen wall as he was banging her against it. It was only after he had slid carefully inside her and begun thrusting deeper and deeper, he realised he needed to find a surface to put her on. It had seemed like a good idea in the throes of lust to hold her against the wall, but he doubted he could get a rhythm going in this position. If she slid down, she would take his dick with her. This realisation required immediate action.

He disengaged, carrying her a couple of feet to the side and placing her on the top of the washing machine. Because his trousers were around his ankles, he had to close one foot into the other and shuffle along, like a teenager learning the Waltz for the first time. It lacked finesse, but it got him across the floor.

It was a clumsy start, but desire finds a way. Once her bare backside felt the coldness of the metal washing machine, Ashley reinserted himself and thrust into her so hard that he must have pressed something with his leg. So, to accompany Ashley's balls, the drum of the washing machine suddenly began to churn its contents. This forced the detective to stifle a grin as he continued to pound.

Mandy grunted and groaned, 'Oh, yeah, fuck yeah,' She leaned forwards, briefly pressing her tongue into his mouth. An interesting mix of tobacco, coffee, and halitosis.

Still, any port in a storm. Ashley always said, far too regularly. She was wet. She was loving it, and if she was loving it, so was he. That's how it worked for him.

The radio was playing golden oldies, and bizarrely even though it was only just November, the DJ took it upon himself to play 'Merry Christmas Everyone' by Slade.

As the washing machine cranked up, so did Ashley's thrusts, somehow in synchronisation with the washing machine. He didn't think he'd make it to the spin cycle. After a few minutes, Mandy's groaning and swearing, her bouncing bosoms, and the situation itself were all too much and, quicker than he hoped, Ashley felt a surge in his balls. He stopped briefly, but he had mistimed it by a microsecond and as they tightened, he ejaculated into the dripping wet pussy of a girl whose second name he couldn't remember, just as Noddy Holder hollered, 'It's Christmas!'

As he pressed deep inside her, he groaned and contemplated whether she might be on the pill or not? It was a bit late to worry about that now, and anyway, Santa's toy laden sleigh and his nine reindeer could not have stopped his hips drilling into her as he orgasmed. That's nature for you. Procreation will override all other emotions given the right setting. She began to scream.

'Ssh! Are you okay?' Ashley said.

'Oh yes, yes!' She screamed again and quickly rubbed herself, letting out a sort of deep woofing sound. Not so much like a dog, but perhaps a Moose on heat.

'Fuck me.' Ashley said as he felt her climax.

Mandy was panting as he slid his cock out and it flopped down, dripping with the mixture of their sex potion. Ashley moved back to avoid it getting on his expensive suit trousers still wrapped around his ankles.

'Use the kitchen sink.' She said, her chest heaving as she caught her breath.

'Okay, thanks.' If nothing else, he was polite.

Ashley washed his member as best he could amidst the teacups and used the off-white tea towel to dry it. The material felt a bit crusty. He pulled his Calvin Klein's and his trousers up and walked, weak legged, into the living room. His head was fuzzy, and he gasped as he sat on the soft chair.

'Jeez.' Of course, he immediately regretted it. Such was the nature of the beast.

'Do you want tea?' Mandy asked quite matter-of-factly. She seemed to have recovered somewhat quicker than he, as he still wrestled with his sexual stupor.

'Erm, sure.'

Mandy took three dirty cups out of the sink, rinsed them briefly under the tap, and wiped them with the same tea towel that bore Ashley's semen. It was indeed a seminal moment.

'Sugar, detective?'

'Two, please.' His voice croaked. He was still a little out of breath, and his heart was pumping.

Mandy came into the living room and bizarrely sat down with no top on, her large breasts fully exposed and her short skirt still partially entangled around her hips, barely pulled down. As she sat, Ashley could see her hairy vagina oozing onto the upholstery.

'Classy.' He thought to himself.

'That's better, isn't it?' She said.

'Definitely. I was a bit quick, but it was pretty hot.'

'I know. You're good; I'll give you that. We can take our time next time. The kettle will be boiled in a minute.'

There was a lull as Mandy sat with a huge smile on her face.

'I'd heard about you from a friend of a friend. She knows you. I told her I fancied you like fuck, and she said you wouldn't turn me down. She told me every little thing about you.'

Ashley laughed. 'Every *little* thing? Blimey, She's been spoiled.'

'Every big thing, then.' She laughed.

'Who's that?'

'Bernice.'

Ashley looked puzzled. 'Bernice? Are you sure I've had her?'

'Yeah, Bernice Leivers, she lives up Snape Wood. Apparently, you haven't been up to see her for months, which she didn't seem too happy about, by the way.'

'I don't remember her, off the top of my head.'

'She's slim, not got much up top. Always wears black false nails and false eyelashes. She's attractive, though. Well, I think she is.'

'Oh, yes, I know who you mean. I have been meaning to call and see her. Her husband works funny shifts, I think.'

'Yeah, he's a lorry driver. Gordon, his name is. Don't let him catch you.'

'I think I will survive, somehow, Mandy.'

'I couldn't believe it when she told me you'd fucked her.'

'Don't believe everything you hear, Mandy.'

'Oh, yeah, she just guessed about the size of your donkey dick, did she?'

'She must have.' Ashley grinned. He would have to stop doing this. What was wrong with him?

'Anyway, if you've got time to call round to see her, you need to come here instead.'

'Maybe.'

Mandy smiled strangely. 'Only kidding. You can do what you want. It's none of my business.'

Ashley laughed. 'Thanks, I'll bear that in mind. That's very kind of you.'

'Don't take it funny. I was just saying.'

'I know.'

'When are you coming back, though?'

Ashley laughed and shook his head. 'I don't know.'

'But you are coming back.'

'Bloody hell, Mandy.'

'Sorry.'

Ashley smiled smugly. There was a pronounced click from the kitchen. 'There we go. That's the kettle.' Mandy said.

'Thank Christ.' Ashley thought to himself.

Ashley listened to her pour the water into mugs, and the post climactic downer started to infiltrate him. Maybe he should have shown some restraint? She seems a bit loose mouthed. Sitting there with her tits out was a bit of a turn off as well. Nice pussy, though.

Mandy returned with three mugs.

'Three mugs?' Ashley looked puzzled. 'Are you expecting someone?'

'One's for my hubby.'

'What?'

'It's all right, he's in bed upstairs.'

Ashley almost choked as he sipped his tea.

'Don't worry. He can't come down, Ashley, he's bedridden. He's not got long left. Luckily he's got me to look after him.'

'Yeah, lucky him.' Ashley shook his head. His face bore an expression of incredulity. 'In bed upstairs dying. Bloody hell, Mandy, you could have told me.'

'It might have put you off.'

'You're fucking right it might.'

'Well, now you've had me, it won't bother you.'

'Christ, Mandy. That is bloody cruel.'

'No, it's not. He's out of it most of the time. He won't know anything happened, don't worry. He's a bastard anyway, he's knocked me about for years before he got ill. Fuck him.'

Ashley laughed instinctively. 'I thought I was bad.'

Within a minute or so, Mandy and her bare breasts returned and settled back onto her chair. She noticed the wetness.

'Aargh, you dirty sod!'

'Me? I think you will find that is you, Mandy.'

'Oh, well. It'll dry.'

'I take it you're on the pill?' Ashley asked.

'Yes, lucky for you, judging by the mess you've made. I didn't think you were going to stop.'

'It's been a while. Well, a couple of days.'

There was a brief lull with the two of them staring into space for a minute or so. Still a little out of breath, Ashley asked whether Mandy had any information for him. It was, after all, the initial reason for his visit. He struggled to talk to her face with her breasts hanging, and he noticed a bead of sweat trickle down her decolletage in between her ample bosoms.

'Mandy lit up a cigarette and threw one at Ashley. See how good I am to you.'

'I'm forever grateful, Mandy.'

'Well, I wasn't going to say owt cos it's a bit risky, the info is, I mean, but I might just tell you.'

'Don't you think what I've just done is a bit risky?' Ashley asked.

'True.'

'Come on, then let's hear it.'

'Well, you haven't heard it from me. Do you know about that woman who got slashed by the Browns?'

'What woman is this?'

'Her name is Jane summat; I don't know her last name. Snitches get stitches, isn't it.'

'Go on. I don't know anything about it. It's news to me.'

'Sharon Brown did her the other night.'

'Oh, hang on, there was a wounding reported, thinking about it. It was on the briefing sheet. What's that got to do with the Browns, though?'

'Don't you dare tell anyone, Ashley.'

'We don't work like that. I won't if you won't.'

'Won't what? Oh, tell anyone about what just happened. I see what you mean. Fair enough. Well, Sharon slashed her with a razor. That's the gossip anyway, and it's all-around Bulwell.'

'Why? Why would Sharon Brown do that, Mandy?'

'It's all to do with a bust-up they had in the Co-op on Highbury Vale the other morning, and this Jane put Sharon on her backside.'

'Oh dear, not a good idea.'

'That's what I said.'

'Anyway, it is Sharon Brown who did it. Is that all right for you? Happy now? Worth coming back for?'

'That is more than all right, Mandy.' Ashley raised his mug of semen tea to acknowledge it as if it might be a champagne flute.

'So, when are you coming round again?'

'Blimey, give me a chance. I haven't left yet.'

'I know, but it would be nice to know when you are coming round again. Roughly.'

'We'll see. I'm a busy man, Mandy. I can't say when, but I'll be back, I promise.'

'You better had. I will have some more info for you by, shall we say Friday?'

'We'll see.'

*

DC Charlie Carter turned left into Saxondale Drive in Bulwell. Stark sat in the passenger seat of the Ford Escort, CID car. He had forgotten just how uncomfortable the old nail was. They should have taken Stark's car; it was much more comfortable, and it was nearly 40 pence a mile on casual users' mileage. It soon added up. Anyway, it was too late, now, and he winced every time they went over these stupid bloody road humps that had sprung up all over the place. They nearly ripped the exhaust off any car going over ten miles an hour and were a literal pain in the backside.

'Thanks for coming boss, I know you're busy.' Charlie said.

'No problem. Apart from these pissing sleeping policemen, everywhere you go. It's getting beyond a joke.'

'These new road humps, you mean?'

'Yes, it's ridiculous. How are we supposed to get anywhere in a hurry?'

'We're not, I guess.'

'How many lives have been lost with ambulances taking twice as long to get there?'

'Exactly, but I don't think they bothered with all that. Once they could claim they were doing something about all these TWOC'ers racing around, they went for it.'

'It's a joke. It really is. Anyway, who's this woman we're going to see?'

'She's not a bad informant, is Rita, I've known her years. She tends to come in fits and starts. I haven't seen her for months, and then she calls me. I've wanted to pay her for a couple of days now. You know I need a DI to witness the payment, so I wanted to grab you as soon as you could make it.'

'A hundred quid is a bit hefty, ain't it. How did you get Headquarters to authorise it?'

'You signed it through, boss.'

'Yes, I suppose I did, but I expected HQ to knock it down a bit. A burglar doesn't warrant that much, I know.'

'Not just any burglar, Dave, it was Scratchy Potter, remember?'

'Yes, I was about to say, thinking about it, I remember it now, how many did he cough to in the end.'

'More than fifty, fifty-three, in the end, I think it was. Over a year, like.'

'One a week.'

Charlie laughed, 'I suppose it is, and one for his nob.'

'I've not met this one, have I?'

'You're in for a treat with the lovely Rita.'

'Oh, Christ.'

The house was pretty well appointed, and the garden neat and tidy. 'Coming.' Stark heard the woman shout and watched her hazy figure approach through the opaque glass of the front door.

'Hiya, Charlie, love.'

Rita Hayes was in her early sixties. She was slender, with shoulder-length dark hair, and heavily made up. Rita wore a pink leisure suit and gold jewellery dripped off her wrists and neck, which she had accumulated over the years.

Rita and Charlie embraced, 'Sorry it's been so long, Rita.'

'I've forgotten what you look like.' She rubbed Charlie's arm, genuinely pleased to see him.

'This is Detective Inspector Stark, Rita,' Charlie said.

'The big cheese, eh?' She put out her hand, and Stark shook it. Rita inexplicably did a tiny curtsey as she shook his hand and nudged Charlie. 'Eh, he's a bit of all right.' She snorted out a laugh which turned into a smoker's cough, and Stark noticed for the first time that all her teeth were completely black and rotted to stumps. It took him by surprise. There was no need for it. Why not get them sorted out?

'Look at me being rude.' She put on a posh accent. 'Please do come in.' She said to Stark, who was grinning.

Rita seemed pleased with the company. The two detectives sat on the floral settee.

'Ouch, ya bugger!' Charlie let out a cry and rubbed at his knee.

'It's about time you got that knee sorted out, Charlie.' Rita winked at Stark, who shrugged out a laugh.

Rita sat to one side of the two gentlemen, and they began the slightly awkward process of paying an informant.

'Let's get this out of the way, then Rita. I have the princely sum of one hundred pounds for you.' Charlie said.

'Ooh, that's nice.' Rita rubbed her hands together.

Charlie counted it out in ten-pound notes onto the glass coffee table, and Stark signed the papers, as a witness to payment, along with Rita as the recipient and Charlie as the handler. Rita scooped up the loot and went to put it in a porcelain pot amongst four or five Capodimonte figurines on a corner shelf.

'That'll help with Christmas, that will.'

'Well, you earned it, Rita.' Stark smiled.

'It's money for old rope when you think about it.' She said as she placed herself delicately onto the armchair.

'It can be, but let's face it, Rita, it's vital to us. It doesn't matter how easy or hard it is for you; it can be gold dust for us.' Stark said. 'Anyway, how does a lovely lady like yourself get to know about the activities of the criminal underworld?'

'Did you hear that, Charlie? Lovely lady. He's a charmer, isn't he?'

Charlie looked at his boss. 'I've always found him to be so.'

Stark laughed. 'Why, thank you, Charlie. So, how come, Rita?'

Rita leaned forward and opened an Onyx topped box full of cigarettes, which she passed around to Charlie and Stark, taking one for herself.

'Well, I'm a mobile hairdresser, Mr Stark, and I get to hear all the gossip from the wives and girlfriends of these criminals. They don't care who hears it.' She produced a small cigarette holder and inserted the cigarette carefully. Stark leaned forward and lit it for her.

'Thank you. Such a gentleman. Anyway, they live like bloody Queen's half on 'em. And my prices aren't cheap. I just think about the poor folks on the other end of it all. The victims of it. Most of 'em are elderly, you know. Some have lost their life savings to these little buggers.'

'I know.' Stark nodded.

'Well, that's why I talk to Charlie. We go back years, don't we, duckie?'

'We sure do, Rita.' Charlie smiled and reached out and held her hand for a moment.

'I can remember him when he was a young detective at the 360 Club in Bulwell. Mind you he was a lot thinner then.'

'Thanks. Rita. I love you too.' Charlie laughed.

She smacked Charlie on the arm, perhaps a little too hard. 'Only kidding.'

'It is true, in fairness.' Charlie bit his lip and didn't mention that she also had all her bloody teeth in those days.

DI Stark's radio crackled. 'Dc McIntyre to DI Stark.'

Stark spoke to Rita. 'Excuse me a second.' He then picked his radio up. 'Go ahead, Jim.'

'Anywhere I can ring you, boss?'

'Standby.' Stark again addressed Rita. 'Is it okay if someone rings me here, Rita?'

'Yes, of course.'

Stark repeated the phone number two figures at a time to Jim, and within thirty seconds, the phone rang in the hallway, and Stark went to answer it, closing the living room door behind him.

'Hello, Jim, what's up?'

'Och, it's gone bloody mental here, boss. I don't know whether to shit, shave, or shampoo.'

Stark laughed. He had never known a time when Jim did not claim to be overwhelmed with work.

'You can cope, Jim, a man of your calibre. Go on then, let's hear it.'

'Young Ashley's been on the blower and said that Sharon Brown did the wounding on that girl Jane Cooper.'

'Wounding?'

'The one on the briefing I mentioned.'

'Oh, yes, of course, I've got you now. It's not been referred yet. Sharon Brown? Dougie's Mrs? You're kidding me.'

'I'm not. Apparently, according to Ash, they had some sort of argument in the supermarket, and Dougie's Mrs took exception to it.'

'How does he know this?'

'Some informant he's fucking I think.'

'Now, Jim, don't be like that.'

'Anyway, an informant told him this morning.'

'Interesting. What's her address? The I.P. I mean.'

'Squires Avenue, 23.'

'Me and Charlie will call and see her. It could be an 'in' to the Browns if we play our cards right.'

'Aye, that's what I thought. Before you do though, boss, someone else has rung in and said that he has seen that wristwatch on the offender for the armed robbery, for sale at a pawnbroker on Mansfield Road, in town. Samsons. He saw it on the news.'

'Bollocks!'

'That's a good thing, isn't it?'

'No, it isn't, because we have to tie it to the Browns and they have realised because of that prat Mole, that they need to get rid, sharpish. It wouldn't surprise me if he hadn't rung them personally and told them. Anyway, don't get me started on him, but it just shows that he has scotched any chance of us getting a bloody warrant at the Browns. He is so full of shit, he really is.'

'That's if it's the same watch.'

'It will be.'

'The pawnbroker might give you details.'

'I won't hold my breath, Jim. Anything else?'

'Do you want me to send Ash up to the pawnbrokers or are you and Charlie going?'

'Yes, go on then, he is on the robbery posse, tell Nobby, first, he might want to go with him.'

'Aye.'

'Me and Charlie will go and see this, Jane Cooper.'

'Nae bother.'

'See you later, Jim. Keep attacking.'

'Aye, cheers, boss.'

*

The Browns living room was standing room only. The youths who called in most days were in a cluster laughing and joking and judging by their actions, reconstructing some sort of punch-up. Smoke lay in a cloud just below the yellowing nicotine-stained Artex ceiling. The whole room needed a revamp. All Dougie had to do was mention to a painter and decorator that it needed doing and it would be done without charge the next day. He just hadn't got round to it, that was all. He had enough on without having to sort the decorating out. Sharon would get around to it one day. Sharon thought the same about Dougie.

Big Trixie and her friend were sitting at the dining table smoking and sorting through a load of makeup and skincare products from the latest shoplifting haul at Boots the Chemist. They read the ingredients of lotions and potions as if they had a chemistry degree.

Dougie and Len 'the bitch' Brown sat on the settee, and Sharon rested her head on her hand on the armchair near the window. Dougie was reading the newspaper, and there was an article about the armed robbery.

'Here listen to this Len, our blagging was in the Evening Post last night; *Local businessman and owner, Bernard Squires, said, 'It was terrifying, I think they were from out of town. It's awful for my customers, and the police don't seem to have a clue. Why can't they protect us, law-abiding citizens, from these sort of crimes?'*

Lennie laughed. 'Good old Bernie. We'll have to treat him.'

Dougie folded up the paper and threw it onto the coffee table. He stretched.

There was a hum of noise and chatter above a comfortable level. It was like the taproom of a spit and sawdust pub, and there were too many people in there.

Len leaned into Dougie's ear. 'Are we ready to talk business? Cos, this lot are doing my fucking head in.'

'Ready when you are, brother.'

Lennie clapped his hands together a couple of times and shouted above the noise. 'Oi up. Oi! Quiet!'

Silence fell.

'Dougie and I have some business to discuss, and so you lot need to disappear for an hour. Come on, chop, chop!'

There was a hint of a groan from the youths; one of whom asked,

'Are we alright in the kitchen, Len? I'm supposed to be doing security today.'

'No, out, right out the house. Come back in an hour minimum. You know how this works, Chaf, come on, sort it.'

'Just checking, Len, that's all.'

They began to shuffle out.

'You too, Trixie.' Dougie shouted. 'Blood only for this one.'

The girls heaved themselves unceremoniously from the dining chairs and began to sort through the goodies from Boots, deciding what to take and what to dispose of in the pub later.

'Leave all of that shit. Do it later.' Dougie said. 'Come on, fuck me, move your fat arses. Out!'

The two girls tutted and waddled out, throwing their hair back as they did.

Sharon scarcely acknowledged what was happening. She seemed to be in a world of her own, staring into the garden beyond the dormant raindrops on the window to the rusting quad bikes and motorcycles accumulated there over the months and years.

After what seemed like an eternity and once the door had slammed, Len started the conversation.

'I'd hate to be behind them fat fuckers in a fire.'

Dougie laughed.

Sharon shot a dirty look towards Len. It was ignored.

'I just wanted to sort out where we are with this co-op business and Sharon. Are we happy now that Sharon has messed up that silly bitch on Squires Avenue? Are we happy we are even now? Are we done with it?' Len asked.

Dougie shifted in his seat, moving to the edge of the settee.

'Maybe, Len. She's scarred for life now, and honour has been restored, I guess.'

'Has it, though?'

'What do you mean, Len?'

'I'm just asking the question. It damaged us quite a bit, Dougie, and the fucking Grants and Conways have been taking the piss apparently.'

'What do you mean? How come I don't know about this? I should be the first to know, not the fucking last. What they been up to?'

'It's no big deal, bro. Just being leery apparently, Little Big Man was in the Fox and Grapes, and Georgie Grant was laughing that we had lost our touch and couldn't be taken serious anymore.'

'Cheeky cunt. What, even after Sharon had slashed the bitch?' Dougie tapped out a cigarette from a packet of Bensons on the table, and Len produced a lighter and lit the end for his brother. 'Cheers, Len.'

'So he says, but maybe word hadn't gone out. They must know we would act on it. As if we would let that go by and do nowt.'

'As if. Course they do. What have the Conway's been saying then?'

'Word is they reckon we're busted, can't protect our own women, that sort of bullshit.'

'That's a fucking laugh; look at Sammy Conway's mother. Doing two years for pisspot shop lifting and he reckons we can't look after our women. Fuck 'em, Len, it's just bullshit.'

'I know, mate, I'm just saying what I've heard. That's why I'm asking the question if we think Sharon slashing the bitch is enough, that's all.'

Dougie seemed to be weighing it up in his mind. He shrugged. 'I reckon it probably is, don't forget our little tickle at Bernie Squires has caused some ripples. Some of this will be jealousy after us pulling off that job at Bernie's. I think maybe leave it. Taking her out isn't really an eye for an eye, it's not really code, Len, is it?'

There was a brief lull. It seemed to rest uneasily with Len. 'We need to fuck up one of the Slack brother's crew out at Newark, then.'

'How come?'

'Since all this kicked off, Slacky junior has been in one the Amusement Arcades at Bulwell, checking out how much they pay us.'

'Fuck off!'

'He has. Jean, what's her name? She works weekends.'

'Storey.'

'Yeah, Jean Storey told Piggy Moyes about it.'

'So, let's do the same to theirs then.'

Len looked unconvinced. 'It's not just that, Dougie.'

'Go on.'

'That Mandingo bloke went and worked one of their doors. They've been chatting him up, adding a bit of muscle.'

'He's ours, isn't he?'

'*Was* ours, Dougie. Looks like he's moved over to them.'

'I think we need a word with the black cunt. I told you about having them black fuckers on board, no loyalty, Len. I don't like having fucking nig nogs on board; you know that. They've got their own shit. We don't bother them, and they don't bother us. End of story.'

'I'm just saying it feels like our position has been weakened, that's all.'

'You're right, but how long does that take to resolve? Not long. A show of strength is needed; it's just tit-for-tat bollocks. They will always try to take liberties. They are just testing us.'

'True.'

'Topping that bint on Squires Avenue is a serious move, that's all, we only do that shit as a last resort.'

'Yeah, but…'

'But what?'

'Dougie, think back to how we got here. We didn't get here by pussy footing around and umming and ah-ing about this and fucking that. We would *annihilate* any fucker that stepped on our toes. Anyone. Destroy the bastards. The whole fucking bag of mashings. Remember as well, you told half the crew you was gonna do her, and now we're not?'

'I was mad, and I just question whether it's an eye for an eye, Len.' Dougie sighed, gently shaking his head as he took in Len's words.

Sharon suddenly stood up, throwing her mug across the room. Tears were in her eyes.

'What the fuck?' Dougie said.

'Not an eye for a fucking eye?' She yelled. 'How dare you, Dougie Brown!'

'Now, what's up?'

'You seem to have forgotten that we probably can't have kids because of her.'

Dougie grimaced. 'I hadn't forgotten, I was just coming to that.'

'No, you were not, Doug, all you were worried about was your fucking ego and whether honour had been restored or whatever it was you said. What about me? What about us? That don't matter do it? No, I thought not.'

'Sit down, Sharon. You will need to clean that fucking tea up in a minute. Just calm down. We're talking it through, aren't we?'

Sharon resumed her seat, sniffling. 'What is there to talk through, Dougie?'

'It's a serious step, Shaz. Cos if I do it, I do it properly…'

'*We* do it.' Len corrected him.

'Sorry, Len, yeah, you're right, *we* do it properly, no pissing about, torture, the works.'

'As long as she pays, I don't care. Just do her in, Dougie. That is if you care about us.'

'Behave, Shaz, of course, I care about us.'

'Do you? Why aren't you mad about what's happened? It's just like a business deal to you. It's like you're talking about the bleeding weather. This is me. Your Mrs and you're gonna let her get away with it?'

'She hasn't got away with anything, Shaz. You've done her up proper, you said.'

'I have scarred the bitch, but she hasn't suffered like I'm suffering. In case you hadn't noticed, I am suffering Douglas Brown. Me. Your wife. I could have lost everything here. I can't believe you are so bloody calm about it.'

'We will get you the best doctors if we need to, but we don't know for certain there is any permanent damage now, do we?'

Sharon wiped away a tear. 'I know it, Doug, trust me, I can *feel* it. And what's more, how come she can just make me feel all this pain and you, not me, you don't even lift a finger. I can't believe it. I've done my bit. Maybe the Conway's are right.'

Dougie stood up and hit out at Sharon. Smacking her across the head. 'Watch your fucking mouth, or you'll be in a fucking black bag yourself! Never say shit like that. Understand?'

Sharon was crying, and she realised she had probably overstepped the mark.

'Understand!' Dougie bore down on her, raising his fist this time.

'Yes. I understand. I didn't mean it, but what are you going to do about it, Dougie. You're my man.' Sharon wailed.

Dougie looked at Len, who shrugged.

'Yes?'

'Fuck it, let's do it.' They clasped hands. 'Just me and you, Len, I don't want the others being involved, just you and me, yeah.'

'Absolutely. Just you and me, our kid. Like old times. Blood brothers.'

'Blood brothers.'

Sharon smiled through her tears.

8

'Zen teaches that once we can open up to the inevitability of our demise, we can begin to transform that situation and lighten up about it.'

– Allen Klein.

It was a stroke of luck that Aunty had turned up at the school to pick Daisy up, explaining to the relieved Jane.

'I couldn't remember whether you were picking her up or if I'd said I would. I didn't want to take a chance.'

The group of youths had backed off when Jane came around the corner with some woman accompanying her. The Browns told them no witnesses, and they would not risk getting on the wrong side of the brothers. As darkness was falling, it didn't take long for Jane and Aunty to be home and the kettle to be steaming.

Daisy had run upstairs to play almost immediately, enabling Jane and Aunty to have a more intimate chat.

'Like I said, Aunty, they tripped me up. I felt a right berk.'

'Little sods. They want a good hiding. Fancy doing that to a defenceless woman.'

'They don't care, Aunty. They don't give a damn.' Jane put her fingers in her mouth and chomped at her fingernails. She tutted. 'This is another thing I've started, biting my bloody nails, and I've not done that since I was twelve years old. I swear I am regressing into childhood again.'

'It's not nice, duckie. I feel for you. I really do. I wish I could help you.'

'Don't be daft, you help me more than anyone. I would be lost without you, Aunty.'

The two synchronised sipping at their respective mugs of tea. Aunty broke the silence.

'I've been thinking.'

'What about?'

'Our Brandon?'

'He's your nephew, isn't he? What about him?'

'I was thinking he could come around for a few days and sit with you.'

'I'm not with you, Aunty?'

'He's a big lad, a rugby player. He's a real hard nut, but don't get me wrong, he's a really nice lad, Jane. It might make you feel a bit safer, duckie.'

Jane sighed. 'Oh, I don't know, Aunty, I don't want to put anyone out.'

'I'm sure he wouldn't mind; in fact, I've mentioned…'

There was a tapping at the back door.

'Who's that?' Jane asked, her eyes widening.

'I don't know. Are you expecting anyone?' Aunty, too looked concerned.

'No. Just ignore it.'

The tapping came again, harder, a bit more insistent.

'Let me go and answer it.' Aunty said. 'If it's them lads, I will say you are out.'

'I don't know. I'm scared. This is what happened the other night.'

The tapping came again, and Aunty got off the settee at the second attempt. 'You can't live like this, Jane.' When she got to the door, she shouted;

'Hello?'

'Police.'

'How do I know?'

'If you open the door, Jane, we can show our ID; we're from the CID.'

Aunty turned to Jane. 'What do you think?'

'They sound old. Have a peek through the door.'

Aunty turned the key, opened the door a couple of inches, and peered through the gap. She saw two well-built men in suits and overcoats. One was holding a wallet up to her face with an identification card in the plastic window.

'DC Charlie Carter, and this is Detective Inspector Stark.'

'It is safe to open up, Jane.' Stark said with a smile.

Aunty opened the door, and Charlie and Stark walked in. Aunty quickly closed and locked the door behind them.

'It's definitely getting chilly out there.' Charlie said. 'Are you Jane…'

'Cooper.' Stark finished the sentence for Charlie.

A head appeared from behind the settee. 'No. I am.'

'Oh hello, we're from the CID. We've come to talk about what happened the other night with Sharon Brown.'

A huge wave of relief swept through Jane's body, and she audibly gasped.

'Thank God. I thought you were never coming.'

'Well, we're here now.' Charlie said with a smile. 'Is that the kettle I can smell?'

'I'll make a drink.' Aunty said.

Stark and Charlie removed their overcoats and settled on the settee while Aunty made a drink. Stark asked.

'I take it your appearance from behind the settee is because of the Browns?'

'Yes, I'm sorry about that. This is what it does to you.' She gave out a nervous laugh and put her hand to her mouth.

'No need to apologise, Jane. That's why we're here, to try to sort it out for you. We specialise in tempting people out from behind settees.' Stark smiled warmly.

Jane laughed. 'You seem pretty good at it.'

Jane told them about the Co-op and the misunderstanding and how Sharon had come round and tricked her way in. There were tears and a clear sense of exasperation as she told them about the gang of lads intimidating her.

'It seems like you are their number one target.' Stark said as he supped his mug of tea.

'But what can I do about it?' Jane asked.

'Charlie here will get a statement from you about when Sharon came around and your injuries. We can then arrest Sharon Brown.'

Jane was biting her lip. 'Aunty, what should I do? I don't want to upset them any more than I already have. No disrespect Detective Stark.'

Stark leaned forward. 'None taken, Jane. Let me be honest with you. I have been in this job a long time, and the chances of the Browns stopping here are remote, I'm afraid. I've met these types many times, and the Browns are just about the worst people you can upset. I'm just telling you like it is, that's all.'

'That's what I mean. I just want it to go away, and I don't want to make them any madder than they already are.'

'I totally understand, Jane. But if they know they can come and do whatever they like to you and you won't report it to the police, do you think that will help to stop it?'

'No, when you put it like that, but they might just forget it now.'

'They might.' Charlie said. 'But what if next time it is Dougie or his brother Len? They could do some real damage. It isn't going to stop, Jane. Sorry to say that, but it won't stop, if like you say, Sharon and Dougie can no longer have kids because of you, then you could be in real danger. They will want payback, big-time.'

'But it wasn't my fault. This is the thing that bugs me. It wasn't anything to do with me, I was just minding my own business, and she came charging at me. She did it herself.' The tears could be heard in her voice.

'They don't bother about things like that, I'm afraid.' Stark said. 'The more I hear about it, if I were you, I would seriously think about moving house, Jane. It's not just you to consider, it is your daughter too.'

'Daisy.'

'We have to think about little Daisy too.' Stark said.

'I know. But why should I have to move because of them?'

Charlie was fatalistic. 'You don't *have* to move, and you don't *have* to make a statement, Jane, you don't *have* to do anything you don't want to. All we can do is offer our advice.'

'Is it a council house?' Stark asked.

'Yes.'

'In that case, we can make it happen really quickly for you. You can be out the house in a day or two.'

Jane shook her head and muttered, 'I know you are trying to help, but I don't want to move.' She glanced at Aunty, who smiled sympathetically at her. 'I've put so much into making this a home for Daisy and me, and it's not been easy.'

'Don't forget there is our Brandon.' Aunty said.

'Who is Brandon?' Stark asked.

'He is my nephew. He's a rugby player. I said that he wouldn't mind coming around for a few nights, just to make her feel a bit safer until it blows over, duckie.'

'We can't condone having a sort of private bodyguard, Jane. That is a matter for you, really. We can get you a Home Office alarm as a definite.'

'What's that?'

'It is a special alarm which, if triggered, comes straight over police radios, and everyone immediately travels to the location. There is no middleman or control centre. It is immediate. I'm happy to authorise one under these circumstances.'

'I want one. Can you do it now?' Jane said.

Stark laughed. 'Not right now. We don't carry them around with us, Jane. I can get someone here in the next couple of hours, though. How's that?'

'That would be great.' Jane smiled with relief, and Aunty held her hand. 'Thank you. Thank you so much.'

'What about this statement?' Charlie asked.

Jane nodded. 'Okay. Okay, I'll do it.'

*

Nobby and Ashley strode through the door of Sawyers pawnbrokers on Mansfield Road. It was an inconspicuous looking place. Small and fusty, and dark and dusty. The proprietor was a middle-aged man with dandruff and a dark complexion. His hair was swept back, giving him an oily look. He was the sort of man who made you want to wipe your hand after you had shaken his.

Nobby already had his wallet out and flashed his warrant card to the owner.

'We're from the CID.'

'I thought you might be. Gerald Keavney, by the way, manager.'

Nobby shook his hand and then wiped it on his trousers. 'Detective Sergeant Clarke.'

Ashley stood just behind the broad shoulders of his DS, moving slightly to one side for fear of being obscured. He was happy for him to do the talking.

'We want to speak to you about a watch that is for sale, a big chunky thing, in fact, that is it there, I believe, under the glass. The black one with that white shape on the face.'

'Ah, the Tag Heur.'

'The what?'

'That's the make, Tag Heur. One of the best. Did you want to purchase it?'

Nobby grimaced. 'No, I want to know who you brought it off and when.'

'It's just come in this morning, a chap from Newcastle, I think.'

'Newcastle?'

'That's what he said.'

'Did he have a Geordie accent?'

'No, I don't believe so. He didn't say much.'

'What's his name?'

'I couldn't tell you off the top of my head.'

'You must keep records, Gerald.'

'I do. They need getting up to date, though.'

'Well, it would be rather wonderful if you were to get them so you can stop guessing and tell me exactly what happened.' Nobby was getting a little impatient.

Gerald shuffled into the back and DS Clarke shot a glance to Ashley who looked sideways. 'He's being an arse.'

'I noticed.'

Gerald returned with a large book full of loose leaves and scraps of paper. He licked at his thumb and began turning pages, pausing intermittently to read various entries.

'It was only this morning, man; surely it's the top page?' Nobby said.

'Yes, you're right, of course. Here we are. John Smith, Newcastle, there. Always happy to help the local constabulary.'

'Yes, that is a terrific help, Gerald. Thank you so much.' Nobby was being ironic.

'My pleasure.' Gerald returned.

'How much did you pay him?'

'Five hundred on the nose.'

'Five hundred pounds!'

'It is worth double that, Sergeant Clarke.'

'I think I'm in the wrong job.'

Gerald laughed. 'It is a lovely watch.'

'Let me see it, please.' Nobby asked.

Gerald fiddled about with a bunch of keys and opened the glass display case. He handed the watch to DS Clarke. 'There you are, top quality.'

Ashley reached over DS Clarke and handed him a small plastic evidence bag, and Nobby threw it in, handling only the leather strap.

'Okay, well, we will be in touch, Gerald.'

'What are you doing?'

'Seizing the watch. It needs to be forensically examined. I have a feeling Mr Smith from Newcastle might be somebody else, don't you?'

'Come off it. I've just spent five hundred knicker on that watch. You can't do that.'

'Can't I? I think you will find I can. You will get it back at some stage.'

'When can I have it back? Will it be today?'

'Oh, goodness me, no. It could be weeks or months.'

'That's not fair.'

'You know, Gerald, life's not fair. But rest assured, if someone comes in your shop and points a sawn-off shotgun at you, the police will leave no stone unturned to track down the perpetrator.'

Ashley chimed in. 'Have you ever heard of a Douglas Brown, Gerald?'

'Dougie Brown. Dougie Brown, erm, mmm, not really.'

'Not really?'

'No, Should I have?'

Nobby smiled. 'Thanks very much, Gerald. We'll be in touch.'

'Wait, when will I get it back?'

The two detectives walked out of the shop, Gerald's protests ringing in their ears. It was a grey day, and dusk was descending. They paused on the pavement.

'I know it is probably a waste of time, it will be wiped clean, but let's go through the motions, you never know, young Ashley. Let's see if SOCO can get anything from it.'

*

It was unusual for Stark to feel uncomfortable briefing his team, and he wondered if it was just general stress that was causing him to feel a little sticky. Maybe tiredness. After all, it was not the flop sweats and the giddiness that had previously overwhelmed him at major conferences in the recent past. He was among friends, and it was pretty informal, although all eyes were on him as he sat at the front of the CID office.

He cut into the low undercurrent of conversation among the detectives 'Thanks for getting back on time, everyone.' He began, and the chatter fell to a silence.

'I just want us to mull a few things over about the armed robbery and talk about another case that has come in that may need to take precedence, but which is very much connected to the Browns…who, let's face it we know did our armed robbery. Feel free to chip in if you have an observation to make. Don't hang on to the thought or you will lose it or decide it's not relevant. Everything is relevant because we have various imponderables, so everything should be aired. Okay?'

Charlie raised a hand. 'What's an imponderable.'

'Shut up, Charlie.' Stark said.

There was laughter and muttering from Stark's team who were scattered around the CID office. Charlie looked like he was ready to doze off as he leaned back in his chair. The younger ones tended to be leaning forward, at their desks, attentive. Nobby had drawn a chair up next to Stark and had a notepad ready, along with various 'lever arch' files on the floor, containing action sheets and statements.

'Should I close the door, sir?' Cynthia asked.

'Yes, please, Cynthia.'

All eyes were on her as she sashayed to the door and wiggled her way back. The closing of the door revealed a Page 3 topless picture someone had pinned behind the door.

Stark coughed. 'Beautifully done, Cynthia.'

'Thank you, sir.'

Stark lit a cigarette as he shuffled his notes. 'Right. I want to keep it brief, hence the name briefing.' There were polite chuckles and shifting in seats.

'There have been a couple of developments that I think are going to need some prioritisation.' He turned to his Detective Sergeant, 'Nobby, can you kick us off with your findings at the pawnshop?'

'Yeah, sure.' Nobby leaned forward, his shirt straining at his large biceps hewn as a young man in the army. His hands were large and gnarled from his boxing days. 'Ashley and me went to Sawyers pawn shop on Mansfield Road after an anonymous tip-off that the watch worn by one of the armed robbers was for sale there.'

He held the clear bag up to display said watch. 'It was, and we have seized it.'

'Any sellers name, Sarge?' Steph asked. It seemed strange to hear her say Sarge to her lover, but it was good to keep up appearances.

'Yes.'

'Great.'

'A Mr John Smith, from Newcastle.'

'Ah.'

'It's a bogus name, obviously, and the bloke there wasn't exactly helpful, although he was pretending to be. We will get it fingerprinted, but it seems unlikely there will be anything for us. Still, we will go through the process, stranger things have happened.'

'What's the make, Nobby?' Charlie asked.

'It's a Tag Heur. I've never heard of it, but apparently, they are top drawer watches. The guy reckons he paid five hundred for it. He's not best pleased that we took it from him but there you go. We couldn't just leave it there.'

'So, is it *the* watch, do we know, Sarge?' Steph asked.

'It certainly looks like it, although it wouldn't stand up in a court of law, the white design on the face is a distinctive shape, and it looks the same. Also, this bullshit about John Smith at Newcastle tends to back up its dodginess. It is just another bit of something. It would have been nice to have found it on a warrant at the Browns house, but that ship has sailed, I'm afraid.'

Stark interjected. 'Just on that point, and not to go outside this room. I want us to be careful if Lee Mole and Carl Davidson start snooping around.'

'Aren't we always, boss?' Ashley said.

'Well, yes, I suppose so, but I have an uncomfortable feeling with this one. It was such a strange thing for him to put that video out when he knew it was our job and had nothing to do with him. It was like a warning to the Browns. Just bear in mind if Mole is asking questions or wants to get involved, you must ask me first. I want to know if they fart within a mile of Dougie Brown or any part of this enquiry.' Stark noticed the trainee detective Steve Aston scribbling at his pad. 'No need to write that down, Steve. Just remember it.'

There were some mutterings, and looks were exchanged. Steve flushed with embarrassment and put his pen down. He felt some screwed up paper hit the bag of his head. It was Ashley's bullseye, but Steve refused to turn around.

Stark continued. 'Now heaven forbid, I would never suggest that Mr Mole or DS Davidson are in the Browns pockets. Good heavens, no. But…anyway, enough said. Let's not dwell on it.'

'Nothing would surprise me with that pair.' Charlie said with a sneer.

Stark did not react but ploughed on.

'Anyway, if it is that good a watch, let's make some enquiries with the manufacturer, there will be a serial number on it and who they sold it to, and we can start a chain to see if it lands at the Brown's door before they sold it on to the pawnbroker. Nobby?'

'Yes, boss. Ashley?'

'Yes, Sarge, Steve?'

Nobby spoke. 'Oi!'

'Only kidding. Yes, no problem, leave it with me, Sarge.' Ash said.

'The other issue that has arisen is a wounding on Squires Avenue, at Bulwell, one Jane Cooper was slashed across the face as she answered the door a couple of nights ago.'

'What's that got to do with the armed robbery, then boss?' Steph asked.

'Well, young Ashley has a female informant who has fingered Sharon Brown as the offender for the slashing, so there is some bad blood there.'

'I bet that's not the only thing that was fingered.' Charlie said, causing much laughter.

'Behave, Charlie, don't judge me by your own standards.' Ashley said as Steph looked at him and slowly shook her head. Ashley shrugged, grinning.

'Okay.' Stark said. 'The connection relates to an altercation in the Co-op supermarket on Highbury Vale the other morning resulting in Jane Cooper putting Sharon Brown on her backside covered in eggs and flour.'

More laughter ensued. 'Oh, dear.' Steph grinned. 'Does that deserve a slashing, though?'

'Does anything? But I know what you mean; apparently, the word is that Sharon Brown injured her ovaries as she collided with the metal trolley, and it has damaged them. She has been told they might not be able to have children.'

'It gets worse.' Steph said. 'I wouldn't wish that on anybody, mind.'

Charlie laughed. 'You say that Steph, but think of the crime figures in fifteen years. Much lower.'

'I always said she was off her trolley.' Ash said. It failed.

Stark sipped at his tea. 'Anyway, we have a situation where it looks like the Browns have sworn to do a full number on Jane Cooper. It's the usual intimidation, gangs of youths, petty assaults, and a slashing. They will ramp it up, and this might be something we can exploit.'

'How so, sir?' Cynthia said with a huge smile.

'Perhaps we can give a degree of protection, get a Home Office alarm installed and catch the Browns at it. If we can catch them actually in the act, they've shot it. Even they will struggle to get off it at Court.'

'That's if they do it themselves.' Charlie said, lighting a cigar.

'True, but when it is a personal slight such as Dougie's own wife, there is more of an expectation that they would do it themselves.'

'Expectation by whom, sir?' Cynthia asked.

'I don't know, the different gangs around the region, I suppose. Bravado. Mucho macho shit. All that stuff.' Stark said.

'Anyway, it is a consideration, serious possibility, maybe even a probability that they will do the deed themselves. So, for once, we can predict what they might be up to. For once, be one step ahead instead of one step behind. That's what I mean when I say we can potentially exploit the situation.'

There was some nodding by one or two in the team.

'The problem I will have is manpower. Persuading old Waggy that we might need to devote some time and staff on being at Jane Cooper's place, twiddling their thumbs, waiting for a potential attack. That is my problem, though, not yours.' Stark took another drink of tea and shuffled his notes, ticking off the first item on his agenda.

'Okay, the other thing I want to do is arrest Sharon Brown for the wounding of Jane Cooper.'

There was an audible gasp. 'What evidence?' Ashley asked.

Charlie interrupted. 'From the girl, am I right, boss?' Stark nodded. 'What Mr Stark means is that we are going to take Sharon Brown hostage. That's the old school term.'

'Hostage?' Ashley asked.

Stark took over again. 'Have a play with her, there might not be enough to charge her, but there is to arrest her. It will send a message out to the criminal community that there are consequences for disfiguring members of the bloody public. There is enough to nick her and get the house searched, without the need for a warrant, under section 32 of PACE. Mole might think that he has prevented us from getting a warrant to search the place by exposing the watch, but he hasn't got the brains to think we might nick Sharon and search the place anyway.'

'Looking for the razor.' Nobby said.

'And if you happen to find a large number of banknotes or a sawn-off shotgun at the same time, happy days.' Stark said with a grin.

'Clever.' Cynthia muttered.

'I doubt the guns will be kept there, but hey, you never know your luck on a dark night. Steph and Cynthia can have the pleasure of bringing Sharon in, with any backup needed, of course.'

Steph and Cynthia nodded at each other.

'One thing I want to say is that I am genuinely concerned about Jane Cooper. The Browns might just be glorified toerags, but they don't mess about, and this is a young woman who has done nothing wrong and deserves our protection. I wouldn't put anything past Dougie and Len the bitch, and she could be in serious danger.'

Stark puffed at his cigarette and stubbed it out in the ashtray wincing as the smoke tickled at his eyes. He closed one eye as the smoke stung, but as he focussed with his good eye, he realised he was looking right at Cynthia. She winked back at him.

He muttered inaudibly, 'Oh shit.' Then chuckled to himself.

Stark carried on addressing the team, 'With that in mind, I want to go and give Dougie and Len the bitch Brown the gypsies warning.'

Cynthia looked puzzled. 'Gypsies warning. What's that?' She winked at him again, but Stark ignored it.

'Me and Nobby, and maybe Charlie, need to pay Dougie another visit. I want him to know that we know about the Jane Cooper thing. It may help him temper any knee jerk reaction to what's happened if he knows he is heading into a shit storm with us. Regardless of his hard man reputation, he is no fool, and so having a whisper in his shell-like might just give Jane a better chance. It's a long shot, but it can work every now and then.'

'But then it's harder to catch them in the act, though?' Ashley said.

'Maybe, maybe not, but we have to do everything we can to protect the victim, Ashley. That has to be the priority.'

'Fair enough. Shall I come as well, boss? A show of force.' Ashley offered.

'Sure.'

'And me, sir?' Steve Aston said, reaching for his corduroy jacket.

'Erm, no, you stay here, Steve, I don't want to go too OTT. Thanks, anyway.'

Steve seemed hurt. An awkwardness briefly descended on the room.

'Yeah, of course. No problem.' Steve said dejectedly.

'Okay, Golden Ball, here we come.' Stark said. 'Unless anyone else has any more questions?

*

A pub is rarely in complete silence, and yet this was the case at the Golden Ball as a wall of besuited CID shoulders ran the length of the wooden bar.

Stark ordered the drinks and turned to survey the scene. His three detectives stood in a circle around him. They knew how to act. Relaxed, jokey, don't give a toss, type of attitude. In truth, they were not frightened by the likes of Dougie and Len the bitch, not least his cronies, who were mostly teenage boys trying to be grown up. Stark and his crew had met and locked up Dougie's ilk before, and they knew that he knew, that they knew, that he knew, who was most fearful of whom. They knew.

That did not mean they were not on added alert. They were fully aware that Dougie Brown and his brother were dangerous and that given the right scenario, he was unpredictable and murderous. It was not Dougie Brown's default position, though, and there was a game to be played first.

It didn't take long before the Brown brothers came over to the detectives. As always, it was Dougie doing the talking.

'This is becoming something of a habit, Inspector Stark.'

'Well, you know, Dougie, you made us feel so welcome last time that we thought we might make it our regular watering hole.'

'I wouldn't do that if I were you,'

'Well, guess what? You aren't me. Anyway, nice to see you, Dougie; got any info for us?'

'Get fucked.'

'Rude.' Stark said.

'What is it that you want, Inspector? How can I help you?' There was an edge to Dougie's tone.

'What do I want? A little chat, that's all.'

'Go for it.'

'I was thinking somewhere a little more discreet, maybe the car park.'

'Are you offering me outside?'

'No, you soft prat, I want to have a bloody conversation without half of Bulwell listening in.'

'Oh right. Fair enough. Me and Len only, and just you. Yeah?'

'Just me and my Detective Sergeant. I think you've already met Sergeant Clarke.'

'Alright?' Nobby grinned. His weathered face matched his stature, finest oak.

'Sweet.' Dougie smiled in return at the giant of a man.

Leaving Charlie and Ashley to cover the gang of youths inside the pub, the four crime leaders trooped outside into the darkness. There was a chill in the air, and two floodlights at the edge of the car park made the pow-wow even shadier than it already was. Long shadows and short shrift. Stark didn't waste any time.

'Let's talk straight to each other, Dougie.'

'That depends on what we are talking about.' He thrust his hands in his pockets and toyed with the knife he always kept there.

'What does the name Jane Cooper mean to you?' Stark asked.

Dougie glanced at Len. 'Jane Cooper? Never heard of her. Have you Len?'

'Never.'

'Who is she?' Dougie asked unconvincingly.

'Okay, let's not talk straight.' Stark said.

'You asked, I answered.'

'Look, Dougie, and you too Len…'

Len was busy eyeing up Nobby Clarke, giving him the thousand-yard stare at ten paces. Stark snapped his fingers in front of Len's face. 'You too, Len. Wakey, wakey.'

'What?'

Stark continued. 'This is for you too, Lennie. I know what the setup is with this Jane Cooper, and I think you have made your point. I'm happy to call it quits if you are.'

'I really don't know what you mean, Inspector Stark.' Dougie said. 'Do you Len?'

'No idea what he is going on about, mate.'

'Fine, let's do the cryptic version.' Stark said. 'Back off from Jane Cooper – you've made a gesture. Fair enough. She's suffered. She's scarred. You have your work to do, and I have mine. If you don't back off, though, gentlemen, we are just going to end up hurting each other. Is it worth inviting a load of shit your way? Can I make it any clearer than that?' Stark thought he probably could have made it a lot clearer.

'Are you threatening me, Inspector Stark? Cos me and Len don't take too well to that, do we, Len?'

'No, we don't, Dougie.' Len said, puffing his chest out and strangely widening his arms from the side of his torso.

Nobby laughed. Len grimaced and went up to his face, almost touching noses. 'Something funny, pig?'

'Yeah, you. Now do yourself a favour and wind your fucking neck in, or I am going to embarrass you in front of all your little boy friends in the pub.'

'Is that so?'

'Or would you like them to see your bare arse spanked in the middle of the fucking bar?'

'You wouldn't dare.'

'Wouldn't I? Give it a whirl, big boy. See how you get on.'

Len scrutinised Nobbys' impassive steely glare. They were the eyes of a man who had seen battle, who had killed and had long since spent any fear he had in the blood of Mossad terrorists and fear no longer made up any element of his soul.

Discretion being the better part of valour, Len swallowed hard and stepped back, fighting the image in his mind that Nobby had irreverently placed there.

'Just be warned.' Len pointed a finger.

'Terrifying.' Nobby grinned. 'Remember, spanky, spanky…bitch.'

Len looked at Dougie a little sheepishly. It had been a long time since anyone had stood up to them like this, and it felt strange. They were certainly out of their comfort zone.

'I've listened to what you've said, Inspector, but you know, sometimes these conversations happen a little too late in the day.'

'I'm sorry to hear that, Dougie, but you know I always say that it is never too late.'

'How can I put this. Look, it has taken many years for me and my brother to build up our little business, and we don't intend to lose our fine reputation any time soon. We don't march to anyone else's tune.'

Dougie hesitated and looked off into the distance momentarily. He sighed before continuing.

'You know my old grandad worked in a hosiery factory in Hucknall for thirty fucking years for two bob an hour. The day he retired. Nothing. Not a by your leave or kiss my arse. Not even a goodbye from the boss. He just walked out the door. When me and Len heard about it, we swore never to take orders from any man, no matter what. We work for no one but ourselves, always have and always will.'

'I get that.'

'And that includes you.'

'It's not an order, Dougie. It's a piece of friendly advice.' Stark said.

'Anything else? Any other friendly advice you want to offer us?' Dougie asked.

'No, I think that covers it. Just do yourself a favour, Doug, you do have a business to protect, and the last thing you want is a load of attention from us. I'd hate you to go bust. We can be ever so thorough. Talking of which, how's Sharon, by the way?'

'She's fine. Never been better as it happens.' Dougie was nodding knowingly at the reference by Stark.

'I heard she had a bit of tummy trouble.'

'No. Thanks for the concern. I can see you are a family man, Inspector. We all have family, now, don't we?'

'That's true, but just remember that my gang is bigger than your gang, Dougie.'

'I know, but sometimes, Mr Stark, we have to go into battle, and there's nothing we can do about it. Sometimes circumstances force us to take action, just like you, Inspector. Just like you.'

'Do yourself a favour, Dougie, I can't say any more than I have. I know you ain't stupid.'

'Trust me, I'm not.'

'Well, I guess I will be seeing you.'

'Maybe. Maybe not.'

'See you later, Dougie, Len.'

With that, Stark walked towards his car, and Nobby veered off and shouted Ashley and Charlie to come outside.

The Brown brothers lit up cigarettes and watched the detectives saunter to their vehicles some distance away in the car park before they stopped, chatting to each other. They were too far away to be heard.

For once, Len was the first to speak. 'The gypsies warning, huh.'

'The gypsies warning, Len.'

'What you gonna do?'

'What do you think I'm gonna do. Carry on. Fuck him. It's gonna cost us, though, Len. There is something about that pig Stark that gives me the shits.'

'Can't we go above him?'

'Like who? Since Derek Posnanski retired, we don't have anyone high up. I tell you what, get Mole over for a pint. Let's see what that prat can tell us about this Stark character. There must be something we can do. I don't like his attitude. He worries me.'

9

'There is a condition worse than blindness, and that is, seeing something that isn't there.' – Thomas Hardy.

Jane Cooper sat on the settee, bolt upright. Her favourite soap, Coronation Street, was on the television, but she turned down the sound. She had lost interest. Real-life had knocked on her door and turned her world upside down. Her thoughts were dominated by one subject, but they were many and varied. They ranged from getting tooled up to fight her way out to whether she should move house, to moving in with her parents, to just ignoring everything. She was going around in circles in her mind. It was just her brain trying to solve the unsolvable, but it would keep going unless and until Jane commanded her thoughts to stop or at least steer them in another direction. Allowing thoughts to repeatedly go back to the start, trying to fix something that you simply cannot, is the road to madness, and she already felt like she was losing her mind. She was constantly distracted, always a repeated word away from acknowledging anything said to her, and a glazed eye away from recognition of anything she had known before.

Her friends had not telephoned her. Worse than that, when she rang them, the phone would be slammed down on her as soon as she said hello. It was cruel and hurtful to Jane and a harsh lesson in the fickle nature of even the closest of friends when danger comes to call. Maybe it goes back to caveman times, every man, or in this case woman, for herself. It was certainly the default in a sinking ship or a fire in a nightclub, and the same applied when the danger was perceived and not visible. It was a 'screw you, I'm getting out of here' mentality. It added to Jane's sense of loneliness, though.

Thank God she had Aunty and her Mum and Dad. That strange shift from parent to child had occurred whereby Jane, as the child, wanted to protect the parent, which prevented her from talking too much to her mother about it. In any case, she didn't trust herself to be able to speak without breaking down, and she was reticent to pile this onto the shoulders of elderly people in the last years of their life. Particularly when her mother had enough on her plate, with Dad becoming so frail so quickly, they shouldn't have to be concerned with all of this. If her Mum felt it was overstated, and a stiff upper lip was all that was required to front out these bullies, then so be it. Blissful ignorance has its appeal.

Jane's thought soup was interrupted by the sound of the bin moving in the alleyway. Her breath stopped along with her heart as every sense collaborated to listen more intensely. She glanced at the button for the Home Office alarm. Should she press it? No. Wait. Listen. Footsteps?

Suddenly a banging on the door made her jump out of her seat and restarted her heart, which was now beating at 150 beats per minute and seemingly pounding a hole in her rib cage like a diligent woodpecker running late.

'Jane, it's me, Brandon.' A voice shouted, and a blurry face appeared in the window.

Relief swept over her as she instantly remembered Aunty had arranged for the muscle-bound rugby player to come and 'babysit' her that evening.

Jane was muttering incomprehensively to herself as she unlocked and unbolted the front door.

'I'm so sorry, Brandon, I had forgotten all about it.' Her face reddened with embarrassment.

'That's okay. I hope I didn't startle you too much. I thought it better to shout, so you knew it was me.'

'That is very considerate. But a fly landing on my knee startles me now, Brandon, come on in. My you are a big boy. Aunty was right.'

Brandon laughed. 'You could say that.' The young man took his large frame into the living room after depositing his coat on the back of the chair. He wore a skintight T-shirt and jeans.

'Can I get you a drink, Brandon?' Jane asked.

'I'm okay for now, thanks. Maybe in a bit.'

'What about something to eat?' She asked.

Brandon smiled. 'I'm fine, honestly. Don't think you have to look after me, Jane, I'm just trying to help. Relax, that's the whole point of me being here.'

'I doubt anyone will come near you, Brandon, looking at the size of you.'

'They've got two choices, Jane.' He grinned.

After a stumbling start and a little awkwardness, the two settled into a night of playing Monopoly on the kitchen table. Jane had suggested a board game to take her mind off things. Brandon was quite happy to go along with it. He was a big lad, but he was still a lad in his early twenties, not what Jane would call a grown man. He had various childlike qualities to him, but she found this quite endearing regardless. He was a wall of solid muscle; his neck looked thicker than her waist. For the first time in a long time, she felt safe.

Had she known that Dougie, Len, and a couple of their entourage were sitting in a car watching their every move, she might not have felt so relaxed. The big lad that turned up just as they were about to make their move had caused them to have a rethink, and Dougie sent young Rob on an errand, postponing the attack for a little while. It was an insurance policy for the Browns, and as always, the odds had to be very much in their favour before making a move. It was basics. Create a winning situation before making your play. It looked like she had hired her own muscle, so he must be removed in that case.

Jane was laughing at Brandon's frustration as he was suffering heavy monetary losses after landing on Park Lane.

'You are taking one hell of a beating, Brandon.' She laughed.

'It's never over until the fat lady sings, Jane. It's all part of the plan.'

'What plan?' She laughed.

'You will see, I'm just about to…'

He stopped in mid-sentence as they both heard the unmistakable noise of the creaking gate that Brandon had closed behind him in the alleyway.

'Someone is outside.' He said.

'I know.'

'Are you expecting anyone?'

'No.'

'Well, someone is outside, I'm sure of it. Let me go and check for you.' Brandon flexed as he stood tall. He peered through the kitchen window but could not see anything, just darkness and his own reflection staring back.

*

Stark was annoyed to see Lee Mole in with Detective Superintendent Wagstaff. He wanted to discuss Jane Cooper's security measures. The last person he wanted present when doing so was Lee Mole, particularly after they argued over the release of the armed robbery video. Stark just did not trust the guy.

'It's fine; I'll call back later.' Stark said.

'No, I'm already late. Sit down. You can talk in front of Lee, can't he?'

'Absolutely. Take a seat, David.' Mole was grinning widely.

'No, seriously, it will wait.'

'Sit down, David.' Wagstaff insisted.

Stark sat down reluctantly.

Wagstaff held court at his desk with the two detective inspectors, each in a chair facing him. They couldn't be more different. Stark, smart in suit and tie and Mole looking bedraggled with a pulled down tie, ill-fitting shiny brown suit covered in stains and cheap shoes with a hole in one of the soles. A clump of sleep hair stood upright at the crown of his head.

Wagstaff, a man of military bearing and full of bluster, stroked at his handlebar moustache as Stark explained the connection between Jane Cooper and the Browns.

'So, it was a complete accident that Sharon Brown ends up on her backside after charging into Jane Cooper's shopping trolley. That's the irony of it.' Stark said.

Mole commented. 'So, she says.'

'Shut up, Lee.' Stark said.

'So, the Browns have got it in for the poor woman?' Wagstaff said through slack jowled concern.

'They have, I'm afraid; you can imagine in their thick skulls they think it is all Jane Cooper's fault that they might be childless.' Stark said,

'Isn't it?' Mole said.

'As I said, thick as pig shit.' Stark said without acknowledging Mole's comment directly.

Wagstaff sighed yet again, seeing what he believed to be childish bickering between two of his detective inspectors.

'What have you got in mind, David. What do you want from me?'

'Haven't you got some work to do, Lee?' Stark asked.

'Yes, with Mr Wagstaff. It's you who came in here unannounced when we were in the middle of strategic planning.'

'Strategic planning. God help us.' Stark rubbed his hand through his hair, hesitant to go into details in front of Mole.

'Come on, let's hear it. You're among friends here, David.' Wagstaff naively said.

'She has a Home Office alarm fitted.' Stark said.

'Surely, that's enough?' Mole said. 'That costs a fortune, as it is.'

Wagstaff nodded. 'True.'

Stark continued unabated, 'But I think she is in danger. I think they are going to do something serious, and I want some of my men to give her protection.'

'All that will do is delay the inevitable.' Mole chimed in once more.

'Lee's probably right, isn't he?' Wagstaff said.

'No, he probably isn't right. It gives us time to work on the armed robbery, and maybe they will discover that Sharon Brown is just milking this baby stuff and get the all-clear from the doctors. Then they might lose interest, might they not?'

'Mmm. Possibly, or go completely berserk if it turns out to be true.' Wagstaff said.

'Yeah, good point, boss.' Mole said.

'Do we have to wait for a knife in her ribs before we are seen to act?' Stark asked with an edge, and he found the situation exasperating.

'Of course not! Watch your tone, David. We have protection measures in place, with the alarm, for heaven's sake.'

Mole was tight-lipped and shaking his head. He looked disappointed in Stark.

Stark continued. 'I know that, but sir, I think if she is left to her own devices, she is going to get seriously hurt, or worse, particularly when Dougie finds out we have nicked his Mrs for slashing her. He's going to be stomping all over the patch.'

'You can't do that. You can't nick Sharon, where's the evidence? How can you nick Sharon Brown?' Mole protested.

Stark ignored him and spoke directly to Wagstaff. 'Don't you find it a little odd that one of your DI's is doing everything to leave Jane Cooper as easy meat for the Browns?'

'That's bang out of order, sir. I'm just playing devil's advocate, that's all.' Mole said.

Wagstaff raised a hand to Stark as if to calm him. 'Just stop it with the paranoia, David. We are playing around with scenarios, and we are all on the same side here.'

'Thank you, sir.' Mole said.

'Well, we are going to nick Sharon Brown as a hostage for the slashing.' Stark insisted.

Wagstaff shrugged. 'Fine, but I can't give any more coverage protection wise, not as things stand, David. Special Ops are at Newark helping on a murder-suicide, and I cannot sanction an open-ended operation on the off chance some toe-rag gets the hump.'

'Let me give it an end date then. I can get a couple of lads down there in the next ten minutes.'

Wagstaff clearly disagreed. 'That's silly. How can you give it an end date? Anyway, they are trained detectives, not bloody bodyguards, for Christ's sake. Are you telling me they are not that busy with other cases, that they have time to go and handhold some woman for weeks on end?'

'Of course not. I'm just concerned for the girl.' Stark felt it slipping away from him.

'We all share that concern.' Mole nodded, straight-faced.

Stark ignored the arse once more. 'Dougie is going to get the hump when we nick his Mrs, we know that, and as he can't hit out at us, guess who it will be? Jane Cooper.'

'None of us has a crystal ball, David.' Wagstaff said.

Mole grinned. 'That's not true sir, my Aunty Rita had one. She kept it on the shelf in the kitchen.'

Wagstaff laughed. 'Good one, Lee. Very amusing. Aunty Rita, Hmm. Yes, a good one that. I will tell Mrs Wagstaff that one. Ha.'

'Can't you take a hike, Lee? You're not helping.' Stark said.

'I do need to nip out actually, thinking about it.' Mole said, glancing at his watch.

'Off you trot.' Stark said.

'I'll be back in a bit, sir. Ten or fifteen minutes, okay?' Mole said.

'That's fine. Thanks, Lee.'

Once the door closed, Stark realised why he had left. 'He's off to phone the Browns no doubt to tell them we are coming for Sharon.'

Wagstaff sighed and shook his head. 'David, you have got to stop this. I am getting sick of these sarcastic comments, and they are not doing you any favours.'

'It is not sarcasm, and I'm not kidding. It is a genuine concern.'

'Do you not trust my judgement with my own detective inspectors? Do you think I'm a bloody old fool, is that it?'

'Of course, I do…trust your judgement, I mean, but I just find it…'

'Then, please, shut up about Mole and get this matter sorted. Have you not given the Browns the gypsies warning?'

'Yes, but I reckon it fell on deaf ears. They are a bit beyond that. These guys are big hitters, boss. They aren't frightened of us. They know how to avoid prosecution. People are more scared of them than they are of us, you know that.'

'Okay, well, I cannot justify using detectives to protect the girl, not *after* an attack, it is like closing the stable door after the horse has bolted, isn't it? Plus, the overtime budget is already well over the month's allocation, and I want us cutting back on it, not adding to it.'

'That attack by Sharon is not the end of it, not by a long chalk. That's just the teaser, trust me.'

'We are surmising, David. We have to deal with facts. Let us just see how things go. I'm not saying never. I'm just saying not now. Sorry, David.'

'Me too, sir. That's a shame.'

'Right, well off you trot.' Wagstaff smiled.

Stark jumped out of the chair and quickly left the office, leaving the door open.

He heard Wagstaff bellow behind him. 'Lee!'

*

DC's Stephanie Dawson and Cynthia Walker had thought the best time to go and arrest Sharon Brown would be during the evening when the brothers would be at the boozer. The point of least resistance. They were surprised to see her car not there and the house in darkness when they arrived. The word was that Sharon only went out at the weekends. It seemed odd she was not at home, but criminal families lead chaotic lives, so maybe it was just one of those things. They did not give up there, she must be somewhere, and she was a creature of habit.

Intelligence on Sharon showed that she was a regular at a couple of pubs in the town. There were not too many options for them to consider, with 'going to the pub' being the most likely; in fact it was the only option they could come up with – Bible studies was on a Thursday. A search of the local hostelries eventually revealed Sharon's car, and they decided to wait for a little while rather than try to make the arrest inside the pub itself. That could be a recipe for disaster. They might need to call for backup after all, but they were reluctant to do so. They wanted to prove a point that they were quite capable of making an arrest, no matter who it was, especially as it was another female: Brown or no Brown.

The experienced Steph was in the driver's seat of the ramshackle CID car, a dark blue Ford Escort and young Cynthia warmed the passenger seat. Steph had parked across the street from The Bull and Butcher and had a good enough view coupled with the ability to get across the road and intercept Sharon when she came out of the pub. A slight drizzle forced Steph to twist the windscreen wipers on every now and then. She had the heater on high to try to calm the misting windscreen. It was an incessant battle and a regular scourge for officers doing observations.

They had been chatting for twenty minutes or so now; tittle-tattle that inevitably grew a little more to the point as boredom overtook the pair of them.

'What's it like going out with a supervisor, Steph. You know, you and Nobby. Is it difficult?' Cynthia asked.

'It can be, but we are getting better at it. We have to separate work and home life. It is not always that easy, though. He is always the boss at work, and I am at home.'

Cynthia laughed. 'I believe you. You're not living together, though? Or are you? Tell me to shut up if I'm being too nosey.'

'No, we aren't shacked up just yet. Have you still got your eye on Mr Stark then? Is that why you're asking?' Steph smiled at her in the dim light.

'Don't be daft. He wouldn't look twice at me. Who says I am interested in him, anyway? He's a lot older than me, Steph. He's an old man to me.' Cynthia began playing with the strands of her hair.

'Cynthia, you would have to be blind not to see it. You've got the hots for the boss. It's obvious to anyone. Just admit it.'

'No, I have not!'

'Er, you have.'

'It isn't that obvious, is it?'

''Fraid so, Cynthia.'

'Damn!'

'Just be careful. That's all I would say.' Steph said.

'In what way? What do you mean?'

'He's married for a start, and I don't think he's the kind of bloke who would do that to his wife. That's all. No disrespect, Cynthia. But, hey, I've been wrong before, the mysterious power of the penis and all that.'

'I know he's not a shagger, and that's partly why I like him. I can't help how I feel though, Steph.'

'That's what they all say. Look, I'm not judging you, that would be hypocritical, bearing in mind some of the escapades I have got mixed up in, but my tip would be to wait a while and concentrate on getting into the CID fully, first. Stark isn't going to entertain you while you are a CID trainee, Cynthia. I doubt it anyway. Who knows, I'm not a bloke, but I can't see it.'

'But he might in a few months?'

'He's a man, isn't he? I mean, look at you. You're bloody gorgeous…you fucking bitch.'

Cynthia laughed. 'I don't see it, but thanks.'

'You're welcome. Just take your time, that's all. Don't get in too deep that you can't swim out.'

'I'll try. I can't seem to help myself. Common sense just goes out the window.'

'You've got it bad, kiddo.'

'I think I have. I've never been like this.' Cynthia said.

'Well, it's nothing to do with me.'

'Don't tell Nobby, will you, Steph?'

'Of course not. Although thinking about it, I suspect that he, like half the CID, already know, anyway.'

'Damn. Do you think Mr Stark knows?'

'He knows alright.'

'For definite? Do you know that for definite?'

'I don't know for definite. But he's no fool, is he, and you shoving your tits in him every verse end the other night might have given him a clue.'

'Oops. I thought I was being subtle.'

Steph laughed. 'Subtle as a brick.'

'I'm not as experienced as you in these matters.'

'What are you saying, I'm a dirty whore?'

'No, I didn't' mean…'

'I'm only joking, Cynthia. We're all whores when we want to be.'

'Thanks for the advice, Steph. I do appreciate it. You've been really kind to me, and it can't be easy when another woman comes into the office.'

'I think I'm a bit too long in the tooth for petty jealousies, Cynthia. Anyway, you seem a nice kid, so it's my pleasure.'

The squeaking of the wiper blade eased the quiet as Cynthia processed what Steph had told her. Steph nudged her.

'Talking of whores. See that old guy there?' Steph asked.

'The bloke with the Zimmer frame?'

'Yes.'

'What about him?' Cynthia asked.

'He's had some women.'

Cynthia laughed. 'Shut up, Steph, what are you talking about?'

'He used to own the butchers on Bulwell Market. I'm talking years ago, mind.'

'Okay. So, what has that to do with his sexual proclivity?'

'He hasn't always been in his seventies, you know.'

'I'm sure he hasn't. I still don't get you.'

'During the war, things were scarce, and…this is according to Edith Evans in the old folk's home…and the ladies would…you know, be 'friendly' to him to get an extra sausage or two.'

Cynthia laughed. 'Get knotted. Seriously?'

'Absolutely, gobble one sausage and get two in return.' Steph laughed too.

Cynthia giggled. 'Steph, you are incorrigible.'

'It's true. Just cos he's an old bugger now, he used to dish it out like there was no tomorrow, probably because they thought there was no tomorrow.'

'I suppose. It's funny, though, isn't it? When you see them now, I mean? All old and that.'

'It is, bless him. He's in Church every Sunday morning now, back in 1943, he was in Edith's mouth every Friday lunchtime in the outside loo.'

'It gives me the shivers.'

'It gave her the shivers too; she reckons he's very well hung.'

'Aargh! Stop it.'

Steph was laughing. 'What? It's true.'

'You sick bugger.'

'What's sick about it? Just because he's knocking on? Don't be daft; they are just people like us. We didn't invent sex, you know. Wait until you're that age. They are just people with a few wrinkles and a weak bladder, but that's not their fault. They've got a tale to tell.'

'I guess so. But doing that for an extra sausage or two, bloody hell!'

'Imagine what she did for a steak!'

Cynthia snorted as she laughed.

Steph grabbed her partners' arm. 'Hang on, that's Sharon. Isn't it?'

The mood changed. 'Yes, you're right. She's with that Trixie and someone else, and she looks drunk as a skunk.'

'Yes, she's pissed. She's all over the place, and that gives me an idea.' Steph put the car into gear and shot across the road into the pub car park.

As she drew up next to her, Steph shouted out the window. 'Taxi for Sharon Brown?'

Sharon got in the back seat without thinking, and the two detectives drove off towards the cells. Steph could see Trixie in her rear-view mirror, scratching at her tufts of hair, confused.

Cynthia turned and spoke to Sharon in the back seat. 'Sharon, we are from the CID; you are under arrest for the wounding...'

'Don't bother Cynthia, she's asleep. Comatose by the looks of it.'

'That was easier than it could have been.'

'You have to use your noggin sometimes, Cynthia.' Steph grinned.

*

Brandon saw the lone youth standing outside the door with his hands crossed behind his back. The youth had a nervous grin on his face. He was wiry but not a threat to Brandon. He did not see the others lurking in the shadows, however. He was too young to realise that not everyone plays fair.

Brandon opened Jane's door quickly, and the youth had a hammer raised above his head in a second. Brandon immediately throated the youth before he got a chance to do anything, pressing his scrawny neck against the fence. The youth was powerless to resist and could do nothing but gargle. He struggled to breathe with the rugby player's strong grip crushing his windpipe. The youth was more interested in prising away the grasp than hitting anyone with a hammer.

Dougie Brown was at the back looking on. He seemed calm. Len stepped up and punched the back of Brandon's head, causing him to stumble. It hurt more than it should. Len had a solid metal knuckleduster wrapped around his fist, giving weight to the blow, cutting skin and chipping bone.

As Brandon staggered to one side, Len caught him once in the face, and the metal squashed the lad's nose and peeled away part of the nostril. The third blow by Len nearly ripped Brandon's nose off, and flapping skin and snot flayed around as Brandon tried to orientate himself and return the fight. Len swung again, but instinct helped Brandon block the blow, and with a tumultuous effort, he charged at the man. The now released youth swung the hammer but thankfully missed and struck Brandon's shoulder. He felt nothing, but Len did as Brandon compressed his stomach with a powerful blow against the brick wall of next door's house.

Jane was frozen in terror. The kitchen door was wide open, and she could see everything. She was a foot away from the Home Office alarm, on the table, all she had to do was press it, but all of that went out of the window as Brandon fought to protect her. The stark nature of the violence shocked her into a stupour. She felt numb, and she could not move.

Brandon quickly realised this was no rugby match; this was dirty stuff, this was street fighting. It was a dog fight, and it was three against one, and they were tooled up. He was in trouble.

Dougie had seen enough and emptied a bottle of bleach over Brandon's head as he tried to stand up as soon as Len was well clear. It had no impact at first, but then the burn began in Brandon's eyeballs, and his vision blurred. The bleach also trickled into the cut skin around his nose, which burned. He tumbled to the floor.

'Press the alarm, Jane!' he shouted. 'Press the fucking alarm!'

Jane snapped out of her malaise and pressed the button. Dougie leaned into the kitchen.

He could hear the noise saying 'Alarm…alarm…' They had to get out of there, sharpish.

'We will be back, Jane Cooper. You are going to die in fucking agony. Enjoy the wait.'

Jane hugged the wall, turning away from the man, snarling at her.

With the threat complete and Brandon a mess on the floor it was time for the men to go. They knew there was a police alarm, and it was obvious she had pressed it. The attackers walked calmly away but not before the spindly youth had smacked Brandon over the head with a sucker punch hammer blow.

'That's for me fucking neck!'

The hammer knocked Brandon unconscious and prevented any glimmer of him diminishing the bleach with water. As he lay on the doorstep the tissues of his eyes were being eaten by the toxins of the bleach, layer by layer. He hadn't seen the hammer blow coming, nor the bleach that Doug Brown had put in his eyes. It had blinded him, not only for the fight but sadly, for the rest of his days. He would never play rugby again. He would never marry. He would never have a job. And he would never see his loved ones again. His life had just changed forever. Still, he meant well.

10

**'In the face of an obstacle which is impossible to overcome, stubbornness is stupid.' –
Simone de Beauvoir.**

Being young and fit, Brandon had come round after three or four minutes. He was screaming in pain and horror at what had happened, pacing around the kitchen area, holding a towel to his face. It soaked up blood and bleach. Jane was crying incessantly, following him around and wanting to help but not knowing quite how to do so.

'I'm sorry, I'm sorry, Brandon.' She kept saying.

'Just get an ambulance here.' Brandon groaned.

'I've rung, they're coming. They'll be here any minute.'

'How long. Christ!'

'I don't know. Soon. I hope.' She said through tears.

Detective Sergeant Nobby Clarke had jumped into a CID car with DC Ashley Stevens and TDC Steve Aston as soon as the Home Office alarm pips came over the radio, followed by the robot voice saying 'alarm…alarm.' They arrived within just four or five minutes and before any ambulance.

Detective Sergeant Nobby Clarke walked straight through the door into the kitchen, followed by the two detectives. The light from the kitchen door had thrown a spotlight on pools of blood in the small yard area outside. The detectives had avoided stepping into it the best they could. They had heard shouts of distress and crying as they approached and hurried into a run as they reached the alleyway. Was it too much to hope the offenders were still present?

'Have they gone?' Was Nobby's first question.

'They've gone. Thank God you're here. They have thrown something in his face. Some fluid, and I think it's bleach or something like it. It's burning him.' Jane said. 'Help him, please.'

'It's burning. I can't see properly!' Brandon was straining every sinew, fighting the pain, and he was grunting and beginning to hyperventilate. Nobby went straight to the kitchen sink and filled a jug with cold water.

'Lie down.' He commanded. 'Get on the floor.'

Brandon got onto the kitchen floor. He was still clutching the bloodied towel tight to his eyes, and Nobby threw water in his face forcing the young man to cry out in surprise.

'It's just water. Move the bloody towel out the way.' Nobby said. 'Let me get some more, and I'm going to pour it directly into your eyes this time. Wait there.'

Nobby returned and pulled hard at Brandon's arms to get the towel away from his face within four or five seconds. 'Don't fight me.' Nobby said. Thankfully Nobby was as strong and using his forearm to press down on Brandon's chest, he forced the lad's eyelids open and poured water in both. He was screaming, but Nobby ignored it. In truth, he did not know whether it would help, but he had to do something, and surely water must dilute whatever is in there?

Blood from Brandon's other injuries washed down onto the floor, pooling around Ashley's expensive shoes.

'Watch the blood, Sarge. He could have AIDS.' Ashley said, concerned.

'It's a bit late for that, lad.' Nobby said.

With great relief, Ashley shouted. 'Ambulance is here, boss,'

A young woman with a blonde ponytail and an older man came into the kitchen in their green attire, carrying several first aid bags and equipment.

The young woman pushed Nobby to one side or tried to; she rebounded off his bulk. 'Let me through, please.' She said curtly.

Nobby quickly stepped to one side.

Ashley chimed in. 'We think he's had bleach thrown in his face, and it's gone in his eyes, and he can't see.'

'I've thrown water in his eyes.' Nobby said quietly.

'Give me some space, please!' The woman said, hitting Nobby's shins with her knuckles as she knelt next to Brandon's head.

'Ouch! Alright, come on everyone, into the living room, out the way.' Nobby said.

Everyone was breathing heavily. Jane was distraught and collapsed onto the settee sobbing, burying her head into a cushion.

Steve Aston sat next to her and placed a comforting arm on her shoulder. 'He'll be okay, Jane. How are you? Are *you* injured?'

'No, they never got to me, thanks to Brandon.' She began sobbing again. She seemed inconsolable.

They all sat in silence, pierced only by Jane's sobbing and heaving. In any case, there was nothing to say. They heard the activities of the ambulance crew working on Brandon. They were all passengers at this point. All had concerned expressions on their faces, with the detectives exchanging tight lipped glances. It didn't look good for the lad.

They heard the ambulance personnel leave with Brandon as quickly as they came, and the silence continued for a couple of minutes in their absence until the loud siren and blue lights tore it to shreds. All that was left were fluids on the kitchen floor, remnants of gel, a bloodied towel, and an array of packaging from whatever equipment the crew had deployed on the helpless youth.

Jane's face was still buried in the settee, with Steve Aston soothing her. She was close to hysterical, blaming herself. 'What have I done? What have I done?'

Nobby tapped Steve on the shoulder, his deep voice quiet but still resonating around the room.

'Go and put the kettle on, Steve. Just watch where you are treading. Also, we will need Scenes of Crime here sharpish.'

'Sure.' Steve got up and headed towards the kitchen.

Ashley said. 'I'll get SOCO here, Sarge.' He followed Steve towards the kitchen area, speaking into his radio.

Nobby patted Jane on the shoulder. 'Come on, come on. Sit up. Sit up, Jane.'

She complied, her face red with tears and contorted in shock at what she had witnessed.

'Will he be blinded?' She sobbed.

'Let's hope not, eh. He's in good hands now, Jane.'

'Should I go to the hospital? Shit! I need to tell Aunty, that's his…that's his aunty. Let me ring her. I need to ring her.'

'Just hang on a minute, Jane. My lads will sort everything out for you in a second. Let's get you a cuppa and compose ourselves, yes? There is nothing that you need to do. We'll sort everything out.'

Her head was jerking as she took in jagged gulps of air. 'I'll try.'

'Where does Aunty live?'

'42. 42 Ravensworth Road. It's just at the top there.' She pointed at the wall.

'I know it. I will get one of my detectives to tell her what's happened and take her to the hospital, if necessary, don't worry. We will sort it.'

She began screaming as anger cascaded out of her. 'Who are these absolute bastards! They are bastards! Why don't you arrest them? What the hell is going on here? For God's sake!'

Nobby stayed calm. 'We will, Jane, don't worry, give us time, we need a statement from you. Brandon won't be able to give one for at least a day or two. The doctors won't let him, for a start.'

'Great. But what can I say? I don't…I don't even know the Browns. I don't know what they look like. Was it them? Yes, I think it was, but I don't…actually know them. I can't swear to it can I? They'd got caps on and scarves. I don't think I would recognise them. What good is all of this? What good is it going to do? Just go and arrest them, please.'

'We will. It's not quite as easy as that, Jane. Trust us to do our job. The first thing is to preserve the scene, and I will get a statement from you, and we can decide what we do from there, my love.'

'This is bloody ridiculous.'

'I know it seems that way.'

Jane had become a shadow of her former confident self. They had done this to her. She just wasn't the same person. She felt like she could not move. Lift an arm even. Her arms were leaden. She was in shock. Now staring into space. She felt physically sick, which was not helped by the stench of bleach everywhere.

Steve came over with a tray of mugs. Ashley too re-joined them.

'Thanks, Steve,' Nobby said. 'Can you nip around to 42 Ravensworth Road and inform Brandon's aunty what has happened? If necessary, take her to the hospital, whatever she needs. Also, take possession of Brandon's clothing from the hospital for forensic and arrange for SOCO to get photos of his injuries at the hospital. It will be tomorrow now, I would think, but let's request it now.'

'Okay, Sarge.'

'Are you taking all this in, Steve?' Nobby asked.

'Yes, sure, Sarge. Why?'

'Cos, you've got that bloody gormless look on your face, lad.'

'No, no. I've got it - Aunty, clothes, SOCO, pics.'

'Try and get a basic written statement off some medical person so we can categorise the level of injury. If his sight is affected, it's going to be a section 18 GBH.'

'No problem. Got it. Aunty, clothes, SOCO pics and statement.'

'Just write it down, Steve,' Nobby said. 'You don't half make things difficult for yourself.'

'Okay, fine, but I can remember it.'

Ashley tore off a piece of paper from his pad, with the handwritten notes on. 'Take this as a reminder.'

'Alright, thanks, Ash. See you later.'

'Keep me updated.' Nobby said.

'Will do, Sarge.'

'Get Jane's phone number so you can ring me from the hospital.'

'What is it?'

'I've taken it off the phone and written it on there for you, Steve. It's already on there, mate.' Ashley said.

'Oh, okay, thanks.' Steve turned and headed through to the kitchen, and Nobby shouted to him.

'Steve?'

'What?'

'Just watch where you are walking. It is a crime scene, remember.'

'Yes, no problem. Of course. Speak to you in a bit.'

'In a bit.'

Steve shoved the bit of paper into his trouser pocket and headed out into the cold, tiptoeing around the blood outside. As he got to the car, he heard a shout.

'Are you there, lad?'

'Yes? Hello?' He turned and saw a man secreted behind a wall two doors down.

'Can you come over here a minute?'

Steve was puzzled but made his way to the man behind the stone façade. 'Are you alright?'

'Yes. I don't want anyone to see me, that's all. I don't want to get involved.'

'Erm. Okay.'

The elderly man held out a scrap of paper. 'That's the reg number of the car those blokes were in. Them that's caused all the trouble tonight. I wrote it down for you. I'm not getting involved, mind. Take it or leave it.'

'I'll take it, thanks.'

Steve snatched the bit of paper and put that in his trouser pocket also.

*

Detective Inspector Lee Mole was mooching around the corridors of the police station after hours. He often did a bit of a walk around. He looked at documents in Stark's office and other detectives' desks. It had become something of a ritual for him before going to the pub on occasion. Not every night, just once a week or so. Now, with the focus on the Browns, he felt he needed to know more, and Stark was being all cagey about it so, he would have to have a sneaky look around for himself.

Mole opened the door to the CID corridor quietly, and as he softly and slowly moved down towards the main office, he heard Stark's voice, so he shot into an adjacent office. He could hear the one-sided conversation that Stark was having on the telephone, and while he couldn't hear what Nobby Clarke was saying, he could fill in the gaps.

'Are you at the house, now, then, Nobby?'

'Good.'

'So, Steve's doing the hospital stuff, and you and Ashley are taking the statement and advising SOCO, yes?'

'What about Jane's clothing?'

'Is she certain?'

'Take it anyway. There could be hair or fibres. We're not going to lose anything by doing it.'

'Yes. Just give her the bags to put them in if you like.'

'Have you checked on the kid?'

'Get Ash to do it while you're on the phone to me.'

'Do you want me to hurry SOCO up?'

'Fair enough.'

'No.'

'Not life-threatening?'

'I know.'

'Supposedly.'

'She can't stay there, Nobby.'

'She can't, mate. What about her parent's house? Wollaton, isn't it? I reckon so.'

'Ask her.'

'That's crazy.'

'It's not as simple as that. It's not just about her, is it?'

'Fast asleep. That's something at least.'

'Yeah, but she can't…'

'I know you can't, but…'

'I tell you what, Nobby, let me grab Cynthia. She and Steph are booking Sharon Brown in downstairs, and we'll come round.'

'No, she can't, mate.'

'I know you can't, but…I mean, what is wrong with the woman?'

'Give me ten mins or so, and I'll come over. Yep. See you shortly.'

'Cheers.'

Stark put the phone down and shook his head. He rubbed at his eyes and groaned. He'd hoped to be in the pub by now. This was escalating just as he knew it would.

He heard a noise. The corridor door? He got out of his chair and looked down the corridor. Nothing. He checked the offices on either side. All empty. It was eerily quiet, and the noise of the door closing had served only to emphasise it. Stark went into the main CID office. He hadn't noticed that in the far corner, around the L shaped office,DC Jim McIntyre was writing using a desk lamp. Jim coughed, startling the Inspector.

'Bloody hell, Jim. You gave me the bleeding shits there, mate.'

Jim laughed. 'All right, boss?'

'Yes. What are you doing here at this time of night?'

'Last-minute Crown Court file. It does my head in.'

'Anybody else been in here in the last few minutes, Jim?'

'No. Nobody. Not that I've noticed anyway, and I think I would have known. It's like the Mary Celeste.'

'I must be imagining things.'

'You hear all sorts of things in here late at night, sir.'

Stark laughed. 'It's probably the ghost of bloody Wagstaff past, coming to haunt me, and he ain't even dead yet.'

Jim laughed. 'Could be boss. Could be.'

*

Cynthia was happy to be asked to go over to Jane Cooper's by Mr Stark, although she got all tongue-tied being in the car on her own with him. It was the first time this had happened. She was so busy thinking what to say to him that she scarcely said anything at all. Her mind was racing, and she found herself just periodically glancing towards him and grinning inanely. Steph was booking Sharon Brown into custody, who was far too drunk to be interviewed until the following morning at the earliest. It would mean more hours in the cell for her, and if they needed an extension of custody, they could perhaps play on the fact that she was unable to be interviewed because of her condition, wasting a good portion of the allotted 24 hours before release or charge.

When Stark and Cynthia got to Jane's house, Stark sat next to Jane, and Cynthia sat on the chair at the side. Nobby and Ashley went outside on the road for a smoke so they wouldn't crowd her.

Jane was upset but now quite defiant. It was a mix of fear and unhealthy stoicism. She was angry and struggling to keep a lid on her emotions which seemed to go from one extreme to the other, each time overcompensating as they tried to find an equilibrium.

'It's not me being awkward.'

'Of course not, Jane.' Stark smiled sympathetically. 'I wouldn't suggest it was.'

'I just don't see why I should have to move. Please don't take this the wrong way, but I expect the police to protect me. I thought that's what you did, and I mean, is that too much to ask?'

'I know, and we will, but we do have limits, I'm afraid. I'm not going to pretend otherwise, Jane. That would be unfair. In my view, the safest option is to move to a new house or, if necessary, your parents, just until we see how this is going to pan out.'

'I cannot go to my parents; I really can't. My Dad is frail, and we think he has Alzheimer's, and so while Mum is putting a brave face on it, I know she is struggling. I can't put her through all of this. Police and detectives at the door every day. The fear of someone knocking, twitching at every noise outside. It's too much for me, never mind them.'

'Is there anywhere else you could go, Jane?' Cynthia asked. 'Friends, maybe?'

'Ha! My friends seem to have disappeared since all this trouble started. Don't ever think you have friends, because you don't. Don't make the same mistake I did.'

Stark leaned forward. 'Let me explain what we can arrange for you. Within one or two days, I can have you out of here into a shiny new council house.'

'It sounds great, but…'

'Let me finish, Jane. And you can still have your alarm, and you, and more importantly Daisy, will be safe. No one will know where you are, and you can put all of this behind you.'

Jane was unsure. 'Would I be able to decide where it was?'

'We can try. Where have you got in mind?'

'Wollaton is nice.'

'It is very nice, and it would be closer to your parents. My worry would be the availability of any council houses in Wollaton. And it is still a bit close to where you are now. Are there any council houses in Wollaton that you know about?'

'Balloon Woods?' Cynthia said.

Jane gasped. 'Oh my God, no, thank you. No way! I know you all mean well, but I will not end up in a shit hole in Balloon Woods. I will stop here, thank you very much.'

Stark glanced disdainfully at Cynthia, and she bit at her lower lip, embarrassed that she had inadvertently thrown a spanner in the works by mentioning the vile estate known as Balloon Woods.

'There will be plenty of other places, Jane.' Stark said.

'But this is our home. I can't imagine they want to do any more than they have. Hopefully, this is the end of it all. Isn't it?'

Stark sighed. 'Jane, I can't impress on you enough what these bloody arseholes are like. They are not like you and me. They have no limits, no boundaries. It is the law of the jungle for them. These people are relentless. They thrive off this sort of stuff. They love it. It is their whole life. Until they get distracted on to something else, you're it, I'm afraid. I wouldn't bet on this being the end, my love. I really wouldn't.'

'I know. I get it. I don't know how to explain it. This is our home. I'm sorry I can't move. I just can't. It would kill me. And there is Daisy's school and her friends to think about. She's an innocent in all of this.'

Stark glanced at Cynthia. 'Okay, look, let me see what I can do getting some detectives to stay with you for a while, even if it's for a few days. I can't promise anything, but I don't want you to feel abandoned.'

The DI stood up and went outside to Nobby and Ashley while Cynthia stayed with Jane. Stark lit up a cigarette and joined in the incongruous shuffling of feet that they all seemed in the habit of doing.

'She's not having it.' Stark said.

'I told you that, boss.' Nobby said.

'I know, but I thought it was worth a pop. We're going to have to try to babysit her as best we can for now.'

Nobby shrugged. 'Fuck her. If she won't move house, why should we put ourselves out?'

'Have you ever thought of a career with the Samaritans, Nobby?'

'Well, it's true.'

'Let's not forget that she is the bloody victim here. She isn't the baddy.' Stark said.

'No, I know that, but if people won't help themselves....'

'I don't mind babysitting her, boss. She's not too bad.' Ashley said with a smirk.

'Behave, Ashley. The last thing she wants is you dropping your keks on her.' Nobby said.

'I suppose, and I don't want any SNAF throwing bleach over my perfect features, thinking about it.'

'What a puff.' Nobby said.

Stark had made his mind up, so it was not open to debate. 'Okay, if you two stay with her this evening and I will try to figure out how the hell I can work around this. It might mean doing it for time owing rather than paid overtime.'

'The lads won't mind, for so long, anyway. Not if it's a chance to put the Browns behind bars.' Ashley said.

'Leave it with me.' Stark said.

'Are we not having a beer then, boss?' Nobby asked.

'Not tonight, Nobby.'

'What about Cynthia? Can't she stay with Ashley here and then me, and you can have a cheeky one.'

'No, I don't want, Cynthia…'

'Don't want Cynthia what, sir?' Cynthia said, appearing in the doorway.

'Oh, hello. I don't want you staying here with Ashley protecting Jane.'

'Why?'

'Because I don't.'

Cynthia looked puzzled. 'Okay, I just wondered why that's all. No problem, sir.'

'You're dealing with Sharon Brown, aren't you?' Stark said.

'Yes, I suppose so.'

'There you are then. Even you can't be in two places at once, Cynthia.' Stark smiled a little unconvincingly.

'What about Wagstaff? He will go ballistic if he finds out we are doing protection. You said he had turned it down earlier.' Nobby said.

'Leave Waggy to me. If anything happens when you are here, just tell him for now that you were making enquiries at the time and you happened to be here. Nobody needs to know its protection.'

'Okay, but on your head be it.'

'No, Nobby, on Jane's head be it, if we don't.'

*

Detective Inspector Mole looked more like an unemployed scarecrow than a detective inspector as he walked into The Golden Ball pub with his detective sergeant Carl Davidson. Mole's suit was two sizes too big, and his off-white shirt's cuffs were fraying and contrasting with the yellow nicotine on his bony fingers.

DS Carl Davidson was slightly more presentable but seemed stuck in the styles of the 1970s with an open neck, rounded collared paisley shirt under his wide lapelled suit.

'Moley!' Dougie Brown shouted over to him.

Lee waved over as Dougie walked over to the bar with a big smile on his face. 'Bring the drinks over, Terry. What are we having, gentlemen?'

'G&T', Mole said.

'Pint of bitter, thanks.' Carl uttered.

Dougie led the two cops over to their contoured seat and some of the lads got up to make a space.

They settled in, and Len nodded a greeting at the detectives. He was always uncomfortable around police, even with the likes of Mole and Davidson.

'Thanks for calling in, Lee.' Dougie shouted towards the bar. 'Terry! Where's them fucking drinks?'

'Coming, Dougie.' Terry called back in a panic.

Mole spoke. 'No problem, Dougie. Let me guess, Stark has been giving you grief. Is that why you wanted to have a word?'

'How did you guess? Who is this prat?'

'He's a wanker Dougie, ignore the fool. He's a no mark.'

'You say that, but he's getting fucking boring now, mate. He's making me twitch a little, you know what I mean.'

'Ignore him; he's small fry. He's not as hard as he thinks he is.'

'What's his game then? Have you got anything on him?'

'Not really. He's a big family man, I know that. Boring fucker, you know the sort.'

'Where does he live?'

'That I'm not sure of. Leave it with me, I'll see if I can find out for you.'

'Sweet. What did I tell you, Len? Proper detectives, these fellas.'

'Aye.' Len sniffed.

'You know he's nicked our Sharon? I've just had word come through. Is he trying to piss me off or what?'

'Yes, that's exactly what he's trying to do.' Mole said, puffing on his cigarette and squinting through the smoke.

'Well fuck him. If he's taking her hostage, I will take a hostage as well. We can all play that fucking game.'

'That's your business, Dougie. I don't want to get involved, my friend. I'll pretend I didn't hear that. Did you hear that, Carl?'

'Hear what, boss?' They laughed a little too heartily at the lame joke. Dougie and Len were not laughing, however.

'But you are involved, Moley.' He grabbed the Detective Inspector's cheek and pulled at it. 'You are as involved as I say you are.'

The youths thought this very funny. Terry arrived with the drinks, and Mole quickly took a gulp.

'Cheers, Dougie. Bottoms up.'

'All right, lads, leave us to talk business. Go on piss off.' Dougie ordered his hangers-on to make themselves scarce, and they slowly meandered over to the bar area. He waited until they were out of earshot.

'So what have you got me, Detective Inspector Mole?'

'I said leave it with me, didn't I? I never disappoint.'

'Well, come on then, Clouseau, what's the news.'

'That Jane Cooper is going to stay at her parents' house. How about that?'

'I fucking knew it!' Dougie slapped the table making the glasses clink together. 'Where do they live?'

'I think it's Wollaton somewhere. I don't know exactly where.' Mole said.

'Fuck me, half a job, eh? Only kidding. Only kidding.' He straightened Moles unkempt knot on his tie. It was intimidatory, but Mole couldn't see it, he thought he had an honoured position at the table, but there was no respect for a bent copper and certainly not for one as dense as this bloke was. They were taking liberties, and he was too thick to know it.

'He's gone too far nicking our Sharon.' Dougie said.

'Who, Stark?' Mole said.

'No, Joseph Locke. Who do you think I mean?' Dougie had no idea who Joseph Locke was, but he had heard the expression before. 'It's a declaration of war, Lee. Does he even know that?'

'Course he does. He ain't bothered. He thinks he's some sort of a fucking hero when he's just a goody-two-shoes, stuck up arsehole, who don't know the streets like we do.'

'Not like you do, eh. Moley?' Dougie winked at Len, who shrugged out a laugh.

'Absolutely. He doesn't know how to talk to people. That's his trouble.'

'Who's that pillock, Nobby Clarke?' Len asked.

'Oh, don't mess with him, Len. He's evil shit. Former Regimental Sergeant Major in the Paras, special forces stuff. Seriously hard, Len. He's a killer.'

Len threw a glass at Mole, and it smashed on the table in front of him. Len was on his feet and had Mole by the shirt, and he dribbled on him as he spoke.

'You saying I can't handle some old fart fucking squaddie?'

'No. No, of course not Len. You'd eat him for breakfast, man.'

'Watch your fucking mouth, then.' Len suddenly grinned. Aware that all eyes were on him. He kissed Mole on the forehead. 'I know, you didn't mean nuffing, Inspector.'

Everyone laughed. Davidson downed his pint. 'We're going to have to go, boss.'

'Don't go on my account, Carl.' Len said with a sick grin.

'No, it's not that, we've got...'

Dougie cut across him. 'You go when we say you go, mate. Anyway, is that all you have for me, that she's staying at her Mum and Dad's. Is that the best you can do?'

'What else is there to know?'

'You tell me.'

'That's it, Dougie, honest mate. And they have been denied permission to protect her. I know that as well. She's on her own, and they can't afford to pay cops to sit with her every hour of the day. Thanks to yours truly.'

'What do you mean.'

'Stark was trying to get permission from our Detective Superintendent to put cops in to protect her, but he wouldn't have it, not when I told him it was a waste of time.' Mole laughed and did a bit of shoulder work as if he was the bee's knees.

'Nice one, Moley!' Dougie snarled. 'So she's on her own, is she? At her Mother's. Easy pickings.'

'Looks like it. Is there anything else, Doug, cos like Carl says, we've got to shoot, mate?'

'Get your arse over to the cells and get our Sharon out for a start.'

Len shrugged out a laugh.

'I can't do that, Dougie, you know that. I would if I could. Times have changed. Some things I can't do and anyway we want to keep our friendship away from prying eyes, don't we?'

'I don't give a shit, mate. Is that Wagstaff fella worth bringing over for a pint?'

'No. He's too strait-laced, Doug. He wouldn't appreciate our little friendship.'

'You sure?'

'Positive. Trust me.'

'Trust you? I wouldn't trust any fucker, not least you Moley.' This time he patted the Detective Inspector's face with the palm of his hand. 'Go on sling your hook.' Dougie slotted a hundred pounds in Mole's suit pocket. 'Have an early Christmas present, Mr Mole.'

'Cheers, Dougie. Very kind. See you later, yeah?'

'See you later, kid.'

Dougie watched the two miscreant detectives leave the bar and wave as they left. They were pathetic, but it was their only route into what was going on. The good news was that Mole was very close to Stark, and he could find things out for them. That was really useful. The information about Jane Cooper staying at her parents was gold dust, though. What a strange little man Lee Mole was.

'He's gonna nick us. Len, you know that, don't you?'

'Who?'

'That Stark fella. He's trying to prove a point, and I know how his mind works. He wants to show who runs the streets, and all that crap. We're gonna get nicked, bro.'

'What for?'

'He'll think of something. Kicking shit out of that youth probably.'

'He can't prove nowt.

'Course he can't, but we need Mac and the lads over to clear the house out. Thinking about it they might even do it tonight on a section 32.'

'Why, because of our Sharon being locked up? Shit! That is a point you've got there, Len.'

'Just saying.'

'It's no sweat, Len. There's nowt there anyway, is there? Let them knock themselves out, mate. It's clean. Shooters are buried again, aren't they?'

'Several feet under.'

'Sweet. What do you reckon, Len? What are we gonna do with this pillock, David Stark?' Dougie sipped at his pint.

'Like you said, it's fucking war. Who does he think he is nicking our Sharon?'

'This Stark geezer, I can't figure him out, though, Len. He don't play the game. He thinks we are just pieces of shit on his shoe. Him and his DS don't seem to be concerned about the Brown brothers.'

'What are you thinking? His family?'

'No, fuck that. That's the last resort, Len. Always do the opposite of what they want. I reckon he needs to have his face rubbed in it a bit. Let's embarrass him. He's taken our Sharon hostage. Why don't we take Jane Cooper hostage? Only she won't be getting no bail, like our Sharon will.'

11

'It is well for the heart to be naïve and the mind not to be.'

Anatole France.

There was no element of surprise when Stark and his team tapped on Dougie Brown's front door at 7.22 am.

Dougie answered promptly, saying, 'I was expecting you. You're late.'

Dougie always said when he was arrested because he wanted to convey that he knew they were coming even if he didn't. It wasn't just a control thing; it was to mitigate any house search following the arrest. Police officers can be just as gullible as anybody else and if they think that the offender will have already removed anything dodgy then any search can become perfunctory.

Not so, Nobby Clarke. He was too long in the tooth for it. As soon as they got Dougie out of the way, they would do a proper job.

'Good news travels fast. How *is* Mr Mole?' Stark asked.

Dougie laughed. 'Nice one. I just need my roll-ups. Hang on.'

Stark took hold of the handcuffs hanging from the back of his belt as he stepped into the house.

Dougie spotted them. 'Hold up, Inspector, no handcuffs. You don't need 'em. I could have done a runner before you even got here if I wanted.'

'I get that, Dougie, but I have to think of everyone's safety, not just mine. Anyway, I always feel twitchy with a violent maniac sitting behind me. Call me old fashioned.'

'I ain't gonna do nowt. Come off it, man.'

Stark spoke matter-of-factly. 'Look, Dougie, let me give you a little bit of advice. I don't doubt that you will be as good as gold, but you will leave this house wearing these handcuffs. If you want to fight, that is a matter for you, but you will be adding police assault to the charge sheet. What do you want to do?'

Nobby took a step over towards Stark.

'Alright fuck me, though. It's ridiculous. I get it, but shit…' He put his hands out in front of him, his tobacco pouch and lighter in one hand.

'No behind your back.' Stark said. He put Dougie's arms behind him and clicked on the cuffs. 'There. That was painless, wasn't it?'

Dougie grunted as Stark and Steve Aston walked him outside to the CID car. Stark was driving, and Steve sat in the back with Dougie. As ever, child locks were on the doors, so they could not be opened from the inside.

When someone was arrested on just enough evidence to creep over the line of 'reasonable suspicion' but not much else, the expression often used was that it was 'a bit thin'. In the Brown brothers' case, it was certainly a bit thin. They had a neighbour who would not give a formal statement but saw some men sitting in a car, who got out and went down the side of Jane's house. The neighbour took the number, and it turned out the car was registered to Dougie's house, albeit under Sharon's name. It was the closest they would come as nothing was registered directly to Dougie or Len Brown. According to the neighbour, the same men then came running out a couple of minutes later and sped off.

The team also had the threat made to Jane by a man, which in the broader context and motive fitted Dougie, as did Jane's very basic description when the man shouted his threats at her from the kitchen door. She was pretty much hysterical by that time, however, and so an identification parade would probably be a waste of time.

The arrest was tactical at best, and to some extent, nothing was lost because if they had to release the brothers but then found more evidence, they could arrest them again on a new 24-hour clock. And then again, ad infinitum, in theory at least.

Another team brought in Len 'the bitch' Brown, who lived just a few doors down the street.

Maybe something could be found at the search tying them in to Jane or the armed robbery at Bernie Squires even though they had not been arrested for that particular crime. If, while legally on premises, an officer discovers an item they consider to be evidence of a crime, he may seize it, regardless of whether it is for that crime or another.

Stark also hoped against hope that the re-introduction to cell walls might prompt the realisation that they would have to suffer if they continued messing with Jane Cooper. There would be consequences, and this was not a free pass. The newfound focus they had brought upon themselves might make the Browns call it quits against Jane. He knew it was a long shot because the more he was learning about these two, the less he thought it might actually happen.

The next step for Stark was to persuade the custody sergeant that there was enough preliminary evidence to detain them in custody for the purpose of obtaining further evidence by enquiries, house searching, and questioning.

Stark chatted to Dougie as he drove over to Hucknall Police Station. DC Steve Aston was so innocuous he might as well not have been there. He was like a chameleon blending into whatever surroundings presented themselves. He spent most of his time staring out of the window and avoiding eye contact with Dougie.

'Don't you get sick of it, Dougie?' Stark asked as he turned right on to Highbury Vale, the indicator clicking, confirming his intention.

'Christ, yeah, of course, but what can you do?' Dougie said.

'Can't you just stack your hand in, Doug? Can't you just piss off somewhere and make a new start?' Stark asked.

Dougie laughed. 'Maybe if we went to some desert island or some dead and alive hole in fucking Cuba or somewhere. Anyway, your enemies find you, no matter where you go. You want to remember that, Mr Stark.'

Stark laughed. 'Oh, stop it Dougie, you daft sod. I'm trying to talk to you like a grown-up. Give it up, man.'

Much of Stark's approach was a front, just as much as Dougie's. Stark knew that the Brown brothers were a rare breed and dangerous. While Dougie came across as the talkative, more affable brother, Stark was well aware of his psychotic outbursts. It took a particular type of mentality to be able to break someone's leg by stamping on it as they lay across the pavement against the kerb. Or gouging someone's eye out, or cutting a couple of fingers off with pliers, all of which he knew Dougie had done, but which, as ever, never came to anything in the courts. There was a nasty, sadistic side to both of the Brown brothers.

Dougie stared out the window, the motion of the car having a greater effect than it otherwise might, because of his hands being handcuffed behind his back. His body jerked forwards and backwards, with Stark being a little heavy with the brake pedal.

'It's prison that does my head in.' Dougie said. 'That's why we will never go back.'

'Let's hope you don't get remanded then, Dougie.'

'Nah, no chance. We both know the score Inspector. You think it's going to help someone, but you don't know me very well.'

Stark ignored Dougie's comment, focussing on his disdain for prison instead. 'I wouldn't have thought it would bother you that much, Doug. Prison, I mean, it's an occupational hazard, isn't it? You get looked after in there, don't you?'

'Shit, yeah, man, prison does my head in. You have to be Mr Big every bastard day. There is no let-up. You know, at home, you can chill, just be normal, but inside, you never get a minute. It is a constant act, you know. There is no let-up from it. It's a nightmare, and I can do without it.'

'I see what you mean. Not easy, I wouldn't think.'

'And there is always some drama going on, you know. Someone wants a piece of you, another gang, wanting to flex up, stick you with a shiv, you need eyes in the back of your head, man. If it ain't that, it's someone's Mrs is being fucked while he's in pokey and can I do this that and can I do the other. It's mental.'

'It is people, Dougie. That's what it is. It doesn't matter what the setting is if you are at the top of the hierarchy among a group of people, it means bloody grief.'

Dougie laughed. 'I guess so.'

'I have the same. It's nothing to do with what I'm doing, it's always some bugger else, and then you react to it, and they get mardy, or they have some family problem they bring in to work, or someone is constantly trying to shaft you or knows better than you. We aren't that different, Dougie, trust me.'

'Yeah, we are. You didn't grow up in poverty and had to survive on the streets like I did. You ain't got a clue, man.'

'Says who? Yes, I did. I come from Bulwell, Dougie. We had the square root of sod all in our house. All I had was a hole in my shoe. I'm no different to you, it just turns out you went down one path and me another.'

'Yeah, you say that.'

'I do say that, Dougie, because it's true. You don't have the monopoly on being impoverished as a child, you know. What's up? Don't you believe me?'

'I don't know. I don't know anybody who did good from our school or neighbourhood. What makes you so special?'

'Maybe I'm God's special little pixie, eh, Dougie.'

He laughed. 'Yeah, maybe.'

'Do you know, Billy Click Walters? Carl Block? Polo Hunt?'

'Yeah, fucking idiots, what about 'em?'

'All in my class at school.'

'Fuck off!'

'They were.'

'No shit.'

'True, Dougie. As I say, you and I go back to a similar world. We just never met.'

*

The suave, well dressed Detective Constable Ashley Stevens slowly moved Sharon Browns knickers to one side as he thrust deeper inside. He couldn't go anymore. Ashley gasped slightly with effort as he wrapped his hand around the base of the thick phallus to guide it.

'Look what I've found, Nobby!' He shouted, producing a large pink vibrator moulded as an erect penis.

'It was in Sharon's knicker drawer.' Ashley laughed.

'You dirty tramp put it back; it'll have all her bloody dried-up love juices all over it, you daft sod.'

Ashley dropped it instantly. 'Eeeugh!'

It started to vibrate, on impact with the carpet, and Ashley made a big song and dance about it. 'It's alive!' He was stamping on it and giggling at the same time. Eventually, it shut off.

Nobby was laughing and shaking his head at the same time. 'Keep your mind on the job, Ash.'

'I am, but it took me by surprise, Sarge.'

'I bet it did. I bet it would take Dougie by surprise an all.'

Ashley sighed and looked around the room like a decorator giving a quote. He scratched his head.

'I doubt there will be anything here, Sarge. He was expecting us for Christ's sake.'

'So he says. Keep looking. We might get lucky. Just watch where you are putting your hands.'

Once they had completed the search in the bedrooms, Nobby and Ash did the bathroom, which was always a popular spot to hide things for criminals. Usually in the cistern, behind a cabinet, or behind the bath panel. In this instance, however, it was clear.

The detectives moved downstairs into the living room. Nobby, in search mode, looked into a potted plant on the windowsill as he did.

'It's a cactus, Sarge.'

'Piss off.'

'Just saying.'

'Are we going to Bobbers Mill Cafe after this?' Nobby said.

'For a brekkie? Ooh, I think we deserve one, don't you?'

'Sausage meat sandwich for me, young Ashley.'

'Mmm. God bless you, Sarge. A man of simple means and simple pleasures, but a man after my own heart.'

'Just like Sharon and that massive bloody dildo, that's her simple pleasure.'

Ashley laughed. 'Shit. Don't remind me. I'm trying to erase that memory from my mind.'

'Did you put it back in the drawer?'

'Did I bloody hell. I'm not touching it again. It's too terrifying.'

Nobby laughed. 'Probably wise.'

There was a funk in the living room. A sweaty sock smell and stale smoke. Like the taproom at 8 o'clock in the morning. The Browns might be the kings of the criminal world, but they certainly did not live like it. You can't buy class, and their slovenliness was indoctrinated and borne from idleness.

Nobby walked over towards the window and examined the shelf. Just some dying plant and deader flies. He looked around. He might as well start from there and work his way around. It was no good flitting from one point to another it needed to be done in sections so that nothing was missed.

Nobby opened the drawer of a small table at the side of the settee. Inside it was three small bookmakers' pens, a small notepad, a load of random keys, some coins, a fridge magnet for Skegness, a Nottingham Forest keyring, and some false nails. Nobby shut it and then quickly opened it again.

He gingerly took out the small note pad, no bigger than a packet of cigarettes, and he looked at it against the light from the patio doors, scrutinising the surface as he held it flat to his eye line.

'Hey, Ashley, what do you think that says?'

'It doesn't say anything; it's blank. What are you on about, Sarge?'

'No. I know that. I mean the imprint. I know nothing is written on it now, but whatever was written on the sheet above has made an indentation. Can you see it?'

Ashley similarly manoeuvred the pad to that which his Sergeant had, trying to catch the light.

'Bloody hell!'

'It says 'Squires Avenue, doesn't it?' Nobby said.

'I think it does, Sarge.'

'And where does Jane Cooper live?'

'Squires Avenue. Now there's a thing.'

*

The house with a red door stood on an incline and looked quite imposing. It had been easy enough to find as the elderly occupants were daft enough to still be in the phone book, listing name, telephone number and address. It was detached, and because it was set back, it stood alone from the others on the street that eventually merged into semi-detached dwellings as you moved further along. There was a small garden at the front that was kept tidy, a mown lawn and two bins neatly arranged at the side of the house. It was built in the 1940s, and the replacement double glazing didn't quite fit with the dark brick and arched bay windows evident on the ground and stretching up to the first floor of the building. It was a nice place.

Mac was an experienced burglar but curiously had never actually done prison time for housebreaking, only violent stuff. If he had looked back with any clarity of thought on his criminal career, he would have realised it was always on behalf of others and in the last ten years for the Brown brothers. He had paid a heavy price, but like many of his ilk he liked the street credibility his association with the Browns gave him. It was his only route to having any sort of pride in the shabby life he had led since the age of fourteen. The Browns gave a loser in life something that no one else could, self-esteem. That was why he did it. That was why he carried out their bidding, although he was oblivious to it.

He never did a job cold. He never acted on impulse. That was a mugs game. He was above all of that amateurishness; he cased a joint every time. It made it quicker and easier when he carried the job out, and a plan helped ease his nerves when he was working. He was on autopilot when he worked, methodical, trying not to break stride from the sequence of steps he had planned out in his mind's eye. If the plan changed for any reason, he aborted it. No questions asked. No trying to make it fit, he got the hell away at the slightest interruption or whiff of discovery. This job was going to be slightly different, though. He would be fronting up.

He always did a recce of a burglary during the daytime too. After dark, everything looks suspicious, whereas during the day, strangers are everywhere, delivering parcels and visiting houses, and no one bats an eyelid, and if they do, they explain it away to themselves. It was usually easier to do the actual break-in during the day when most people were at work, but this one was slightly different. This assignment needed the occupants to be in. This one had complications, but his partner in crime for later was a trusted accomplice who had never lost his bottle. They could pull it off, and they would be handsomely rewarded. Whether £500 was worth, a potential ten years for aggravated burglary was a moot point. It was arranged, and anyway, he had no intention of getting caught. He did not like the last-minute element of it in truth, and why Dougie had insisted it had to be that day, he did not know. Maybe he knew something he didn't. Maybe Dougie had set up some sort of alibi for himself?

Mac's burgling experience told him not to break stride, not to hesitate, as he veered off the main drag and up the drive to the side of the house. He carried on through, bold as brass to the rear of the premises. Looking up, he saw no alarm box, and he sought to quickly identify a point of entry. The rear patio doors looked like they had been there a while, maybe five years or more. They looked inexpensive, and the lock was flimsy. They slid along on runners. Easy.

Mac looked behind him and noticed the garden shed. Peering through the window, splashed with flecks of brown varnish, he saw an array of garden tools, garden hose, fork, spade and the like. Plus, a lawnmower and cardboard boxes. It was unlocked. Just a clasp.

As Mac tried to figure out which bedroom was whose, he heard a voice. An elderly woman.

'Hello, can I help you?' The voice was tentative.

He lowered his gaze to see a woman in her seventies standing at the patio doors.

'Ehup, yeah, I was wondering if you needed a window cleaner?' He was beaming a smile as he walked towards the woman.

'No, thank you. We have one that comes every two weeks.'

'Okay, well, fair enough then. I'm doing the rounds that's all.'

'What are you doing in my garden? Why didn't you knock?'

'Just about to. I was sizing up the cost for a house like this. There's a lot of glass. It's a lot of windows, but I can do it for £2. What does your man charge you?'

'A little more than that, but we are happy with him. He does a good job, and he's regular.'

'I can see that. Okay, well, never mind, Mrs?'

'Cooper. Mrs Cooper.'

'Thank you, Mrs Cooper. I'm sorry to have disturbed you, and I hope I didn't give you a fright.' He laughed. 'That's just me being over-keen, that's all.'

'No, that's okay. Thank you for calling. Next door might need a window cleaner they had some sort of dispute with ours over ladder marks on the lawn, apparently.'

'Great. I'll give them a try. Lovely to meet you.'

'You too. Thank you anyway.'

'Bye. Mrs Cooper.'

'Bye, lovey. Good luck.'

'Thanks a lot. And thanks for the lead with next door. Fingers crossed, eh?'

'Fingers crossed.' Mrs Cooper held up her crossed fingers gnarled by arthritis, and she could only cross them at the tip. She was smiling as she shuffled back inside.

'What a lovely chap.' She muttered to herself.

*

The plan was to interview Dougie and Len Brown throughout the day, and even Sharon had sobered up sufficiently to be questioned by Cynthia and Stephanie. Strangely she had not asked for a solicitor. Dougie and Len would disapprove.

'Half of Bulwell knows you've done it, Sharon.' Cynthia said, her long nails wrapped around a small plastic vending machine coffee cup before succumbing to the heat and hurriedly placed it on the table.

'Do they?' Sharon smiled.

'Do you accept that there was an altercation in the Co-op, Sharon?' Cynthia asked.

'Nope.'

'That's silly. Everyone knows what happened. Let's just agree that you were in the shop at the same time as Jane Cooper, yes?'

'Nope.'

'So even though you have a reputation to uphold, you allow someone like this Jane Cooper kick your butt, and she gets away Scot free?'

'I don't even know anyone by that name. Who is she? What's supposed to have gone off?'

'Oh, Sharon, behave yourself.'

Sharon grabbed a cigarette off a communal packet on the table. Steph had told her to help herself. 'Have you got a light?'

Steph lit it for her, and she drew it in like it was the nectar of the Gods. She coughed out an exhale. 'Cheers.'

Steph decided to have a go. 'So you're going to let her get away with it, Sharon?'

'Nope.'

'Exactly "nope." Because you haven't let her get away with it have you? You've cut her up.'

'Nope.'

'She must have done something to you, Sharon. Something really bad for this to all kick-off. I mean, what is it? Unless you tell us, we can't do anything. We think we know, but we need to hear it from you, and then we can investigate it, can't we? What did she do in the supermarket, Sharon? Come on, tell us.'

'Nope.'

'So it is all you, then? You did it all. She is totally innocent, is she?'

'Nope.'

Steph sat back in her chair and glanced at Cynthia.

'If that's how you want to play it. So be it, but she will pick you out in an ID parade, Sharon.'

'How come she ain't sat here. Why am I picked on, it's cos I'm a Brown. She gets away with everything, and I get nicked. How does that work?'

'So you did have a fall out with her?' Cynthia smiled.

'Nope.'

'Christ. It's like pulling teeth.' Steph said.

A similar scene played out in another interview room in the cell complex. Charlie and Steve Aston sat down opposite Dougie Brown and his solicitor, David Armstrong, of Armstrong, Jacobs and Dicker. He was expensive, but it was always worth it.

'Ouch ya, bugger.' Charlie said as he adjusted his seating position, rubbing at his knee.

Steve shuffled some papers.

'Where's Inspector Stark?' Dougie asked.

'He doesn't interview for something this lowly, Doug. He has better things to do. Bigger fish to fry.'

Dougie sneered. He didn't like the phrase nor that he did not qualify for Inspector Stark or even a Detective Sergeant, just two DC's. One looked like a divvy kid and the other like he qualified for a Bus Pass.

'This is Bullshit.' Dougie said.

'Isn't it always, Douglas. Isn't it always?' Charlie grinned.

'This is…what do you call it? Erm, discrimination, yeah, discrimination this is.'

'Oh yes, how come?'

'Cos, it's me, Dougie Brown. If it wasn't me, I wouldn't have even got nicked.'

'I really don't know what you mean, Dougie. I don't know who you think you are, but you are just another criminal to Steve and me. Sorry to disappoint, and we are not guilty of "Dougism," I can assure you.' Charlie mimed the exclamation marks.

'Yeah, right.'

Mr Armstrong touched Dougie's arm and spoke softly. 'Remember what we said, Douglas, don't be drawn.' He glanced at Charlie.

'I'm not, Mr Armstrong. We haven't started yet. He hasn't cautioned me yet. It's just the craic, you know.'

'I am just advising you, Douglas, that is all.'

'I know, I get it. Cheers.'

'So let us caution you then. You do not have to say anything, but anything you do say may be given in evidence.' Charlie said.

'Sweet.'

'Tell us about the fight between your wife, Sharon, and Jane Cooper then, Doug.'

'No comment.'

'Have you heard the name Jane Cooper before, Doug?'

'No comment.'

And so the interview continued as predicted by all and sundry. 'No comment.'

Next, it would be Len, but no amount of skill, looping, reverse psychology, showing exhibits, reasoning, empathising or anything else would change the negative answers. Sometimes there was a breakthrough in such interviews for a myriad of reasons. Maybe a fall-out with the Mrs, or a need to get out urgently, or a willingness to hide something else, it could be anything, but with a solicitor present any hint of sunlight was quickly extinguished before it could be built upon.

Interviews were for novice offenders, crimes of passion or those who did not have a solicitor present, not for hardened, professional criminals with the best lawyer in town within touching distance.

The charade was to go on for a couple more interviews spread throughout the day. It was the nuisance factor that bit at the Browns. They were long past the novelty of getting nicked. It was extremely annoying and degrading to them.

It shone a light on who they were, not what they imagined themselves to be. They had to ask nicely for concessions and cigarettes from the Custody Sergeant, not bark out orders to their minions.

Charlie and Steve made a few inquiries to justify the detention; Jane's neighbour, revisit witness statements and sought clarity from Brandon and his doctors over certain issues. It was a dead rubber; they knew they were just playing the game. An ID parade could be arranged in future weeks, perhaps, for Jane Cooper but it seemed insufficient and likely to fail. It was an option.

Poor Brandon would not get his day in court, nor would he get any glimmer of justice for trying to do the right thing, bless him. He was trying to help someone in need. He would be abandoned to his own devices soon and for the rest of his life. Within a couple of weeks, he would be Brandon, who?

*

Mr and Mrs Cooper lay in bed reading. She preferred the dark nights because they tended to go to bed early, around ten, and read until their eyelids felt heavy. The bedside lamp cast shadows around the bedroom but afforded sufficient light for her book if she tilted it slightly. The shadows cast a hazy border to an arc of light that cocooned them in the warmth of their blankets.

George had always read, but now as dementia and a dodgy ticker began eating away at him, he often just lay staring at the ceiling giving monosyllabic answers to comments and questions that Mary uttered in between chapters. Sometimes he would smile and laugh for no apparent reason. Other times Mary noticed a tear trickle down his wrinkled cheek. He was lost in his memories and lost in a fog that would sweep in and sweep out. The fog grew thicker as his resistance lightened. It stayed longer each night, blowing with it a chilly wind that taunted and tormented the remnants of a once contented soul. Poor George was on a path to delirium, which he would soon crest, opening up into a calmer world as he succumbed, allowing insanity to devour him whole before the blissful respite of death and whatever lay beyond.

The night terrors and hallucinations had yet to begin in earnest, but Mary knew they were approaching, as she would hear him sometimes in the night talking, sometimes like a child, full of both wonder and fear, dependent on the tricks his mind had decided to play on him.

Mary had helped him into his pyjamas and was disturbed by a far-reaching stare that pierced her, as if he was looking through her. It was heartbreaking, but she would not shirk from doing whatever it took to give him the best end-of-life she could, and he would have done the same for her.

He still had motor skills; for example, he could do up the buttons okay, but they were often fastened into the wrong hole, and it was easier and quicker to do it for him.

Her only release was that there were still good days and funny moments, glimpses, still, of the man she loved and the life they shared. They were fleeting but welcome.

Curiously they had bickered less in recent weeks. The niggling annoyances had gone, probably replaced by an understanding that it wasn't George who was leaving the oven on. It wasn't George who left the bath running. It wasn't George who didn't flush the toilet. It was some other character. Someone she did not know. His puppet master: the devil who had slipped inside him uninvited. A monster that could not be defeated, which had slithered in and wouldn't come out until it had killed its host.

As Mary read, her thoughts occasionally overtook her, and while staring at the page, she was lost in her own concerns. She had been worried about Jane since she first mentioned the episode at the supermarket. She had played it down when she mentioned it so as not to worry her daughter, but it did bother her. Jane had become a little distant since the incident, and it was at times such as these, she missed the old George. He had always been a quiet but intelligent man. He was brimming with common sense and good judgement. Everyone went to George for advice in the family, and he dealt with it calmly and assuredly each time. Now his diminished faculties exposed Mary and the rest of them to a colder, more uncertain world. Mary felt lonely and sad, worse than alone; she felt that she was now George's parent. It was only a matter of time before he did not recognise her. But she would recognise him, and she was determined to honour him by never forgetting the man he had always been. This horrid illness would not define his life nor their memory of him. That would be the ultimate betrayal.

If she mentioned the problems Jane was having with George, it would only confuse and disorientate him. He would become agitated and unsettled, and she needed a good night's sleep, not a restless one. His old self and the desire to help would swim to the surface of his consciousness and battle with the raging current pulling him down into the relentless and murky deep.

Mary paused, resting her book and spectacles on the bed covers. She was actively listening. A noise from the back garden? A clink of metal on concrete? It sounded like a spade. Was it her imagination? She listened again.

'What was that, George?'

'Eh?'

'Did you hear a noise in the garden?'

'A noise, heh, heh. There aren't any noises, I don't think, Mary.'

'Listen. Can you hear anything? It sounds like metal on metal or metal on concrete.'

The coolness of the night swept through the house and found its way into the main bedroom and the Coopers. It was a noticeable cold rush of air that made Mary shudder. It was as if a door had been left open, and she was sure she had locked up.

'I heard that, Mary.' George said.

'Ring the police.'

'Where's the phone?'

'Downstairs.'

'Okay.'

'No. Just a minute, love. Look down the stairs and see if you can see or hear anything. first.'

The request was born out of habit. George would always investigate any such noises. He was the man of the house. She had momentarily forgotten that man had all but gone, unfortunately. At least if he went out, she could follow him down to the phone.

George rolled out of bed slowly, slid his slippers onto his feet, and waited a few seconds as he sat on the bed. Allowing everything to settle before standing.

'Hurry up, George.'

He heaved himself to his feet before toddling off onto the landing.

'Put the light on, you daft apeth.' Mary shouted in a sort of whisper.

She would have to get a second phone fitted in the bedroom. These types of eventualities served to expose how vulnerable they were becoming as a couple with George's worsening impediment.

She lay there, listening intently. Her heart was beating fast, and her breath quickened. Maybe she should have gone herself rather than sent George. It was against her better judgement, but in truth, she was frightened. She was convinced someone was breaking in. Hopefully, it was nothing. She was allowed to be vulnerable too.

It had suddenly gone quiet.

'George?'

12

'In life, there is good, evil, love, and hatred. What we desire, choose, and need to pursue is in our hands.' – Dhanush.

George came shuffling back into the bedroom with a strange look on his face. He looked quite pleased with himself.

'Was it anything, George?' Mary asked, relieved to see him return unscathed.

'It's all right. Nothing to worry about. False alarm.'

'Oh, good.' Mary put her book and glasses on the bedside table and pulled back the blankets, ready for George.

'It's my dad come to see us.' He giggled to himself. 'Aye fancy that, my dear old Dad.'

'What? What are you talking about? Your dad has been dead for…'

The intruder followed George into the bedroom and pushed him to the floor. His accomplice was searching other rooms and now stomping around without a care.

'Where's Jane Cooper?' The intruder snarled.

Mary let out a muffled squeal but noticed he was brandishing a carving knife and her heart fell into the pit of her stomach. The man was wearing a ski mask with holes in the eyes and mouth area. It added to the horror. Mary was rigid with fear as she tried to make sense of what was happening. She was rooted to the spot. After a couple of seconds she blurted out,

'What is going on? Who are you? Can you please leave?'

'You heard. I said, where is Jane Cooper?'

'She doesn't live here. She hasn't years. You've got the wrong house.'

'Get out of bed. Move it!' The man barked at her.

'Wait. You're not going to hurt us, are you?' Her voice was timid and quavering, and she now needed the toilet. Mary immediately felt weak, vulnerable, and floppy like a rag doll, unable to move. It was as if all the blood had drained out of her body. It was the sort of naked fear that shakes you to the marrow of your bones.

'I said get on the floor and shut up asking questions, or I *will* fucking hurt you. Move it!' He seemed to be getting angrier.

Mary got out of bed as quickly as she could. 'Jane's not here; she doesn't live here.' She kept saying. 'She's not here. Please don't hurt us.'

'Just get on the floor.'

'I won't be able to get up.' Mary said as she clumsily knelt down and manoeuvred her back side on the floor with a bump using the edge of the bed. She let out a gasp.

George was lying on his side, looking around. He had landed awkwardly and hurt his hip. He was rubbing it, and she grabbed at his hand to try to help him.

'My husband has hurt himself.'

'Shut up!' His voice was garbled by the mask but just about discernible.

The intruder quickly used plastic ties to secure the elderly couples' hands behind their backs and ripped out the bedside lamp, making the room pitch black and changing the dynamic further. Jane Cooper's elderly parents sat on the unforgiving carpet, leaning against each other, trembling with fear. George was confused and staring at Mary for help or guidance or both. Mary couldn't see well without her glasses, but she could hear George puffing and panting at the side of her. He hadn't fully got his balance and was leaning heavily against her as they both sat in the darkness. Mary searched out shadows of movement but was taken aback when the intruder turned on his torch and shone it at the pair, causing Mary to squint. She was crying and whimpering. She was horrified.

'Just take the money. My purse is on the kitchen top.' She said.

She received no reply. A youth could be heard calling from the landing.

'Not here, mate.'

The knifeman walked over to Mary, who cowered in the darkness. He shone the torch in her eyes, and she turned her head away.

'The Brown brothers send their compliments.'

'Who? Who are they? We don't know anyone called Brown, do we, George?'

'Only Eric Brown on Merchant Street, Mary. He's called Brown. His eldest was a joiner, or was he a mechanic?'

'What's up with this prat?' The man said.

'He's got Alzheimer's.' Mary whimpered.

The intruder laughed. 'Silly old prat. What a fucking nutter!'

'Hey, watch your language. No need to swear.' George said. He seemed affronted as if he was suddenly in the present and lucid.

'What would your mother say, coming out with filthy language like that? There's a lady present.'

The old George was back, but it was only a fleeting visit. The knifeman booted George in the face with such force that it knocked him unconscious. He fell sideways into Mary's lap, but she could not soothe him because of the restriction to her hands shackled behind her back by cable ties.

'You bastard! He's an old man!' Mary shouted in temper, but the intruder had gone.

'Oi! You!' She shouted after him.

She felt a warm liquid soaking through her nightdress into her lap. It was blood. George's blood.

Mary couldn't help herself, and she urinated into the carpet as she sobbed. The smell of blood and urine made her heave, and she thought she was going to be sick. Mary couldn't just sit there. She drew in a breath and called out into the darkness.

'Help! Help! Police! We need help!'

*

It had been a long day for DC's Charlie Carter and Steve Aston. A day of interviews and chasing around trying to magic willing witnesses out of thin air.

The two detectives had assembled the Brown family in the cell complex at Nottingham Police Station. It was always cold in there, and the large bricks gave it an austerity worthy of its purpose. The Browns were in a jubilant mood and seemed pleased to see each other, and the swagger had returned. They were bouncing and grinning and making sly comments at every opportunity to one another.

Custody Sergeant Peet was elevated behind a large domineering counter; he was a big man with a large stomach straining the buttons on his blue police shirt. He was open-collared and never wore a tie when he was on nights. A portable television set could be heard in the backroom, and the smell of a Chinese meal wafted through the corridors.

Sergeant Peet was getting close to drawing his pension. He was ready. He had done his bit over the previous thirty years and, just like many in his situation, longed for the good old days to return. It was ever thus, but they never would. 'TJF' was a common phrase from Sergeant Peet, and every officer knew it stood for 'the job's fucked.' At one time, his tunic buttons were shiny, and now it was the backside of his trousers.

Stark had advised Charlie over the phone to release the Browns on police bail at this stage to keep them on their toes, rather than give them a 'refused charge' sheet. After all, it was a live enquiry, and there was always the prospect that they might turn something up. It was a shame that they could not charge them with something and seek bail conditions through the courts to keep away from Jane and her family. Maybe even seek a remand in prison pending the court case. However, Stark had to be realistic; there was not enough to charge. Even the Squires Avenue indentation Nobby had found while corroborative was not going to be enough to prove anything beyond a reasonable doubt. He suggested they consider an identification parade the following week, or at least discuss the pros and cons.

Custody Sergeant Peet was pleased to get three prisoners out of the cellblock, and no doubt enjoy a more peaceful night shift in his home from home – the back office. He handed Dougie his belt and meagre possessions, notably his tobacco and 'skins.'

'I told you, didn't I?' Dougie said to Charlie with a huge stupid grin on his face.

'You did, Dougie, you sure did.'

'What time is it?'

Charlie looked at his watch. 'Ten to midnight. There's a clock up there, Dougie.'

'I know, I just wanted to check the time with you.'

Charlie looked puzzled. What was that about? He had seen this before, it was rare, but a time check sometimes meant an alibi for some other matter. It gave him an uneasy feeling, and he glanced at Steve, who seemed oblivious to the comment. He just stood biting his nails, staring at Dougie fiddling with his belt.

Dougie turned to Steve Aston. 'Won't your Mummy and Daddy be worried you being out at this time of night?'

'Very funny.' Steve muttered.

'You have to look after your parents, you know. They won't be around forever.'

'Is there something you want to tell us, Dougie? What's all this shit you're coming out with?' Charlie asked.

'Just making conversation, that's all. Just being friendly, you know. No hard feelings and all that.'

'Your comments are duly noted.' Charlie said, and Sergeant Peet glanced at Charlie. There was often a mime show between different parties in the tenseness of a cell complex. Knowing glances, facial expressions, and gesticulations for private conversations in the back room between police officers.

'Have you made a note of the time, Custody Sergeant?' Dougie asked.

'Of course. Everything is noted, and the time it happened. You know that, Dougie.'

'That's cool.' Dougie winked at Charlie, doing nothing to ease his concerns. Something was going on, but DC Carter wasn't sure quite what it was.

Steve Aston opened the cellblock door and showed the Brown family out into the chilly air.

'Thank you, my good man.' Dougie said and gestured a kiss towards Steve, who blushed.

'See you again soon, Dougie. Take care, now.' Charlie said as they ambled out of view.

As the door closed, Sergeant Peet said, 'What was that all about, Charlie?'

'Christ knows. It seems he knows something we don't.'

'Alibi?' Sergeant Peet asked.

'Maybe.'

*

George had been silent all this time as Mary sat in the darkness. His breathing was heavy and inconsistent. It seemed to stop, and then suddenly, a prolonged intake of air whistled through his throat, which sounded horrible.

Mary's shouts for help had been fruitless, and now she was exhausted from the yelling, and her voice had pretty much given out on her. Her thoughts had been tortuous. She mainly focused on George and how she could try to stem the blood coming from his nose and ear. She couldn't, and it was pooling on her nightdress in a thickening gloop.

Now and then, she would force herself to shout for help, but the house was set on a slight hill, it was detached, and all the windows were closed. It was futile. In truth Mary was in shock, and it took a while to snap out of the torpor these hideous circumstances had put her in. Periodically shouting into the black was not going to help them. She had to do something. She wasn't convinced George would survive the night, at this rate, if she didn't get assistance of some sort.

She was silently crying, not because the plastic ties were too tight or the viciousness of the attack on them but out of pure concern for George. He did not deserve this. Not in his condition. In some ways, it was a blessing; he was out of it, unaware of the desperate situation they were in. That was her burden. It was on her.

George's head rested on her lap, and his breathing was becoming more and more erratic. Mary wasn't sure how long they had been there, since the man left, maybe two hours? Maybe it was less. There was no way of knowing.

The darkness of the room did not help the sense of helplessness. Mary was annoyed that she could not touch George or soothe him with her hands, but she spoke to him softly.

'It's okay, George. Help is on its way, my love.'

'Not long, now George, hang in there, love. It will soon be morning.'

'Stay with me, George. Think of our Jane.'

She wasn't sure if he could hear her or not, but she persisted. It helped her if nothing else.

Her eyes had adapted to the darkness, and she could see the outline of some of the furniture now. The hall light was off, but she could tell the bedroom door was slightly ajar as there was a faint light permeating from the streetlamps and up the stairs and through the small crack of the door.

However long it had been, Mary could not just sit there forever. Who would ever find them? Even when morning came? George appeared to be getting worse with every passing minute, and he had not regained consciousness from the nasty kick to the head the intruder gave him. She had to do something. She was afraid. She was scared to try to go down those stairs. She didn't feel she had the strength to do it.

The plastic ties restricted her hands behind her back, but her legs were free. She had been trying to figure out whether she could get downstairs to the phone and had resisted at first because of her uncertainty. She kept seeing herself in her mind's eye tumbling down the stairs and breaking her neck with no way to break her fall with her arms tied up behind her. The whole escapade felt dangerous but not impossible. Mary had hoped that her shouts might draw some attention. But no. And now her mouth was dry and her throat sore from her efforts. That was a waste of time. Give it up. Try something else.

The more she pondered her options and as the shock of the incident subsided slightly, affording some clarity of thought, the more she thought that while dangerous, it was her only chance. She felt that if she took her time, moving really slowly, she could shuffle along the carpet to the top of the stairs and then one-by-one go down them. It was a Godsend that the intruders had left the bedroom door slightly ajar because if it had been closed, she would have absolutely no chance of getting out.

Most of George's body was lying on the carpet with just his head and shoulders across her knees. He was gargling with the blood accumulating in his mouth and throat. She gently let George's head roll from her lap onto the floor and had to nudge it slightly with her knee as he was face-first into the carpet. This actually helped the blood come out and ease his breathing. Now, after her gentle nudge, his face was tilted to one side, and he would be able to breathe easier.

Mary stretched her legs out and pulled her backside towards her feet, and she began to make progress moving little by little along the carpet, but it was harder than she had imagined, and she kept falling sideways. Her legs began to shake violently, and she got cramp. There was no way she could get to her feet. Her knees wouldn't stand it, even if she leant against the bed or wall. That was a non-starter. The effort to right herself when she fell sideways, was exhausting but she persevered. Occasionally she stopped to listen for George breathing. The pooled blood on her nightdress was now cooling and sticky, smearing along her thighs and causing her to grimace with revulsion. As she got to the bedroom door, she swiped it open first with the tip of her toe and then with her foot. She paused again to listen but could hear nothing. Maybe she was out of range? She had to see this through.

This was going to be the tricky bit—the top of the stairs. The stairs were steep, but she managed a stair at a time with careful manoeuvring. She was leaning back, which hurt her spine and caused her to slide down two stairs in one go on a couple of occasions. She had figured it would be better to slide down the stairs rather than tilt forward head over heels if she fell. Her nightdress had rolled up, exposing her nakedness, and she kept catching her bound hands on the top of the stair behind her, and this caused her to cry out in pain as it bent her elbows awkwardly and tore at each shoulder. She had tears rolling down her cheeks. What a mess they were in.

After what seemed like an age, she reached the bottom. She used her head to push over the telephone stand, and as the handset had come off the cradle, she managed to align her finger. Hands still tethered behind her back, to the '9' on the dial and, whilst awkward, managed to clumsily rotate it enough, three times. A voice pierced the quiet of the hallway.

'Fire, Police or Ambulance?'

Mary stooped down to get her mouth close to the handset. 'Police and Ambulance. Help! We've been attacked. We are tied up.'

'Putting you through.'

'Nottinghamshire Police.'

'Help, please. We have been attacked; my husband is seriously hurt. We are tied up; come quickly, please.'

'Hello?'

'Yes, hello, please come quick?'

'Can you hear something? It sounds like someone is on the line. I can't hear bugger all. Something faint, maybe. I bet it's those bloody kids again.' The officer was not speaking to Mary but a colleague.

Mary was so hoarse from the shouting her voice had almost completely gone. She leaned as close as she could and tried again. 'Can you hear me?' She croaked.

The strident sound of the call being disconnected made Mary squeal and curse.

'You bloody idiot!'

She sobbed in desperation. The cool air from the broken patio door was giving her the shivers, and it was an option to try to get outside and start yelling again, but she didn't think her voicebox would be able to get anything out.

Mary decided she would try the phone once more. She needed the police to come. She had to get to the telephone and press down one of the buttons that were flattened when the handset was resting on top. This, when released, opened the line back up for another call to be made. She found the dialling even harder this time around, and her fingers were cramping with the effort. She had arthritis in her hands, so trying to manoeuvre them awkwardly like this was painful.

'Police, Fire or Ambulance.'

'Jesus Christ, Police.'

'Putting you through.'

This time it was a female voice. 'Nottinghamshire Police.'

'Please help; we are tied up.' Mary whispered as she lay on her side, her lips almost touching the speaking bit of the phone scoop.

'What is your address?' The woman asked.

'Thank God.' Mary said before giving her details slowly and surely.

'Stay on the line; someone is coming to you straight away. Don't hang up.'

'I won't, hurry up, please. I'm worried for my husband.'

'We will get there as soon as we can, don't worry.'

13

'Sometimes, you get tired of fighting. I think you just sort of come to this realisation that yes, that you will get tired, but that doesn't mean that you can give up the fight.'

– Jesmyn Ward.

Neighbours of Mary and George Cooper awoke to see police tape flapping in the wind and two uniformed officers standing outside the front door. It looked ominous, and something serious had happened.

The two cops were PC's Ged Stent and Ian Carlisle. It was chilly, but they had their long macs and gloves on, and so with the occasional stamping of feet and clapping of hands, it was just about bearable. Beat bobbies were pretty hardy where adverse weather was concerned, and they knew all the tea-spots and could usually wangle a safe haven in bad weather anywhere on their patch. 'A good bobby never gets wet.' It was a regular saying.

'What are we waiting for now?' Ged asked his older companion.

'The D.I. to attend.'

'Can we go then?'

'I doubt it, but maybe after scenes of crime have finished.'

'Christ, that will be hours yet.'

'The Sergeant might switch us over. If we can get to snap time, we can perhaps suggest whoever replaces us can do a reasonable stint too. I don't see why it needs two of us either, for that matter.'

'No. Good idea, though, Ian. See what the Sarge says when we get back to the nick. Is the D.I. on his way, or what?'

'He's here now, by the looks of it.'

Ian nodded towards a car pulling onto the kerb, and the DI and DS got out and walked up the slight hill to the front door.

'Morning, Mr Mole.'

'Morning Ian. What have we got?' Mole immediately lit up a cigarette and handed one to his Detective Sergeant, Carl Davidson.

Ian told his DI all he knew. 'Apparently, all the calls are logged at Control with the relevant times. It's a tie-up job. Burglary: entry and exit via the rear patio door. They've levered the door off the runners with a spade by the looks of it. You'll see it around the back. The female has been taken to hospital. I'm afraid the old guy is deceased in the bedroom.'

'Any motive, or is it just a burglary gone wrong, do we know?'

'No idea, sir.'

'Who are the couple?' Mole sucked in the nicotine.

'A George and Mary Cooper. They've lived here years, according to her next door. Lovely old couple, he was going a bit gaga apparently, but they were both well-liked.'

'Cooper, eh?'

'Yeah, Mr and Mrs Cooper. There's a note on the pad that it is the parents of that Jane Cooper who the Browns have got the knife into. It looks like this might be their handiwork. They've dropped a goolie if it is.'

'Don't start spreading rumours who has done it at this early stage, constable, dangerous talk costs lives, you know.' Mole said, pointing a finger.

'Yeah, I know. I'm just saying...'

'Well, don't.'

'Yes, sir.'

There was an awkward silence as Mole surveyed the outside of the property as he finished his cigarette.

PC Carlisle spoke again. 'We haven't had a murder for a while on this patch, have we? It's all been over on DI Stark's lately.'

'Who says it's a murder, Ian?' Mole said.

'Well, I just assumed…'

'Well, don't. The guy could have died from natural causes for all we know.'

The two PCs exchanged puzzled looks.

'Well, there's a lot of blood in there, sir.'

'Maybe he's had a haemorrhage. Don't jump to conclusions. We don't want you going around telling everyone it's murder before he's even cold, now do we.'

'No, sir.'

'Are SOCO on their way?' Mole asked.

'Yes, Senior SOCO is attending. They should be here any minute.'

'I'll just go and have a gander. Come on, Carl.'

The two walked inside the open front door of the house and immediately noticed the telephone table on its side and the phone on the floor, along with some trinkets presumably off the top of the table, splayed out when it spilt over. They could feel the cold blasting through from the rear patio door being askew. Mole peered through the hallway at the point of entry. 'We'll have a look at that in a bit, Carl.'

'Sure.'

The two detectives went up the stairs together and stopped in the doorway of the bedroom. It was usual for the senior detective to survey the scene even before SOCO arrived to get an impression of what they were dealing with and direct them in what they wanted doing. It would be impractical to wait for SOCO to finish which would be later that evening, no doubt.

They saw George immediately, lying face down in his pyjamas with his head to one side and his eyes and mouth slightly open. The deceased's hands were still bound behind his back. His face was bloodied, and the dark stain on the beige carpet showed further blood loss had occurred.

'Looks like a fractured skull. I wonder what's caused the injury?' DS Davidson said.

'Blunt trauma by the looks of it. He looks like he's had a bit of a pasting. The postmortem is going to tell us more, no doubt.'

'This could be a tricky one to sort out, Lee.' Carl said in a hushed tone. 'What with the connection with you know who.'

'Yes. It's the Brown's, I shouldn't wonder. It's too much of a coincidence.' Mole shook his head. 'They don't make life easy, do they, Carl?'

'No. There is a glimmer of hope because according to the old bat who lives here, his Mrs,' he nodded at George, 'they broke in about 11 to 11.30 pm.'

'So what? It's a bit early, but it depends on what they were trying to do, steal stuff or give them a bit of pain.' Mole said.

'Or both.'

'Or both.'

'The time is important, though, boss, because a little birdy has told me that the Browns were in custody at the time, so it can't be them.'

'You little beauty! You're kidding me?' Mole's little Weasley face filled with glee.

'No, I'm not kidding. Stark had them all nicked yesterday, I hear, for blinding that youth.'

'What a prat. So Stark's given them the alibi?'

'Erm, I suppose he has, boss, yeah.'

'Wait 'til Wagstaff hears about this little gem.'

'It's not best, is it, for Stark and his crew, I mean.'

'What an absolute pri…'

PC Carlisle appeared behind them at the top of the stairs, surprised to see the ribaldry and cheery faces. Mole immediately put on a sterner expression.

'Yes, Ian?'

'Next door has made a brew if you want a cuppa.'

'Nice one, we'll be down in a minute. Two sugars in each, Ian, please.'

'So is it a murder, sir?'

'We don't know yet. He might have stumbled and hit his head when he was tied up. It's too early to say, mate.'

'Oh, erm, righto.'

Davidson chimed in. 'Is she going to get the frying pan on, Ian? A couple of bacon butties would go down a treat.'

'I can ask.'

'Good man. Happy days.'

*

'I know you're busy, sir, but it all makes sense now.' Charlie had spotted Stark in the CID office corridor.

'What does?'

'The Browns, last night when we kicked them out on bail, Dougie especially, he kept going on about what time it was, and then he made some smart-arse comment to Steve about you should always look after your parents. He was obviously referring to Jane's parents.'

'Sounds like it, Charlie. I'll bear it in mind. Look, I've got to meet Wagstaff and Mole in a minute, so I've got to dash. We need to decide who and how this is dealt with.'

''It's got to be us. It's connected.'

'Don't hang your hat on it, Charlie, this is Mole and bloody Wagstaff we are talking about; anything could happen. It's mind-blowing, trust me.'

Charlie laughed, but Stark's face remained impassive. 'By the way, sir, Cynthia and Steph have gone to Jane's to do the death message. Nobby sorted it early doors.'

'Excellent. We need to get her moved out of that address sharpish.'

'Surely after this, she will get out of harm's way.'

'You would think so, wouldn't you?'

'Definitely.'

'Anyway, better shoot. His nibs will be waiting.'

'Good luck, boss.'

'I think I might need it, Charlie.'

Stark entered the room at the far end of the corridor and was greeted by Detective Superintendent Wagstaff.

'Morning, David.'

'Morning, sir.'

'A bit of a funny one, this one.'

'I suppose so, in what sense?'

'Lee was saying he wasn't sure it was a murder.'

'What? Not a murder? This I've got to hear.'

'Hear what?' Mole breezed in. He looked a little frazzled. His air of confidence was brittle and did not fool Stark.

'That it's not a murder.' Stark said.

'It might not be yet.'

'How come?'

'We need the PM doing. He's got blunt trauma to his head, but you have to bear in mind he's also got his hands tied behind his back. He could easily have fallen.'

'Ah, that old chestnut. Is there blood on a table or something then?' Stark asked.

'Not that I can see, but I didn't want to go too deep in before SOCO had done the business.'

'Very wise, Lee.' Wagstaff said, giving him the thumbs up.

'Have we got photos of the scene yet?' Stark asked.

'Not yet, no.'

'So when's the PM? I wouldn't mind coming to that.' Stark said.

Mole averted his gaze. 'Tomorrow morning at 11 am, and the pathologist is coming over from Lincoln.'

'Tomorrow? Can't he get any earlier than that?' Stark asked.

'I don't know, David, perhaps you can give him a ring and ask him what the fucking delay is.' Mole laughed.

'Better not, David.' Wagstaff seemed to jiggle his jowls at the suggestion, not seeing the sarcasm.

Wagstaff's phone rang. 'It's for you, Lee.'

Stark could only hear Lee's side of the conversation. Whatever Carl was saying was inaudible.

'Ehup, Carl. Have you got a statement off her yet?'

'Just notes at the moment. She said the offender mentioned Dougie Brown's name to her and to give his compliments or something like that.'

'Right.' Mole showed no expression but looked at Stark as he listened to his DS. Stark sat down.

'The offender had a knife that he got out the kitchen, and he booted the old guy in the head. A definite assault. Nasty too, full force, and it knocked him clean out. George never woke up after that. It's probably a fractured skull and bleeds on the brain.'

'Okay.'

'What's up, can't you talk?'

'No, mate.'

'Okay. That's the meat of it, anyway. It is an assault leading to death, and the Browns are mentioned, so we're back to square one. Tricky dicky.'

'Hang on to that one, for now, yeah?'

'What the info I've just told you?'

'Yes.'

'Okay, got you. Anything else?'

'Yes, we will catch up later, Carl. Good work, mate. Laters.'

Mole slowly placed the phone back on the cradle, his mind a whirl. He sauntered over to a chair in the silence. Wagstaff sipped at a mug of tea.

'Anything new, Lee?' Wagstaff asked.

'Not really. Carl is trying to make sense of the old woman, but it's all a bit confused apparently.'

'So it's the Browns, then?' Stark said.

Mole shrugged.

Stark continued. 'It's got to be. It is Jane's parents. The Browns have to have done it.'

'They can't have done it, David.' Mole said.

'What do you mean, they can't have done it?'

'From what I've found out, they couldn't have done it because they were locked up here—downstairs in the cells. You've given them their bleeding alibi! Can you believe that, sir?' Mole looked flabbergasted.

'What? I don't understand.' Wagstaff's eyes flitted between the two Detectives. 'We've done what?'

Mole was happy to explain. 'Not we. Him. Yeah. Stark here got them all nicked just to fuck them off, and all he's ended up doing is give them a frigging alibi!'

'Jesus Christ, David.' Wagstaff said.

'They will be behind it. They probably wouldn't do it themselves anyway, whether they were locked up or not.'

'I'm just saying that we shouldn't rush to conclusions. There is no evidence that I know of that points to the Browns. We are just guessing. And that is no way to run an investigation, is it, sir?' Mole said.

'Not it is not, you're right, Lee.' Wagstaff pursed his lips.

'So are you handing it over? It's wrapped up in the Cooper case.' Stark asked, ignoring Mole's sneakiness.

'I've just said we don't know yet.'

Wagstaff coughed into a comment. 'Let Lee carry on with it, for now, David. After all, it is on his patch, and we are just one big team, are we not? Just until we know if it is a murder or whatever the hell it is. We are jumping the gun a bit here. Suppose there is no evidence that the Browns are involved. Let's stick to the facts, not what we surmise to be the case.'

'Fine. I won't even bother arguing it.' Stark folded his arms. He had been down this road before, and he wasn't going to beg.

'If it needs to it will come over to you, David. Rest assured.' Wagstaff said, stroking at his handlebar moustache.

Mole chewed on some gum as he winked at Stark.

'You can trust me to be thorough, David; don't you worry about that.' Mole said.

'Huh.' Stark shrugged out a laugh and shook his head. 'What about protection for her. For Jane, and well, the mother too, I suppose.'

Mole jumped in. 'Hang on, Mr Wagstaff. I was just about to ask for extra staff on this job, and there's a load of work to do we can't have detectives babysitting her twenty-four-seven.'

'So we give the Browns a clean run at her, do we?' Stark said.

'Things have changed somewhat.' Wagstaff was clearly pondering his options.

'They won't have another go after this. It's too hot now.' Mole said.

'Imagine if they did and we had done sod all to protect her.' Stark said.

Wagstaff stood and walked over to the window to buy some thinking time.

'I think David is right on this one. But I want her moved to a safe house. Total secrecy as soon as possible. I will authorise protection for 48 hours, and then we can review it after the post-mortem.'

'I've got somewhere in mind. It's just persuading her, but I doubt she will protest after what has happened to her parents. She will be distraught, bless her.'

'Where will she be moving to then, David?' Mole asked.

'I'm not saying that. You've just heard the gaffer say utmost secrecy, and that's a need-to-know basis, and you don't need to know.'

'I will need to talk to her as part of my enquiry into what happened to her parents.' Mole said.

'If you do. Come through me. And I will arrange a meet.' Stark said.

'Is that necessary, David?' Wagstaff asked.

Stark sighed. 'I haven't even settled on somewhere yet, so I cannot divulge somewhere she *might* go. What's the point in that?'

'Fair enough. Let's meet up again tomorrow after the post-mortem.' Wagstaff said.

They left the office and went their separate ways. No sooner had Stark sat back down at his own desk, but Cynthia came in, tapping at the door with her fingernails as she did.

'Oh, hello, Cynthia. How did she take it?'

'How do you think?'

'Badly, I assume.'

'She didn't say much, to be honest. She was numb, I think. I'm not sure it has sunk in. It's just another massive kick in the teeth for her, and she must be at breaking point.'

'Who is with her now?'

'Charlie came over, and he's there with Steph. I came back to see if you needed us to do anything.'

'No, what did she say about moving house?'

'To be honest, we never broached the subject, and it was distressing enough as it is. Should we have done?'

Stark sighed. 'No, I get it. I just want her in a safe house. Go back and get her to sign up for an address so we can get things moving.'

'Are we still being careful with Mr Mole?'

Stark laughed. 'Yeah, and Ratty, his DS.'

Cynthia laughed too.

'Everything is top secret, Cynthia, just our team. Not even Jim.' Stark said.

'Oh, isn't he on the team?'

'Sort of, but he's office manager, so yes and no. He's a desk Wallah. Just us for now, yes?'

'Yes, of course, sir. Anything you say.'

'Look, even if you have to wrestle her to the damned floor, Jane Cooper needs to be in a new house by this time tomorrow.'

*

Everything about the mess they were in troubled Stark. Mole had free range to do whatever the hell he liked, and he was becoming more and more convinced that the Browns had Mole in their pocket. Mole was a mole. This meant that Jane was in extreme danger. They had already demonstrated their ruthlessness with George Cooper, and Mole had already revealed his leanings in the conversation with Wagstaff. Wagstaff might have a blind spot with Mole, but he was right that they could not sustain detectives sitting with Jane and her mother once she was out of hospital, ad infinitum. He had to take the initiative. He had to get some control over proceedings. While Mole had access to information that could lead to Jane Cooper, he could not be satisfied she was safe or that his officers protecting her were not in grave danger themselves. The attack on Brandon showed that. So he had to come up with a plan, so he called for a team meeting at the Green Dragon pub, next door to the police station. This was a conversation that needed to take place away from the prying eyes and ears.

In order to get all the team together, he arranged with the duty Inspector to get two uniformed officers to babysit Jane and Daisy while they had their conflab. Mary Cooper was with DS Davidson, and God help her.

Stark had said he would pay the uniformed officer's overtime, and he stipulated the cops he wanted. They were tried and tested, and they were to park the police vehicle immediately outside Jane's house as a warning to all comers that they were there waiting.

Stark had captured the back table in the lounge. There was a buzz of excitement in the air along with the stench of cigarette smoke and pints of ale. His detectives could sense something unusual was in the offing, and once their glasses were charged, Stark began the debrief, leaning forward to share the news. Then he would get down to the nitty-gritty and explain the trap he had in mind.

'Give us an update on the house move, Cynthia, please.' Stark said.

'Jane is being moved first thing in the morning at 6 am.' Cynthia explained. 'No one will know, and she will be taken to a house away from the locale.'

'Great, anybody else got anything they want to say?' Stark said.

Nobby reared up in his chair. 'Yeah, me.'

'Okay, Nobby, go for it. I'm all ears.'

'I'll say it if nobody else will. You know they are going to get her, don't you?'

'Nobby…'

'If not now, later, or should I say soon. I'm sorry, boss, but they *are* going to kill her. You know what these nutters are like. It's a given, and they've obviously decreed it.'

'Nobby, she is not going to die.'

'Sir, she is already as good as dead.'

Stark shook his head. 'Okay, she will die, but at the age of ninety-nine and three quarters surrounded by her loving family and friends sitting in a bath chair on a veranda.'

'That's quite explicit, sir.' Cynthia said, smiling.

'Christ, I can't think of anything worse. You know what I mean, though, boss?' Nobby said.

'Of course, I do. That is why we need to get off the back foot and try to make something happen.'

'What have you got in mind?'

'Right, before I go into the why's and wherefores and what we are going to do or not going to do, I want to talk to you all in confidence. I want this to be the sanctum sanctorum.'

'The what?' Nobby asked.

'Sanctum sanctorum. The holy of holies. The central secret place is where access is only allowed to a chosen few.'

'You want us to keep schtum, you mean.' Nobby said.

'Erm, yes, that is the general idea.' Stark grinned.

'Why didn't you say that boss, I don't know what sanctorium is, or whatever the hell it is called.'

'Bloody hell, Nobby.'

'I know what you meant, sir.' Cynthia said.

'Thank you, Cynthia. Look, I am deadly serious with this. I mean it. This is absolutely top secret, confidential, okay?'

Glances were exchanged and mumblings of 'sure' and 'yes, okay.'

'This is not a joke. We must keep this watertight. Now, if anyone does not want to keep this confidence, I would ask that you leave now. No hard feelings, but I do not want this to go anywhere. Is that clear? Don't feel awkward. It's fine, and I don't want any half measures.'

There was a brief silence before Steve Aston spoke in a pitch that was slightly higher than his norm,

'It's nothing untoward, is it, sir?'

'Of course, not Steve. It is just that whatever we discuss here is not discussed with anyone, or even within earshot of anyone, other than our team and by 'our team', I mean those assembled here right now.'

This enabled shrugs and nodding of heads.

'Is everyone comfortable with that, yeah?'

'Yes.' Came the harmonious response.

'Okay, well, it may come as no surprise to many of you that I think Lee Mole and his fucking divvy sidekick Sheriff Davidson are bent.'

There was laughter and comments such as 'Der, yeah.' And 'no shit.'

'Okay, but I mean perhaps even more so than we thought. I think they may be actively working with the Browns. I don't have enough to make my thoughts officially known, but that doesn't help the situation we are in right now. Lives are at stake, here. So it's no good sitting on our hands.'

'Shit.' Steve Aston said, which was not like him.

'So, bearing that in mind, I will not share Jane Cooper's new address with him. Or rather I am, but it will be a false one.'

'Eh?' Nobby seemed confused already.

'Okay, look, I know that Mole pokes around everyone's desk out of hours, the sneaky fucking weasel.'

'Does he? Wait 'til I see him.' Nobby growled.

'Nobby, for Christ's sake, this is just for us, remember.'

'Oh yeah, I know. It's just an expression.

'God help us. Anyway, he does. So I am going to leave a file in my drawer marked "Confidential" with an address in it for Jane Cooper. Only it won't be the real safe house. It will be a different one where we will be waiting. If Mole leaks that to the Browns, we know it is him, but we can also get them nicked, hopefully.'

'Holy shit. This is fucking dynamite. Wagstaff would not like this.' Nobby said, slapping the table.

'Fuck him. He's daft enough to let things slide and not address what is really happening with Lee Mole, and we cannot afford to mess about. If we fail, they will get her, and they will make sure she suffers before topping her. Let's face it they've got form for it. As Nobby says, it's a given.'

There were a few sighs and puffing out of cheeks along with wary glances between those assembled.

'So what do we need to do, sir?' Cynthia asked.

'Who at the Council arranged the move, Cynthia?'

'It's a woman called Pat Payne from Housing she does all the moves. She's sound as a pound.'

'Okay, get another address; an empty Council house, for a bogus name off her, a case that is nothing to do with the Browns or Jane Cooper. Something a million miles away from all that.'

'Then what?' Cynthia asked.

'The bogus address will be the one I will leave for Mole to find in my desk drawer, and when the Browns turn up, they will get more than they bargained for.'

'Yeah, somebody that can fight back.' Nobby said.

'In the meantime, Jane Cooper will be at the proper safehouse out of harm's way and miles away from the Browns.' Cynthia said.

'You've got it.'

'That could work.' Nobby said.

'I'm open to any other suggestions?'

'Sounds good to me. Let's do it.' Nobby seemed fired up.

'If Cynthia sorts something out tonight, I will leave the bogus address in my drawer. I know Mole will be around later; he's champing at the bit to find out where Jane is going to be moved to. He's drooling about it. Then we go there and wait.'

Ashley clapped his hands together. 'This is going to be good.'

'I hope so, young Ashley. I hope so. Now, remember not a bloody word to anyone. The whole success of this depends on the Browns not getting Jane's real address.'

'What if we're wrong about Mole?' Steph asked.

'Then what have we lost?'

'Nothing, I suppose.' Steph nodded. 'Okay. I like it.'

'Absolutely. Now, any questions? Is everybody clear?'

'Yes.'

Stark raised his glass. 'Cheers all.' The glasses met in the middle. 'Sanctorium.' Nobby said with a grin.

'Ashley, can I have a quick word, mate?' Stark said as the general chatter returned around the table.

'Sure boss'

Stark stood, and Ashley followed him over to the bar.

'Nothing wrong, I hope, sir?' Ashley said.

'Me too. Look, I'll be upfront, Ash, it jarred with me, something Charlie said the other day.'

'What's that?'

'About you fingering the informant.'

'Blimey, you've got a good memory, boss. It was only a joke.' Ashley laughed.

'Well, I'm being serious, Ashley, as a friend, not as a boss. I didn't fall off a bloody Christmas Tree, and I know what the temptations are. Just be careful. I'm sure it's all a big joke, and if it isn't, I don't want to bloody know. But please be careful, and if you're getting too close, Ashley, I can guarantee you it will go belly up. It always does, and it's no good coming crying to me.'

'Okay, boss. You've got nothing to worry about, but thanks for the advice. I appreciate it.' Ashley's cheeks seemed a little redder than before.

'You know when I asked you to come and have a word.'

'Yes.'

'Those things that popped into your mind that you worried it could be?'

'Erm.'

'All those things you thought you could be in the shit for?'

'Well, there weren't that many, I mean…'

'Well, they are the things you need to stop doing. It's that easy. Okay.'

Ashley smiled. 'Message understood, sir.'

'It's just between you and me, okay?' Stark said. 'Tell the gang we were talking about your appraisal because we sort of were. Weren't we?'

Ashley swallowed. 'Yes, sure. I get it. No problem.'

'Good lad. It looks like we've got an eventful few days ahead of us.'

'Looks that way, sir.'

Ashley made a move back to the detective's table. Stark shouted after him, 'Don't forget.'

'What's that, boss?'

'Sanctorium.' Stark said, grinning.

Ashley laughed. 'Sanctorium.'

14

'I do everything I think possible or acceptable to escape from this trap.'

– Jacques Derrida.

Stark had arrived at the Queens Medical Centre Hospital around 10 am. He figured that would be plenty of time for the staff to finish breakfast and ablutions of the patients.

He pressed the buzzer on the wall outside ward E12. A middle-aged nurse, the ward sister, peered through the small glass slot and recognised the face. She pressed the release button, and Stark smiled his way in.

'David!'

'Izzie!'

The two old friends embraced.

'How are you?' Stark asked.

'I'm well, but look at you on the CID.'

'Detective Inspector no less. How crazy is that?' Stark grinned.

'Detective Inspector. Wow. They really will have anyone.' She laughed.

'You cheeky, sod, you've not changed, Isobel.'

'Anyway, what are you, Matron? I've seen those Carry-On films. Where's Kenneth Williams and Sid James hiding?'

'Half the time, it's like a bloody Carry-On film in here, David, I can tell you.'

'Where is she?'

'Just up here.' Izzie led the way. Stark was aware of the frenetic activity around the nurses' hub and the sneaky glances of some of the nurses who nudged each other, curious about Sister's guest.

'She's in a bay on her own, so you have some privacy.' Isobel said.

'Thanks for this favour, Izzie. The other cop has gone, you said?'

'Yes, thank God. Where did you dig him up from? Carl Davidson, he said his name was. What a horrible man. I hope they aren't all like that.'

'No, but every job has its idiots, Isobel, you know that. Trust me, every other decent cop hates his guts too. How is Mrs Cooper?'

'She didn't get much sleep. It is mainly the trauma of it all and exhaustion, I think. What a terrible ordeal for her, but we're hoping she shouldn't be in too long.' Isobel stopped at the door to the private bay.

Stark asked in a hushed tone. 'Does she know about her husband?'

'Yes, that pig Davidson just told her outright. No build-up. Nothing.'

Stark shook his head. 'I'm not surprised. Do you want to sit in with me?'

She glanced at the watch on her chest. 'I can, but only for ten or fifteen minutes, I'm afraid.'

'That would be great. I won't be long; there is something I want to ask her, that's all. Just one thing, but it is important, and I cannot trust Davidson to give me the answer.'

'Oh dear, David, is it that bad?'

'It is at the moment, I'm afraid.'

As Izzie opened the door, they could see Mrs Cooper was sleeping. 'Maybe I should come back?'

'No need. I'm awake.' Mrs Cooper said drearily. Her throat sounded dry as she dragged her eyelids open. She sighed and hutched up the bed slightly, which took quite a bit of effort.

Sister Isobel sat on one of the plastic seats at the end of the bed, and Stark pulled up a chair and sat at the side of her. Isobel pressed a button and the bed lowered.

'Hello, Mrs Cooper. I'm Detective Inspector Stark.'

'Oh aye.'

'He's not like that other fellow, Mrs Cooper. I've known David years. He's one of the good guys.' Isobel said.

'I don't know about that.' David smiled. 'Sorry if he was messing you around.'

'I suppose it's got to be done.'

'I'm so sorry for your loss. For George. It must be awful.'

'Thank you.' She closed her eyes briefly and sighed. 'Maybe it's a blessing in disguise for him. I'll miss him so much, and he didn't deserve to go like that.'

'Hopefully, he wouldn't have been aware of too much, Mrs Cooper.'

'Maybe you're right. I hope so too.'

There was a slight lull before Stark blurted out. 'I'm one of the chaps who has been looking after your Jane.'

'So how come she's been hurt?' Mrs Cooper looked straight into his eyes. She didn't mince her words.

Stark winced. 'Because we didn't do it well enough, I suppose. That's the quick answer. We are doing our best, I promise you.'

'She's in danger, Detective. I'm worried for her, and she's all I've got left, you know.'

'I know we're moving her to a new house. She's fine. Don't worry. She will come and see you as soon as she can.' Stark took hold of her hand. 'She thinks the world of you, Mrs Cooper.'

'She's a good girl, bless her. I just want her and Daisy to be safe.'

'I know. They will be, don't worry. I wanted to ask you a couple of questions about the burglary if that's okay.'

'I've already told the Detective with the bad attitude.'

'I know, but was there anything that the burglars said or did that you could connect to the Brown brothers, you know, the ones who have been harassing, Jane?'

'Of course. I told him yesterday. It was one of the first things I wanted him to know.' Mrs Cooper smoothed out the blanket in front of her with her right hand.

'Sorry?' Stark looked a little confused. 'Tell him what?'

'The man, the one who broke in, said something about Derek Brown sends his regards.'

'Derek?'

'I thought that was what he said.'

'Could it be Dougie Brown?'

'I don't know, I thought it was Derek, it was Brown, I know that.'

'And you told the detective this yesterday?'

'Yes, of course, it was one of the first things I said to him. I've just said that.'

Stark remembered the phone call from Carl Davidson to Mole in Wagstaff's office when he said there was nothing to connect the Browns. The lying toerag.

'Was anything else said about them?'

'No, I think that was it.' Mrs Cooper's eyelids looked heavy, and her face relaxed with her mouth open until she jolted back to the room.

'Okay. Well, look, I'm not going to keep you. I just wanted to confirm any connection with the Browns. Let's face it. It is too much of a coincidence not to be.'

Mrs Cooper had closed her eyes and had drifted off to sleep. Stark slid his hand away and crept out with Isobel in tow.

They made their way back to the ward entrance, and David stopped and turned to embrace her again.

'Thank you so much, Izzie. I'm grateful. You know that.'

'Anything to help. It's been nice to see you. Call in again, why don't you?'

'I will, and we can perhaps get a coffee next time. Oh, and by the way..'

'What?'

Stark leaned in to whisper in her ear. 'You still look as fit as anything.'

Isobel smacked his arm. She was smiling. 'Go on, be off with you.'

'Bye, Izzie.'

'Bye, David. Don't be a stranger.'

Stark waved as he walked down the hospital corridor. 'Bye, Izzie. Take care, love.'

*

Dougie and Len sat on their thrones in the Golden Ball public house. Lord of all they surveyed. Which wasn't a lot. A dingy pub with a handful of customers and a jukebox that hadn't been changed for at least ten years.

Dougie had asked the lads to go and play pool so that he and Len could have a 'chinwag.'

'It is time, Len?'

'To do her, you mean. I reckon so. When?'

'How does tonight sound? It was good to use Mac and have an alibi, but you know what. We need to get this by the scruff of the neck. We need to run this show, kid.'

'Sounds good to me.'

'That pig Mole has been in touch; he has got an address where they've moved her.'

'Brill. What's wrong with that?' Len asked.

'Nowt, but he is a cop. Len. Never trust any fucker, remember?'

'I know, but he's too shit scared to mess us about.' Len took a large swig of beer which punctuated the conversation as Dougie couldn't help but focus on Len's adam's-apple bobbing up and down with each gulp.

'I just want to make doubly sure these arseholes are not snowing us.'

'Where is it?'

'Eastwood.'

'Not too far.'

'Exactly.' Dougie said.

'What do you mean?'

'Why move her just a few miles away? What's the point of that?'

Len shrugged. 'Dunno.'

Dougie grimaced. 'I just have a funny feeling about it, Len. Something feels off. Mole reckons he saw the address in Stark's drawer. Would he be that stupid?'

'Dunno, mate.'

'And like you say, Len, it ain't that far away.'

'So you think it's a set-up?'

'No, I'm not saying that. I'm just saying let's be careful.' Dougie took tobacco from a pouch on the wooden table and expertly rolled it into a cigarette.

'It can't be tonight then.'

'It will. In fact, here she is.' Dougie beckoned over a young woman in a leather mini skirt and heavy mascara.

'Eh-up, Pat, me duck, have a seat. This is my brother Len. Len, this is Pat Payne, and she works for the Council.'

Len nodded.

'Sorry about that misunderstanding, Pat. I've sorted it all for you.' Dougie said.

'It frightened me to death. Thanks for sorting it.' She was twitchy, and her head was lowered into her shoulders slightly as if she had ducked to avoid a thrown object and got stuck in the position. She was timid and self-conscious.

Dougy took hold of her hand. 'Degsy can be a little excitable, and he was out of order threatening to burn your house down, just over a little misunderstanding like that. He's bang out of order.'

'It wasn't because I didn't want to help, Doug. I just can't afford to get the sack from there. I've got bills to pay.'

He patted her hand and dropped it back on her lap. 'Let's put all of that behind us. Nothing is going to happen, now, so you're safe....'

'As houses.' Len said, and the two of them laughed. Pat went along with it but was clearly intimidated by the pair. She was the only woman in the place.

'So we're good, yeah?' Dougie said.

'Yes, of course, Doug. Like I said, I was just scared of losing my job. You know me, I'll help anytime.' Pat said.

'What have you got for me then?'

Pat handed him a piece of paper which she took from her coat pocket. Dougie unfolded it and silently read the details of the address written on it.

'That is interesting. How sure are you, Pat?' Doug asked.

'One hundred percent, Doug. I arranged the bloody move; I should know.'

'And it was in the name Jane Cooper?'

'No, it's not in any name. There is never any name given, but it was an urgent witness protection move from Squires Avenue at Bulwell. It has to be her.'

Dougie unfurled a wad of cash. 'I feel bad about Degsy frightening you like that, Pat. Here's a couple of hundred for your trouble. And don't you worry about anything, yeah?'

'Wow. Two hundred pounds! Are you sure?'

'Course, I'm sure. I appreciate your time, Pat.'

'That's brilliant. Thank you so much.' Her face lit up, and she was clearly relieved. This would help with Christmas, and her toils seemed lighter all of a sudden.

'Just keep it between us. Okay?'

'Yeah, of course.'

Dougie pointed a finger to emphasise the point. 'I mean it. You don't tell just one person: your Mum, your best friend, nobody. That is where people go wrong. I wouldn't be pleased, Pat.'

'Don't worry. I won't tell a soul.'

'Good girl.'

As Pat stood to squeeze through the small gap in the tables, Dougie slapped her backside, perhaps a little too hard, causing her to jerk and give out an embarrassed laugh. With a giggle, she wiggled to the door and looked back at the dangerous pair who had observed her every move. Dougie waved to her as she reached the door, and Pat smiled and waved back before scurrying out.

'Worth every penny. You get the shooters, Len. I'll get the rest of the gear.'

*

Stark had decided to have one of his detectives in a van outside the premises, situated around the corner. The remainder would be waiting inside as a reception party for the Browns. The house in Eastwood was located such that the only access was into a cul-de-sac. So the 'spotter' in the van could radio in any activity and prepare them once the Browns arrived. When the Browns came to get Jane Cooper, they would leave it a minute and then come in on foot and do a bit of a pincer manoeuvre.

Unfortunately, Charlie and Steph had to peel off to deal with a rape that had come in, so Stark had put Steve Aston in the van as the spotter while he, Nobby, Ashley, and Cynthia were in the house.

With them being somewhat depleted, Stark had arranged for an armed unit to be on standby and a dog man to patrol the Eastwood area should they need backup.

DI Stark had it in mind that as soon as Steve spotted the Browns, he would call the other units in straight away, so long it was a confirmed sighting. The only likely complication would be if the Browns were tooled up, or they came mob-handed. Stark couldn't see it. They were only expecting Jane and a kid to be at the house. There was no need, and he reckoned that this being personal, family business, they would do it solo to restore a bit of their street cred.

Were that to happen, they should still be able to deal with it; regardless, he couldn't open another box of policemen from the policeman shop. It was all he could muster. They were used to going toe-to-toe.

Of course, Jane Cooper was nowhere near Eastwood. That was the bogus address, the address that Stark was luring the Brown's to. Jane was in a rather nice house in Newark, twenty miles away.

Jane had decided to see her mother at the hospital tomorrow, assuming Inspector Stark said it was okay. She was somewhat annoyed that he had advised against it until she was moved, but she understood the seriousness of the situation she was in. Stark had asked Jane to let him know if she needed to come back into Nottingham for any reason, at least for the foreseeable future.

Jane loved the new house, it was cosy, and she felt much safer, but the loss of her father had completely floored her. Not just the loss, but the way it had happened. Yes, he was at peace now in some ways, but the horror of the whole situation and what her parents had to go through mortified her. She had done little but cried since the policewoman broke the news to her. She felt guilty about it all. As if it was somehow her fault. Her parents didn't deserve all of this at their age or any age. She hated the Browns. She hated hating the Browns. She didn't want to even know of their existence. But she did, and she despised them and their pathetic ways and felt impotent that these animals could turn her entire life upside down and hurt so many people without any consequences. It just wasn't right. Poor Brandon. His life was a complete mess. Her stomach churned at the thought of it all. She had been so trembly lately and thought she could be having a nervous breakdown. Would the death of her father be the end of it? Surely. They weren't that crazy; nobody was that mental. Had they no heart at all? Didn't they care?

Hopefully, this move would bring an end to it all, and she could make a life for her and Daisy. It would mean moving schools, but, in the meantime, Stark had arranged for a taxi to take Daisy to school and bring her back with a social worker. All paid for by the Council as an emergency case. The teachers were made aware of the situation, and the social worker was trained to be surveillance conscious in case they were followed.

Jane was grateful for Stark's help despite everything that had happened, even though the police seemed powerless to do anything. What had they actually done to help her? What exactly were they doing? Anything?

Everything about her life was now filthy. Everything felt unclean and corrosive, like a clinging, sticky cloud of darkness that wrapped around her thumping head and neck—shackling her to her sorrow and low mood. It was awful. Jane felt debilitated and could scarcely bring herself to move. She felt physically sick. She didn't know if she could come through all of this, but something inside of her forged the will to carry on, not for her, not even for her Mum, but for little Daisy.

*

Dougie and Len were dressed all in black. They had got their hands on a hooky van with no windows in the back. They knew where they were going to take her once they got her. It was out of the way and secure, and no one would guess where they were. It was soundproof and secure. They had used it before, a long time ago, and never for something like this.

Dougie still enjoyed the thrill of the caper. It was an adrenalin hit. He wanted to make Jane Cooper suffer. Just like Sharon was suffering at the thought that she might be barren. She had been crying again all night last night, and it was doing his head in. Little stories kept reaching him about others pressing against their territory. This would never have happened before. They needed reminding just who they were dealing with. There were too many people taking too many liberties, and Dougie knew exactly how to deal with it. Just as he had been doing, with an overwhelming and isolating force so that anyone associated with Jane Cooper ended up hurt or damaged in some way. Watch everyone desert them and then move in for the kill. Well, that day had come. Dougie was clear-eyed and focused as he steered the van around the back streets.

Len literally rode shotgun and had the firearm on his lap. It was loaded with two cartridges, and he had two more in his pocket. They didn't expect to use it, only as a last resort. It was probably unnecessary, but it tended to save arguments or anyone getting too brave.

'Why don't we just take her head off with the sawn-off, Dougie?' Len asked.

'No. If we do that, she doesn't suffer anymore, and we leave a body. This way, we can get rid her carcass in the concrete on the motorway excavations.'

'Does Jacko still work the M1?'

'Yeah, he's married to Louise Turner now. It'll be even easier now, he's gaffer apparently.'

'Christ. Things must be desperate.'

Dougie laughed. 'You know the score, Len. She has to suffer, and this will put any doubters minds to rest. We don't fuck about. People need to know that, Len.'

'The last one was over five years ago, Dougie. Can you believe it?'

'Yes, and we are long overdue.'

'What are you doing? Fingers off?'

'Let's get her to the place. Get her bagged up and underground, and then we can do whatever the hell we decide once we get her there. Are you having a go on her, Len?'

'Too right. Anyone messes with you, messes with me, bro. We're in this together.'

'I think this is it. On the left. Black door. You ready?'

Len took hold of the shotgun. 'I'm ready, bro.'

*

'DC Aston to DI Stark.' The radio burst into life. Steve's hand was trembling as he clutched the handset.

'Go ahead.'

'Standby, standby, a vehicle just entered the close, two white males, over. I can't see in. I can't confirm it's them, but it's coming down to you, over.'

'Ten-Four.'

Stark muttered to himself. 'Bloody hell, Steve. You've got one bleeding job.'

The DI stood up, as did Nobby and Ash. All had their wooden truncheons in hand, and they stood at the side of both front and back door. Cynthia had handcuffs at the ready and secreted herself in the corner of the room. It fell quiet. All of them were listening for a sign. Was it them?

They heard a car pull up outside the house, tyres on gravel. Tensions and tendons strained. Teeth were gritted, and lips were tight. It looked like this was game on.

Stark whispered. 'No questions asked, Nobby, just down the fuckers.'

'Straight in, boss. Make'em have it. Keep out the way, Cynthia.'

'Okay, Sarge.'

'Are you listening, Ashley?' Stark said.

'Yeah, got it, boss. Straight into 'em.'

*

Jane had been constantly tired since the news of her father's death. Her pounding headache seemed to be ripping her forehead apart, it made her skin feel dry, and she felt generally unwell and weak. She had a sore throat and sore eyes. Jane had been existing on cups of tea and chocolate, which she had been gorging on. She had lost any inhibitions concerning watching what she ate, and she was essentially eating her feelings—trying anything to lift the spectre of depression that was following her around.

A month ago, she would not have believed something like this was even possible. It was a living hell. A bad dream, worse, night terrors. No dream could capture the infinite tumbling down of her spirits and the loss of her will to fight on. It was unfathomable that she could go from living a quite happy modest existence to being exposed to this pack of hounds. She hated it, and she hated them and their animalistic, ridiculous, pathetic ways. They should be eliminated from the face of the earth. All they did was cause pain in the most brutal, intentional, and grotesque fashion. And she was stuck with it. There was no way out. None, or at least that was the way it seemed. She just wanted it all to go away and get her dad back.

She could feel her eyelids drooping and drawing to a close as she lay on the settee. It wasn't a choice; it was almost as if she had been drugged, a heavy blanket of tiredness too strong to resist. It was the body trying to protect itself, of course. Sleep was the great healer, and she certainly wasn't getting enough of that during the night. Her sleep was punctuated by torment. She was too distressed to relax sufficiently, and when she did for a few minutes, she would start twitching and talking and shouting. She was in a right state. The nervousness ahead of the move had contributed to her insomnia along with the horrible images that invaded her mind. Mainly about her Mum and Dad and the ordeal they had been through. Jane was always there as a silent witness to their ordeal as a bystander but unable to move, unable to help them despite their pleading looks, and while she knew it was just her imagination, it haunted her nonetheless.

When she evaded the twitching and slept for more than a few minutes, she would awake with a start. A sudden jump. As if someone had shaken her awake urgently. As if she had to deal with something quickly. She was unsettled and on edge.

As her head dropped forward again, she awoke, with a start, her heart thumping. Had she been asleep for a minute or an hour?

What was it that woke her up? She listened intently, and there was nothing. She settled her breathing and walked over to the kettle.

She had to somehow think of a way to get over all of this. It was over, and she had to come to accept that was the case. She had to learn to live again and truly believe this was over.

*

The first thing that alarmed Jane was the door being kicked off its hinges, and then she saw the double barrels of a shotgun getting larger and larger as Len ran towards her. It was all she could see. The figures behind were hazy. Her eyes were blurred from the sleep.

A male voice was harsh, nasty in its tone. 'On the floor, bitch!'

Jane rolled onto the carpet, whimpering and crying as the realisation dawned. She was on all floors before she felt a knee in her back knocking her flat face down.

Dougie put her hands behind her back and secured her wrists with a plastic cable tie. It was fiddly, and he struggled for a few seconds as he squashed her ribcage.

'I can't breathe.'

'Good.'

With the ties finally secured, he pulled Jane up with her hair causing her to shout out in pain. The mug on the coffee table went flying as Doug put his mouth close to Jane's ear and, through gritted teeth, said. 'Make any noise, and we will blow your fucking brains out.'

Jane nodded as the tears rolled down her cheeks.

'Where's the kid?'

Jane was stammering. She was incoherent. She couldn't get the words out.

'Speak up!'

She managed to get out. 'School.'

The two bastards marched Jane out the way they had come. At one point, her legs gave way, so Dougie dragged her by the hair, but she started squealing and making a fuss. He stood her up and smacked her across the face, knocking the wind out of her sails, and stunning her into silence.

Within thirty seconds, they threw her into the back of the stolen van that they had backed onto the drive, and they were away.

They had got her. Jane was doomed. She had gone into a sort of hypnotic state, eyes wide but unseeing. She was in shock. She was quiet at first, compliant. Jane had given up and was frozen in fear. She was face down in the van, and her hands bound behind her back made it difficult to stabilise herself as the van swung from side to side. She was thrown around inside by the violent shifting of the van. It was banging her head against the metal floor and sides, causing her to grunt and shout out in pain. Len leaned over the back of his seat and pointed the shotgun at her.

When Dougie braked, she slid up to the front, and Len whacked her with the butt of the shotgun. He was laughing as he did. As Doug accelerated, she slid down the doors end out of reach, but each time he braked, she slid back up towards the madman when he would repeatedly try to bust her face with the wooden end of the gun. He usually missed hitting the floor or slicing at the back of her head. He hit her face a couple of times, ripping her lips open and then busting her nose. She was coughing up snot and blood and trying to twist to avoid the blows. Blood and dirt-smeared over her white top, and grime slid up her jeans from the dirty, gritty floor. Her upper arms were grazed and red, and there was a long way to go.

Jane was in a whole world of trouble. The odds of getting out of this alive seemed slim.

15

'The longer I live, the more convinced I am that this planet is used by other planets as a lunatic asylum.'

– George Bernard Shaw.

The detectives had been waiting silently or two or three minutes. It seemed an age. The tension was high and the focus intense. Sweat was beginning to form in the wooden grooves at the base of the wooden truncheon.

Stark was surprised to hear a knocking on the door; he had expected the door to be booted in. He looked through the kitchen window to see DC Aston's concerned face looking back. His shoulders dropped, and he physically relaxed.

'It's Steve.'

The others groaned, and they too dropped their guard.

Stark opened the door and let him in. The DI walked to the settee to join the others, and Steve followed behind.

'Come on then, Steve, what is it?' Stark asked. 'It'd better be good if you've left your post to come and tell us.'

'I don't know how to tell you this, sir.'

Nobby barked at him. 'Just say it, Steve. Stop being a bloody drama queen.'

'Something has come over VHS about an incident in Newark. Possible kidnapping.'

'You're joking.' Stark said.

'I'm not. I'm afraid. Briar Close?'

'Fuck!' Cynthia put her head in her hands.

'Is that the road?' Steve asked.

'Yes. Jesus Christ! They've got her.' Stark stood up, and the others followed suit.

'It's not one hundred percent, sir.'

'A kidnapping on Briar Close at Newark. How often does that happen? What else do we know?' Stark said clearly agitated.

'A neighbour heard screaming outside and saw a girl being bundled into the back of a van.'

'A girl?'

'Well, I think they said a "young woman" being bundled into a van.'

'Speak precisely, Steve; it's important, man!' Nobby was irritated.'

'Fuck.' Stark was now stunned into monosyllabic swear words.

'Fuck.' Nobby joined in for good measure.

Steve continued the brief. 'No registration number, just that it was a battered old white van with no rear windows. A small van, not a transit, not that big. You know what I mean, like a small plumber's van, something like that. If that makes sense.'

'Any direction of travel?' Ashley asked.

Stark interjected. 'It doesn't matter, Ash, she could be taken anywhere. They've got her. That's the point.'

'Told you she would end up dead.' Nobby said.

'Shut up, Nobby. Let me think.' Stark said.

'Not much we can do, sir, is there?' Ashley asked.

'Let's get it confirmed it's Jane Cooper and get local CID to fax a statement over from the witness. In the meantime, circulate the description of the van and get anything that remotely looks like it pulled over and searched.'

'How did they know?' Nobby asked.

'Christ knows.' Stark said. His face was white. He looked shocked and concerned. He rubbed his face with his hands and groaned. 'Let's get back to the nick and get our heads together. This is going to go down like a bleeding lead balloon. We've got to find them sharpish. We need every damned lockup, every location they've ever been known to use. Every associate, every address, everything.'

'There's only half a dozen of us, boss.' Nobby said.

'That's why we need to prioritise. What do they intend to do with her? Where would you take her to do that? A warehouse? A lock-up? Somewhere out the way in the sticks? Somebody's house? Let's gather in and make a start. Jane's life depends on it.'

'How the hell did they bloody know. We were watertight.' Nobby said despondently.

'Clearly not, Nobby. Someone has told them. They've not just put a pin in a map, have they?' Stark said.

'It won't be any of us.' Ashley said.

'It has to be someone involved in the move.' Stark said, glancing at Cynthia.

'It has to be.' Cynthia said. 'The woman said it was highly confidential, a need-to-know basis.'

'That's going to be a question for another day. Let's not beat ourselves up now. Today is to find her and find her alive.' Stark's face was riddled with concern.

'The clock is ticking, boss.' Nobby said.

*

The clock was not ticking in the great hall of Orridge's old hosiery factory on the outskirts of Hucknall town. At one time, the place had been full of machinery and women feverishly working the cloth with great skill and speed. With giant sewing machines and women's voices chattering, and the room vibrating with the hum of those machines, coupled with the myriad footsteps that scurried from pillar to post, bringing fabric in, bringing wool in, and taking socks and underwear out.

Now the place was long since abandoned. Many of the exterior windows were broken and covered in grime and dust. The floor was made of wood with noticeable splinters exposed here and there. A couple of broken pallets, some rags and a large, caged area that covered a section in one corner were all that remained. The cage door had a lock covered by a metal plate that could only be opened from the inside, and you needed a key to gain access from the outside of it. The cage door was ajar and unmoved for ten or more years.

Dougie manhandled Jane up the outside steps and into the factory while Len pulled a small rug back, revealing a large hatch that had a brass metal ring pull. With a groan, he pulled open the hatch revealing wooden steps into a lower chamber.

'Get the van moved out the way, Len. I'll take her down. Gimme the gun.'

Len handed the shotgun to his brother, and Doug moved Jane down the stairs into the lower space.

It must have been used by a caretaker or boiler man, something along those lines. It was windowless. There was an old desk, a couple of dusty wooden chairs, a coffee table, and two brown coloured mouldy armchairs with the arms exposing the upholstery. Cobwebs abounded in the corners. It smelt a little bit of urine and stale water with a dash of mould. Dust particles in their thousands riddled the air brought alive by the shaft of light coming down the wooden steps from the hatch.

There was even a well-used dartboard still on the wall with three battered old darts sticking in it.

'On the floor and be quiet.' Doug said to Jane quite calmly.

Jane slithered down the wall in the corner and swallowed more blood and mucus. She felt wretched and in pain. The length of Jane's arms was red raw from the grazing during the journey in the van, and her face was a bloody mess from the battering she took from Len. Some of her hair was matted to the wound on her mouth, and she couldn't free it. Her mouth and nose were throbbing and sore. It hurt.

'It's been a while since I've been here. My old grandad worked here for thirty years. And you know when he left, no one even said goodbye to him. Can you believe that?' Doug said.

Jane just looked at him with hatred in her eyes. She couldn't give a toss about his stupid old grandad.

'Don't start looking at me like I'm the fucking bad guy here, cunt. You've caused this, and the only reason we are here is because of you, Jane Cooper. Get that in your thick head.'

Her voice was croaky. 'Can I have a drink?'

'No.'

Jane bowed her head. The refusal of a drink struck her hard, which would have helped so much but without one, her hopes sank to the floor. The blood was blocking her airways a little, and she could feel panic rising inside her. She tried to steady her breathing. She coughed and spat out some blood to one side to clear her throat. This was quickly becoming a matter of survival. She couldn't see a way out of the situation. Her arms were throbbing from the damned grazes, and her face, neck and head ached so much. She felt like her left eye was closing a little as her vision was obscured. She was shaking uncontrollably.

Dougie walked up and down the room, each step making him more emboldened in the knowledge that he now had a plaything. They had made it to their secure chamber, and things were about to get ugly. The control was a buzz for him, and the sadistic side of his nature was bubbling to the surface.

'Your top is filthy.' He leaned forward and, pulling it out of her jeans, raised it up. She had no bra on, and she turned her head away as Dougie slavered over her breasts. 'Nice.'

'Pull my top down, please.' Jane said, feeling embarrassed.

'No fuck it, leave it up.' He looped her top over her head, fully exposing her.

'You don't have a say anymore. Your say is finished. I own you now, Jane fucking Cooper. You are the property of Dougie Brown. Be proud of those tits. Anyway, it gives me something nice to look at while we are in this shithole.'

Jane closed her eyes, just trying to block the whole ordeal out of her mind.

Dougie went over to the dartboard and pulled out the darts. He began to throw at the board and retrieve them. He seemed either agitated or excited, or perhaps both. Almost at a loss as to what to do next. His mind was filled with thoughts.

He heard Len return at the top of the stairs.

'Pull the hatch down, Len, when you come down.' Dougie said. 'I've put the lights on.'

Len did just that, and as Jane came into view, he whooped. 'Woohoo. Nice titties.'

'Nice, huh?' Dougie grinned.

Len leaned down and squeezed Janes bosoms. 'Firm. Very nice.'

'Please don't.' Jane said quietly.

'Fancy a game of darts, Len?'

'Yes, sure.'

'Here, watch this. Double top.'

Dougie threw a dart at Jane's head, and it missed and stuck in her shoulder. The two laughed hysterically.

Jane screamed as it was excruciatingly painful.

Dougie threw another one and another in quick succession.

'One hundred and eighty!'

The first missed, and the second stuck in her arm. She was making a racket, and Doug swiped his hand across her face knocking the dart out her arm.

'Here, lift her face up, Len. See if I can get one in her eyeball.' Dougie pulled out the dart in her shoulder.

She just wanted to die.

*

Stark and the team gathered in the office. Things were tense, and Stark was pacing around. For once, he appeared flustered. He wasn't his usual self, that's for sure. He was smoking and paused only to stare out the window. Most of the team were sitting around waiting for divine inspiration, presumably.

'This is my fault.' Stark said.

'Sir, no, it's not.' Cynthia said. 'It isn't.'

'It is. We should have stayed with her.'

'We didn't have the staff. It's ridiculous to think we can offer any protection anyway. This ain't the bloody movies. There isn't enough of us to babysit someone twenty-four-seven.' Nobby stated the obvious.

'Yeah, the only person that messed this up was whoever leaked the info to the Browns. They want stringing up.' Ashley said.

Stark still faced the window. 'We have to find her, guys. She will be going through hell with these mad bastards.'

Jim McIntyre came across clutching sheets of paper.

'These are the addresses I can find in the intelligence system, sir. It includes known associates, so you might wannae filter it down a wee bit.'

'Thanks, Jim. Do me a favour and contact any cops who have dealt with the Browns or their associates in the last ten years. Speak to them, ask them if they know of a lock-up or warehouse or anywhere that they have used to hide firearms or stolen gear,'

'Really?'

'Really.'

'That's a lot of work for one wee man.'

'Just do it, Jim. We're in shit street here.' Stark said.

Jim walked away, muttering and shaking his head.

Stark addressed the gang. 'Once Nobby has filtered this list down, split up and get out on the streets.' He handed the papers to Nobby, who immediately began scrutinising the information. Stark continued, 'The trigger is going to be that van they used, but don't make it a deal-breaker. They will feel safe in it, though. Maybe it is parked outside or near the premises.'

'They could take her anywhere in the country.' Ashley said tentatively. 'I don't want to sound negative. I'm just saying.'

Nobby threw his mug across the room, smashing it. 'For fuck's sake, Ash, do you think we don't know that!'

'Yeah. I was only saying.'

'Well, fucking don't!'

Stark interjected. 'Alright, come on. Let's keep calm. Keep professional. She depends on us using our brains.'

'I didn't mean anything by it. Christ! I find it upsetting, that's all.' Ashley said.

'Do you want to talk about it, Ash' Cynthia asked.

'No, he doesn't. We haven't got time for that bloody nonsense. We're all upset, but that isn't going to help anyone. Get bloody focussed.' Stark snapped.

Stark wiped his hand through his hair. It was wet with sweat. Cynthia appeared hurt by his sharp tone.

He continued, 'Okay, the description of the van has gone out to all forces countrywide. Anyway, I sense that they will be somewhere local or at least where they feel comfortable. Somewhere they have used before. Get on it, guys. We aren't going to find them in this office, are we?'

Stark walked out the room and down the corridor to the toilet, his pace increasing with every step. He let the door swing behind him, and he dashed into a cubicle and sat on the loo. He held his hand out in front of him. It was trembling. He could feel his chest tighten, and his breathing had become more laboured.

All he could think of was Jane Cooper's mother in the hospital chastising him for not protecting her daughter, and now he had let her down again.

He tried to recall what the therapist had said, something about breathing in for five seconds, holding it for five seconds, and breathing out for 7 seconds. It was something like that.

He failed at the first attempt, and air burst out his lungs while trying to hold it after four seconds. It just made his heart pound even more.

He was sweating again. This was anxiety, but it was the first time he had felt it just because of the situation. It was just a social anxiety thing, talking to crowds, wasn't it?

He had to get his shit together. 'Come on, think. Where would you go?'

He took a deep breath in and breathed out hard.

'Bastards.' He said to no one. He smacked the side of the cubicle with the side of his fist, causing it to shake. 'What an unholy fucking, bollocks, shit, load of absolute fucking...'

A voice shattered his thoughts. 'Are you alright, boss?' It was Nobby's echoing voice from the direction of the urinal.

'Fuck me, Nobby. I never heard you come in. You nearly gave me a bleeding heart attack, man. Yes, I'm fine, mate, just a tricky shit.' He shouted over the cubicle door.

'Christ. It must be with that racket. Really tricky. I followed you in. Tricky shits are the worst. I'd better get out of here sharpish by the sounds of it. See you in a bit. Do you want some super strength IZAL toilet paper passing through?' He laughed.

Stark laughed. 'My grandad had that bloody stuff, and it was like wiping your backside on tracing paper.'

'I'll leave it with you.' Nobby closed the door behind him.

Stark heard him leave and listened to make sure he was actually on his own this time. All was quiet. He closed his eyes and put his trembling hand to his sweaty forehead.

Didn't Dougie Brown say something about *his* grandfather? Something about working at a hosiery factory for thirty years?

*

Len lifted Jane's face up, and Dougie moved closer to aim the dart at her eyeball, but something in his peripheral vision drew his attention. It was a metal coat rack with three empty coat hangers on it.

'Hang on. Len. Get me those pliers off the desk, will ya.'

'What desk?'

'Fuck me, Len, there's only one, that one there look. That thing that looks like a fucking great desk.'

'Alright, keep your hair on.'

Dougie took the metal coat hanger off the rail, and Len handed him the pliers. Dougie pulled at the coat hanger frame, making it circular and placing it over Jane's head and around her neck.

'I want to try something.'

He placed the pliers around the base of the hook and twisted around and around. The metal began to tighten around Jane's neck.

'Please don't. You've had your fun. I'm not going to tell anyone.'

'Shut up. That's what they all say. You're going nowhere.'

The metal drew tight against the skin of her neck. Some of the blood that had dried on her throat flaked away and rested on the sticky sweat of the exposed skin of her breasts.

'There we are that will do for now. Every so often, when I feel like it, I am going to twist that metal just a little bit more. Bit by bit, you are going to be strangled, Jane. Good huh?'

Jane was crying. 'Please don't.'

Dougie smacked her across the face again and a bruise added further colour to her bloodied, swollen face.

'Why don't we do a quiz?' Len asked.

'What the fuck are you talking about?'

'Ask her a question, and if she gets it right, fine, and if she gets it wrong, it gets tightened.'

Dougie clapped his hands together and laughed excitedly. 'Genius, bro.' Dougie got one of the wooden chairs and drew it up in front of the wretched face of Jane Cooper. Len sat in one of the old armchairs to watch proceedings.

'Right, let's think. Erm. Why should I let you live?'

Jane mumbled. 'Because I've done nothing wrong.'

'What? Speak up. I can't hear you.'

She cleared her throat a bit and swallowed more blood. 'Because I've done nothing wrong.'

Dougie made a noise like a buzzer on the popular Family Fortunes television programme. 'Er er! Wrong.'

He tightened the metal noose. He could see it now indenting the skin, and one of the veins in her neck became more pronounced as blood began to be restricted. He grinned.

'Ask her a proper question, Doug, you know, that she can get right or wrong.'

'Alright. Like what?'

'I dunno, you're the brainy one, kiddo.'

'Okay, okay, I've got one.'

'What is the capital of Spain?'

'Madrid.'

'Fuck me, Doug, even I knew that bugger.'

'I've got one. What is the calibre of the most powerful handgun in the world?'

'I don't know.'

'Yes, you do. It's in them "Dirty Harry" films.'

'I don't know.' She sobbed.

'Er er! Wrong.' Dougie put on a whispering Clint Eastwood voice. 'This is a Magnum .45, the most powerful handgun in the world, and it will blow your head clean off. So do you feel lucky, punk?'

Len was laughing and clapping like a seal waiting to catch a fish.

Jane felt sick and thought she might vomit. She felt the metal tighten around her neck once more, this time causing her head to throb and make a rattling noise when she breathed.

'I'm loving this.' Dougie said. 'I wonder if we should just blow her fucking head off, Len? With the shotgun, I mean. What d'ya reckon?'

'It's up to you, mate. It'd be good to see. I've never seen that before.'

'I'd quite like to see that wouldn't you, Jane?'

'Yes.'

'What? So you would prefer to have me blow your brains out right now than play our quiz?'

It was hard to decipher her voice as it was distorted and hoarse by the grip of the metal hanger. 'Just do it. Please. Get it over with.'

'She sounds like the Elephant Man now, Dougie.' Len said.

'She does, doesn't she?' Dougie impersonated the Elephant Man with sucking in air as he spoke. 'Oh, Mr Treves, you've been so very kind.'

They were both in hysterics.

'That's a good question, that is.' Dougie said.

'What is?' Len asked.

'Here we go. When did the Elephant Man come out at the pictures? What year?'

It was getting an effort to speak. 'Eighty-One.' Jane gasped.

'Er er! Wrong! Nineteen eighty.'

He tightened the metal once more, and Jane's chest began to heave as she was really struggling to breathe, and her eyes were closing and flickering. A wrinkled vein at her forehead was straining.

'Look at her tits wobbling!' Len said.

'Wahey!' Dougie started knocking her naked breasts up and down as she struggled to get in air. She manoeuvred her neck to one side, and it seemed to help her breathing slightly, but the rasping persisted.

'Oh, look at them nip nips.' Dougie said as he tightened the pliers around one of her nipples.

'Rip the bastard off, Dougie.' Len was doing his seal impersonation again.

'Do you reckon?'

'Yeah. Rip it right off. Let me have a go.'

'I need the loo.' Jane said in a whisper.

'Fuck off.'

Jane couldn't help it, and she urinated into her jeans, and it began to pool underneath her.

Dougie moved back to avoid the trickle and booted her in the face. 'Dirty cow!'

It knocked her into blissful unconsciousness.

'What did you do that for? It's no good if she can't feel nowt.' Len exclaimed.

'Fucking pissing on me, dirty bitch. Sod that. It nearly went on me trainers!'

*

Stark had heard of Orridge's old factory at the edge of town from the locals on many occasions. Many people had worked there over the decades, but as the area fell into decline in the early seventies, it ended up becoming isolated from the town itself and surrounded by derelict housing it was becoming unfit for purpose. A depressing building in a run-down area. That's when the company moved away and managed to install new machinery with government support and halve the workforce. It took the town years to recover economically.

It must have been the place that Dougie Brown's grandfather worked for. There were no others that had been operative for that long. It was still quite a long shot, so he hadn't mentioned it to the guys who were busy plotting and planning an organised search of potential sites—not just going out on a wing and a prayer, like he was, on a hunch. It just came to him that Dougie had an affinity with his grandad, and....people are strange creatures as well as creatures of habit.

For all Stark knew, Jane Cooper was lying dead in a ditch in Newark, but until he saw her dead body, he would be doing everything he could to find her. As far as he was concerned, she was alive until he placed his hand on her cold dead face.

His best guess was that she would be alive for the next day or two at least. He couldn't see Dougie and Len passing this opportunity by. They wanted to make a statement to the world that you don't mess with them. It was pathetic. He just shuddered to think what the hell they were doing to her.

Stark drove around the outskirts of the disused factory, but he couldn't see a van anywhere, so he wondered whether it was worth bothering with. Maybe he was just wasting time and should head back to the station. This was why he didn't say anything to anybody. Investigations aren't a guessing game; he had said to many young detectives over the years. And here he was ignoring his own advice.

Still, he had driven this far out, so he might as well just have a nosey. He parked his car outside the ramshackle edifice that now merely read 'ridge's hosi.'

He got out and looked around the yard. Did he need his coat? He fancied it would be no warmer inside, so he put it on, closing the car door behind him. The door slamming echoed around what must have once been the car park, now just dust and weeds fighting through the grey tarmac. A bedraggled chain link fence with bits of rubbish hanging off it here and there. Stark listened. He could hear nothing but the slight hum of traffic behind him and the honking of some geese flying nearby heading off to warmer climes. The place was deserted. A shiver ran through him. Maybe he had better shout up on the radio.

'DI Stark to control.'

No reply.

'DI Stark to control, over.'

No reply.

The radio signals were poor. Stark was only going to report his location as a precaution. It looked like a no-go anyway, so he stepped up the five concrete stairs and opened the heavy door. He let it slam behind him, and it was this noise that made Dougie and Len freeze. Thankfully Jane was out of it, but Dougie held both barrels of the shotgun in front of her face in any case. Sweat was forming on Doug's forehead.

Dougie and Len could hear his footsteps on the wooden floor above them. Dougie held a finger to his lips as they both stared towards the top of the stairs and the hatch. Dougie swivelled the shotgun around to point at the entrance to the cellar from the factory floor.

Stark walked around the echoey room and kicked a few rags. He went into the caged area and tested the lock. It must have been used for high-value goods; having a catch on the inside, but a key needed to get in it from the outside.

Stark had a good look around, covering the entire floor space. Down to the far end where there were shells of offices and some further smaller rooms and cupboards. Nothing of note, just detritus. He took his time. It was always best to take your time and get into the vibe of the room to see if anything stood out. Anything different. He wasn't feeling it. Again he stopped at the edge of the factory floor, and his eyes scanned the expanse. He sighed and looked at his watch.

What the hell was he doing? Wasting time.

Stark walked back towards the door and strode outside. He skipped down the steps and back into his car. He turned the ignition and then paused for a moment.

Was he mistaken? As he replayed the view of the factory floor in his mind's eye, it looked like the dust was disturbed heading to the rug in the centre of the floor? But why would it just disappear into the rug and not come out the other side?

'DI Stark to control.' He tried his radio once more.

No reply.

'Bloody signals.' He muttered to himself.

Stark turned the ignition off. He couldn't just leave his question hanging. He needed another look. He pulled at the car handle.

Stark strode back up the stairs and opened the heavy door once more. No. He was not mistaken. If you caught the light in the room right, you could see several tracks heading towards the rug. They appeared just as his own did, only his circled the outside of the room, and they looked recent.

Stark approached the rug and kicked it. He saw a brass strip running some distance along the floor. He kicked the rug further away and exposed the large hatch door and brass ring.

He knelt down and listened intently. Not a sound. But wait! A rasping noise. A rattle of heavy breathing. Was someone asleep? Someone snoring? Something was making the noise.

There was only one way to find out. He put his fingers through the golden ring and pulled it back.

There was a loud explosion, and the top corner of the hatch was destroyed.

Dougie had shot early from the foot of the stairs. The force knocked the hatch out of Stark's hand, and it fell back down, shut tight but with a ruddy great hole in it. Stark ran back towards the old offices at the far end of the factory floor. He hadn't been hit, but he had seconds to get the hell away. He felt blood on his face. Just specks from splinters. He was fine.

Lennie passed the two shotgun cartridges from his jacket pocket to Dougie. He took one and, in his haste, to get up the stairs; the second cartridge fell to the floor. Two rounds in the barrels should suffice. He pulled out the smoking cartridge case and pushed the new one in the empty barrel.

As Dougie peered over the hatch, he could see the abandoned factory floor was empty. Where was Stark?

*

Stark had no way of knowing that Nobby Clarke had indeed heard his original attempt to communicate on the radio when he first arrived at the derelict factory.

It wasn't that they could not hear Stark. He could not hear them replying to him, and despite repeated attempts to get him to pass his message, it was to no avail.

The problem was that Stark had not included his location, just that he was trying to get in touch.

Nobby had got the troops out in their vehicles, instructing them to find the van that the Browns had used in the kidnap and keep an eye out for DI Stark's vehicle.

Thankfully instead of spirally out from the town centre, Nobby had decided to spiral in from the outskirts, concentrating on the outlying properties and old industrial units first.

This meant that it was in relatively quick time that he saw Stark's car parked up and unattended on neglected wasteland with the only likely place he could be was an old hosiery factory.

What was Stark doing there? Was he on to something? Why hadn't he said?

Nobby had a look around for any van that might match the Browns, but he could not see one in the immediate vicinity.

He spoke into his radio. 'DS Clarke to Control.'

No reply.

'DS Clarke to control, over.'

It struck him that when Stark had radioed up, they could hear him, but seemingly he was not receiving signals in return. With that in mind, he tried again,

'DS Clarke to control. I am at the abandoned hosiery factory near the old Brickyard Cottages off Watnall Road. Can you get Ashley Stevens to join me, please?'

No sign of a response yet again.

Should he wait? Should he go down to the old factory? Surely he could wait a few minutes for Ashley to get there as backup?

*

Stark had secreted himself at the rear of one of the offices behind a metal cabinet. He could see an iron crowbar on top of the radiator and a dusty old plastic sandwich box on a window ledge. He could hear Dougie breathing heavily, kicking stuff around, slamming doors, making a noise. Every now and then, he would shout out,

'Show yourself Stark, or I'm going to kill her.'

'This is your fault if she dies.'

There was a panicky tone to Dougie's shouts. He knew that this was probably game over. Unless he made it game over for Stark. But killing a cop was not a good career move.

What choice did he have? Fuck him. They needed to get away, which was not possible while Stark was there.

Stark could hear Dougie getting closer. He had to do something. He couldn't just wait there. He would be a dead man.

Stark made his move. He grabbed the iron bar and silently went to the window ledge and threw the sandwich box out of the window creating a noise outside. He heard Dougie stop and then run at pace outside with the big door slamming behind him. That was Stark's cue to run back towards the hatch, and he was behind it just as Len stepped onto the warehouse floor.

'Have you got him, Dougie?'

Len neither saw nor heard Stark. The closest he got was seeing stars as Stark whacked him from behind with the iron bar, and he sunk to the floor like a sack of potatoes. Stark dragged the unconscious Lennie into the large cage and locked the door behind him from the inside, and he was just in time as Dougie burst back through the main door.

'You fucker! What you done to me brother?'

Stark had managed to get to the far corner of the cage and sat with his back to the cage as he pulled Len's unconscious body over his own as a shield.

'How good a shot are you, Dougie?' Stark said. 'Wanna kill your brother?'

'Fuck you.'

It dawned on Doug that he could not get within 20 feet of Stark and the rigid metal cage had small meshing, thick and tightly woven; far too small for the barrels of a sawn-off to fit through.

'Now what, Dougie?'

'This is stupid. Give it up, Stark.'

'I'm not giving anything up, my friend.'

Dougie held the barrels against the solid mesh. He couldn't fire through it. This was awkward. He stepped back and fired the shotgun at the cage at a different angle to where Stark and his brother lay. The noise shook the dust from the ceiling and echoed through the old building like a hurricane.

Dougie poked the shotgun through the hole he had made in the mesh and aimed it at Stark.

'Are you seriously prepared to kill your own brother, Dougie?'

'Instead of life in prison? Fuck yeah.'

'Think where you are? Your grandad worked here, Dougie. Would he approve?'

'Don't start that bollocks. He's long fucking dead. I don't believe in ghosts.'

In the heat and tension of the situation, it had not yet occurred to Dougie that perhaps he could shoot the lock off the cage to gain access. Now it was too late.

The plating around the locking was large and robust, and he would have to guess the area of the mechanism and hope that the force of the blast was sufficient to open it. Trying to shoot his way in was futile. Why? Because he now had only one cartridge left in the barrels. The remaining one was on the basement floor or in Len's jacket. He didn't know which. On such things is fate decided.

'You can kill me right now, Dougie, but your brother comes too.'

'He won't feel it.'

'Depends how good a shot you are.'

'Good enough to take your fucking head off.'

Should he just run while the going is good? Where did Len park the van? He didn't have the keys, either. It would mean an attempted escape on foot, and he doubted he would get far. No. He was looking into the eyes of his way out. But then there was Jane Cooper. It would mean a dash down the cellar and manhandling her upstairs to hold the gun to her head, and in the meantime, Stark could be out the cage and away.... Fuck. It was all suddenly so complicated.

'Dougie, take a minute to think of the situation you're in. It's over, son.'

Stark's voice was raised suddenly, and he was shouting much louder than before. The reason for this was simply because in his peripheral vision, behind

Dougie Brown, he could see the hulking figure of Detective Sergeant Nobby Clarke slowly and quietly walking towards him.

He steadfastly kept his focus on the face of Dougie Brown, but it was no good. Call it a sixth sense, but Dougie swivelled around and pointed the shotgun at Nobby Clarke.

'It's over, Dougie. Don't be a daft lad.' Nobby said.

'Over for you, you mean.'

'Don't rush into any decisions, Dougie. I'm standing right here, and I'm not going to do anything.'

'Yeah, right.'

'I'm not. I promise. We work it out from here.'

'No. Fuck you. You're the twat that threatened my Len. I've been looking forward to…'

There were two explosions. One was the impact of DI Stark's crowbar smashing into the back of Dougie's head, and the other was the shotgun blasting off as he fell. The blast narrowly missed Nobby Clarke.

Dougie crumpled to the floor, the shotgun clattering at his side.

'What did you do that for, boss? I was just about to take the little fucker down. He could have bloody shot me!'

'He was a second from shooting you anyway.'

'Maybe, but I'd done all the hard work.' Nobby kicked the shotgun away from the prostate Dougie.

'The hard work! I've been talking to the prat for the last ten minutes. What kept you anyway?'

'What kept me? That's gratitude for you, isn't it? I'm the one who crept up on him unarmed.'

'Crept up on him? You were like a herd of bleeding elephants; even when I was shouting, I could hear your size twelves clumping towards him.'

Both men were grinning with relief. Nobby heard a groan from the caged area and walked over to Len, stirring from his unconsciousness. Nobby stroked his hair.

'Wakey, wakey, Len. It's Christmas morning, and I've got a little present for you. A lovely pair of bracelets.'

Nobby secured the handcuffs on Len, and Stark cuffed Dougie, lying him on his front with his head to one side as he snored through his coma.

There was a screech of brakes outside. It was Ashley Stevens.

'Just in time, Ashley.' Stark said as he walked down the hatch steps to find Jane Cooper in the cellar.

Both Nobby and Ashley heard the horror in Stark's voice.

'Oh my God, Jane. Nobby, get an ambulance here, quick!'

16

'We failed, but in the good providence of God apparent failure often proves a blessing.'
– Robert E. Lee

Stark sat in Wagstaff's office with his Detective Superintendent staring at him over the top of his reading glasses.

'A stroke of luck, then?'

'You could say that. All the best ideas come to you in the shower or on the loo, do they not?'

'Funny you should say that. I suppose they do, thinking about it.' Wagstaff appeared thoughtful for a split second.

'The main thing is, Jane Cooper can rebuild her life once she gets out of hospital that is.' Stark said.

'What those bastards did was inhuman, David. Bloody animals they are. If you hadn't got to her, they would have killed her.'

'God knows what they would have done to her. It will take her a long time to get over it, sir. If she ever does.'

'They will be looking at twenty years each for this.'

'At least. They will still run things from prison, so we need to keep a watching brief on things.'

'Anyway, the Chief has moved from incandescent rage to a lovely lily pink.' Wagstaff said, twiddling with his ridiculous moustache.

'That's good to hear, sir. That's my favourite colour.'

Wagstaff shrugged out a laugh heaving himself up from his chair and strode over towards Stark. David stood and Wagstaff shook his hand. 'Well done, David. Fortune favours the brave.'

'Thank you, sir. It was a team effort.' Stark left the office with the imprint of Wagstaff's hand on his back, and walked down the corridor to his own, closing the door behind him.

He picked up the phone and dialled his home number.

'Stark residence.' It was Carol.

'Stark residence? Have we gone up in the world?'

'Oh hello, I wasn't expecting it to be you. No. I don't like to give the telephone number, but then again, I don't like to give my full name either, not while you're after those gangsters.'

Stark laughed. 'Gangsters. Huh. Anyway, you can relax now. They are both behind bars for the next thousand years.'

'You got them?'

'We got them.'

'Yay, Well done you.'

'I hope nobody got hurt.'

'Let's just say it's a long story. My suit is a bit dirty.'

'Oh, David, you only took that to the dry cleaners a couple of weeks ago, didn't you?'

Stark laughed. 'You're right. I did, but a dirty suit is a good result, trust me.'

'Well, I hope the job is going to pay for it to be cleaned again.'

'We get vouchers, look why are we talking about dry cleaning?'

'I don't know. You said you had messed your suit up. Will you be back for tea?'

'Back for tea. Listen, will you do me a favour?'

'What's that?'

'Ring that therapist and book me in another appointment for tomorrow, will you?'

'Wow. I never thought I would hear you say that. Was it that bad?'

'It was that bad.'

*

Ashley smoked into his smile as Stark's team sat around the tables feeling good about themselves.

'I see they are all coming out the woodwork now.' Ashley said.

Charlie grinned, his buttons on his shirt stretching as he reached forward to pat some cigarette ash into the ashtray on the desk.

'You mean all the witnesses; now the Browns are locked up. That's the way it works, Ash. They suddenly want to become good citizens now the coast is clear.'

'Still, it's going to make life easier. We already know the shotgun blast from their shotgun caused the hole in Bernie's bookmakers during the armed robbery.' Ashley said.

'Forensics confirmed that already, huh. That's good news, kiddo.'

'Yeah, and did you hear that Steph took a call from a youth who reckons he was on the burglary where Mr Cooper died. He reckons he was forced into it.'

'He's trying to get a lighter sentence before he's bloody caught.' Charlie laughed.

'He says he didn't expect anyone to get hurt. He reckons it was somebody called Mac, and it looks like it is Scot MacKenzie from Top Valley, one of the Brown gang, of course.'

'Mac, was it? I dealt with him as a kid. I always knew he would go places.'

'There's only one place he's going, Charlie.' Ashley's gold chain clinked against the tin ashtray as he stubbed his cigarette out.

'Maybe Mac will drop the Browns into that one as well, you know, for organising it. I'll have to have a word with him. Conspiracy to kidnap on top of everything else.'

'Christ, they might as well throw the key away, Charlie.'

'It's looking that way.'

The telephone rang, and Ashley threw it to his ear.

'CID, DC Stevens.'

'Hello, is that CID?'

'Yes, CID, DC Stevens.'

'My name's Trixie, and I want to tell you where the razor is that Sharon Brown used to slash that, Jane Cooper.'

'Why would you want to do that, Trixie?'

'Because I was with her when she did it, but I didn't do nowt. I don't want to get in trouble for it, though, if I tell you.'

'Aren't you Sharon's mate, Trixie?'

'Yeah, but they been treating us like shit lately, and we're all sick of it. Now they are locked up they can't thingy, they can't do nowt, can they?'

'So where is it, this razor?' Ashley grabbed a pen and was poised nib over the paper.

'So I won't be in trouble then?'

'Doesn't sound like it to me, Trixie. Where is the razor?' Ash was non-committal.

'It's at the back of a shed in the garden of 26 Saxondale Drive, Bulwell.'

Ashley scribbled onto his pad.

'How do you know?' He asked.

'Course I know cos, thingy, I was with her when she dropped it between the fence and the shed.'

'And how will we know it was the razor used on Jane?'

'Dunno, but she didn't wipe it or owt, so it will have her blood on it and maybe Sharon's thingy, Sharon's fingerprints. She didn't wear gloves. I don't think she did anyway.'

'Proper little amateur detective, aren't you, Trixie?'

'What, oh yeah.' She giggled. 'Thanks.'

'Come in and see me tomorrow at 11 am, yeah? My name's Ashley Stevens, and I will get a statement from you.'

'Okay. I'm going to have to go though, cos thingy, I ain't got any more change, and the pips will go in a minute.'

'Make sure you come and see me, Trixie, or we will have to come looking for you, and then you will be in big trouble, yeah.' Ashley winked at Charlie, who was listening.

'Okay. What's your name again.'

'Ashley Stevens.'

'Okay, bye.'

'Bye.'

Trixie put the phone down in the telephone kiosk and walked in the Autumn breeze towards the Browns abode. She kept repeating the name Ashley Stevens, Ashley Stevens, Ashley Stevens.

As she reached the gate, she clashed with the postman also reaching for the hasp.

'It's okay I will take those in.'

The postman gave her a couple of letters and went on his way.

'Shit what was that coppers name?' Trixie muttered as she went down the path. Instead of waiting she walked straight through Sharon's front door after the briefest of knocks. It was less hassle now that Dougie was behind bars, and Sharon needed her friendship for once.

'Postman gave me these.' She threw them on Sharon's lap and sat down on the vacant armchair.

'Cheers, Trixie. You're a good friend, sweetie.'

'Thanks.

Sharon ripped open the white envelope marked NHS and read the contents in a whisper, rushing down to the final paragraph.

The result is that **no** damage was caused to either ovary, but there was some localised bruising to the stomach wall. Miss Sharon Brown's ovaries are functioning normally, and there is no need for any follow-up appointment.

Yours….

Mr S. Chaudry MB, ChB, FRCS(Eng)

Sharon jumped out of her chair. 'Woohoo! I've had the all clear! I can have kids, Trixie. It's all okay. My ovaries are fine. Thank God for that.'

Sharon and Trixie embraced. Trixie was smiling. 'I told you, the only way is up, Shaz.'

'I need to let our Dougie know. I need my conjugal rights visits at the prison.'

'Ooh.' Trixie winced.

'What?'

'They don't allow them, Shaz.'

'Yes, they do. I've seen it on telly.'

'Nah, that's thingy, that's America. They don't do that here. It's going to be fifteen-twenty years before you have kids, Shaz. That is if you want them with your Dougie, and I doubt he would be too happy if you have them with anyone else.'

'Oh fuck!'

THE END

Printed in Great Britain
by Amazon

75821966R00180